A LUST FOR BLOOD

REALM OF CURSES
BOOK 1

K.C. SMITH

Phantom House
Press

This is a work of fiction. Names, characters, places, and incidents either are the product of the author's imagination or are used fictitiously. Any resemblance to actual persons, living or dead, events, or locales is entirely coincidental.

Copyright © 2022 by K.C. Smith

All rights reserved.

No portion of this book may be reproduced or used in any in any form without written permission from the publisher or author, except for use of quotations in a book review.

Published by Phantom House Press

Cover Design by TS95 Studios

Editing by Alyse Bailey

ISBN (Paperback): 9798986459004

CONTENT WARNING

This novel contains graphic scenes of death, gore, blood, self harm, attempted suicide and sexual situations. If these issues could be considered triggering for you, please take note.

A LUST FOR BLOOD

K.C. SMITH

To those who dare to break free and become who they were always meant to be.

PART ONE

ORIGINS

I

ORIANA

31ST DAY OF THE TWELFTH MONTH, 1099

A shrill scream ripped through the air. Oriana opened her eyes. The full moon peered down from above, its blood-red glow casting an eerie haze into the field around her.

Disoriented, she sat up. Tall grass brushed coarsely against her bare arms as a cool breeze whispered its way around her, rustling the field, giving the grass the appearance of rippling water. From her seated position, the blades met just above her waist, sharp to the touch, with frost sparkling on the tips. She couldn't see where she was, couldn't remember how she had even gotten there. A robust, metallic tang filled the air, mingling with the pungent scent of upturned earth.

She pushed herself to her feet just in time to see a woman—the one who must have been screaming—standing at the edge of the field, lantern in hand, wide-eyed, and deathly pale. She jerked the lantern in Oriana's direction, drawing a shaking hand up to her mouth as she gasped, screamed once more, and took off toward a small town gleaming in the distance.

Dazed, Oriana stumbled after her. "Wait!" she called out, "Stop! What is going on?" Lantern flames winked in and out of the swift breeze like tiny fireflies. Chimney smoke pulled above the rooftops of the town, illuminated by the ghostly scarlet beams of moonlight. It spread out as if creating a shield to protect from any terrors the night might have to offer.

Oriana had only made it a handful of steps toward the town and the fleeing woman when her foot brushed against something cold and solid. She glanced down to see a large, dark form lying in the grass beside her. The moon's dim glow left barely enough light to see. Crouching, she brushed a hand across the form. It felt distinctly like a body. Her fingers met with the rough stubble of an unkempt beard. It was a male body, and it was cold as ice.

She inhaled deeply, and something primal roused inside her. A thrill at the scent. Her entire body tingled with exhilaration as she stroked a pointed fingernail along the dead man's cheek, digging into flesh, leaving behind a bloodless gash that gapped. She closed her eyes, breathing in the scent of death and feeling a satisfied smile spread across her lips.

"Beautiful," she purred through teeth that no longer felt like her own.

No! Her mind screamed as she shook off the morbidly blissful sensations that had begun to course through her, gradually coming back into herself. *What are you doing?* She inwardly chastised, an uneasiness suddenly settling over her.

She felt the man's neck for a sign of life, hoping that her growing suspicions and nagging unease were false. Her hand came away wet. There was no mistaking the feel and scent of the substance as she rubbed it between her thumb and forefinger.

Blood.

She felt the earth surrounding him further. Her hands then traveled over his body in search of a wound from which the blood could be leaking from. She felt nothing, no pool of blood puddling beneath him and no indication of how his body was void of its life source.

Her stomach grew queasy, bile rising in her throat as her mind urged her to move up and feel his neck again.

Oriana swallowed hard as she gently brushed trembling fingers back across his throat to the spot where the last ounce of his blood had been, and there, just where the tender flesh of his neck met the harder muscular structure of his shoulder, was a set of punctures.

This man was not only dead, but completely drained—an empty husk. Yet, the metallic scent of blood hung heavy in the air. More death lingered nearby. *What had happened here?* Mind reeling, she searched for an explanation other than the one she refused to face. But it couldn't be. She had always held complete control over her hunger.

Oriana gingerly ran her fingers further along the punctures before snatching them back, gasping in shock. She fell back, the frosted grass crunching beneath her weight. "No, it cannot be." she breathed, head pounding as she continued to push away the creeping thoughts.

Something, she thought–ignoring the fact that her mind was screaming *someone*–had bitten him. The marks on his neck were not from an animal. An animal would have ripped and torn through flesh, and the marks would have been larger and deeper. These were most definitely something else. The punctures nearly created a perfect circle with two bigger, gaping holes just where the major pulsing artery along the column of his neck lay. To the unknowing eye, it would have looked almost like a human bite, but Oriana knew better.

She stood, skin prickling as the evening wind swirled around her, and took off for the spot where the screaming woman had been standing. Another dark shape lay just on the outside of the field, this one smaller. Oriana stepped reluctantly closer until she loomed above the figure, breath hitching.

This is where the woman with the lantern had run from. This is what had made her go so deathly pale and had caused her to pierce the night with her ear-splitting scream. A petite woman was lying in a crumpled heap. Her chest rose and fell with weak breaths. Still alive, but barely. The moonlight's ghostly beams revealed a trickle of blood leaking from her neck. The punctures were a twin to those she had found on the man lying dead in the field. Oriana knelt before her, so close she could almost taste the blood slowly seeping from the woman's wound. A dizzying sensation overtook her, something like want, no...it was need. An urge so extreme, so insistent.

Oriana's fingers ached to dig deep into the woman's chest and stroke her slowly beating heart. The very thought had her arm moving on its own accord, reaching out until her slender fingers hovered barely a whisper above the woman's weak, heaving chest.

Tears sprang to her eyes. "No!" she wailed, attempting to push herself away from the girl, but the feeling only grew more tenacious. Oriana grabbed her own head, ripping at her face and hair. A guttural cry of anguish burst forth from deep within her. But she couldn't stop it, couldn't control it. She pushed as hard as she could against the repulsive force slithering through her body, seizing hold of her limbs one by one. She cried out in torment once more before finally conceding to the monster.

Oriana yanked the small woman up by her hair, placing her other hand on the woman's shoulder, twisting her head and smiling as she heard the pop of the woman's neck snapping before pulling the pulsing artery to meet her waiting lips. A satisfied groan escaped her as she slowly sank her teeth into the soft tissue and drank deeply. Closing her eyes, she reveled in the taste and feel of the woman's thick blood gliding down her throat. An intense warmth coursed through her with each swallow. She couldn't remember the last time she had felt absolute ecstasy like this.

It wasn't until the poor woman was dry, cold, and white as a clean linen sheet that Oriana pushed back into herself for only a moment. She scrambled backward, fingers digging into the rich soil as she kicked with her feet and forced herself away from the lifeless corpse.

Oriana's breath quickened. What was happening? Why was this happening? She hadn't been able to stop herself, hadn't been in control of her own faculties. And worse, she had enjoyed it, delighted in the life slowly draining from the woman. She felt exhilarated as she heard the woman's heart pulse out its last beat.

Oriana shot to her feet, racing back into the field of tall grass, the moon still casting the world in a crimson haze. Squinting through the darkness, she pushed the blades aside, searching. She found four more bodies, three male and one female. All were dead, two completely drained of their life's blood. The other two had their heads severed from their bodies, blood sprayed across the ice-covered grass. She whimpered, sinking to her knees in the center of the field, burying her head into her hands. This couldn't be happening.

But she knew the corpses scattered like fallen leaves in the field were connected to her. Her teeth had slid far too easily into the exposed ripe flesh of the woman's neck. It had to be some kind of sick dream. She would never hurt these people, never do these things! This wasn't her. She had always suppressed the thirst for violence. She had always been able to control the monster that lurked beneath her skin. But it wasn't a dream. She knew from the gore soaking through her gown, sticking to her skin, and the icy blades of grass beneath her feet like shards of glass digging into her flesh.

Even now, all she could think of were the bodies around her and how she wished to rip them apart further, flay the skin from their bones, and spread their ribs apart one by one to look like the wings of a great bird. An impish smile spread across her face at the thought.

"No!" she yelled again, beating the palms of her hands against her head as if she could knock the thoughts and urges from her mind. "Stop it! Stop! You have control. You don't want to do these things. Keep it separate, lock it down deep." She began chanting the words to herself, slowing her breathing, but it didn't work. She snarled, releasing an animalistic sound into the fleeting night. Her head spun to the center of the field. There was a rhythm like the sound of a drum, constant but dying, growing softer with each beat.

A primal growl rumbled from within, and she prowled towards the rhythmic sound until she was standing over it–or rather, him. A man, chest rising and falling with wheezing breaths, stared up at her, eyes frantically darting back and forth. He weakly tried to move away from her, desperately searching for something–anything–to help him. To save him.

Oriana graced him with a feral smile before she tore into his chest. His screams of agony were a symphony to her ears. She heard someone's laugh, cold and callous, and realized suddenly that it was her own.

As she ripped out the man's still-beating heart, his screams silenced. His inert eyes remained set on her, full of terror. She held the bleeding organ up to the moon, only to see that the moon had fallen from its place in the night sky, replaced by the golden light of the sun as it slowly rose from its slumber and bathed the blood-strewn field in its warmth.

As if its shining rays had sparked her mind, setting it ablaze with memory, everything came crashing back. It was Anthes. He had done this to her. The memory of his venomous red eyes bore into her, white plaited locks whipping in the wind like errant snakes, and the burning embers of what used to be her home illuminating the axe slung across his back. The scene would be forever etched in her mind.

He was a vile brute that feasted on the utter despair of those who wronged him. He was a trickster and a warrior who exacted revenge no matter the cost. After all these years, he had finally found her, and he had brought his wrath down upon her.

Oriana looked down at herself. Blood dripped down her arm, her hand still gripping the heart she had savagely ripped from the nameless man's chest. She dropped it as if it were a hot coal. Its weight *thunked* to the grassy earth with a soft gurgle as the last bit of its blood squirted across her feet.

As the morning illuminated the horrifying massacre surrounding her, the tears began to fall, streaking lines through the gore that coated her face.

The monster had been set free, and it was Anthes's doing.

Oriana threw her head back, a bellow of fury erupting from her as the glacial wind surged around her, frosting over the pool of her victim's blood puddled at her feet.

2

GARREN

30TH DAY OF THE TENTH MONTH, 1774

G arren was in a foul mood. After traveling north on the King's Road for a fortnight, he had finally made it to Randier, which sat at the road's end. It was a petite village at the junction of three major roads–a resting place for weary travelers. The King's Road from the south, the Loch Road from the west, and the Daylight Road from the east. To the north, it bordered the Bone Loch, beyond which sat the White Giants, the largest and harshest mountain range in all of Svakland. Any attempt to cross the Giants was a death sentence. If the pure freezing conditions didn't kill you first, an avalanche, wolves, or snow lions would claim you long before you ever reached the other side. He had been heading towards a forest known as the Phantom Wood, and Randier was to be his last stop before that ultimate destination.

Garren's eyes were heavy with exhaustion from days of travel with little food and restless sleep. All he really wanted was a hot meal and a soft bed to rest his weary head. But good things never came easy. He had barely purchased a room to stay for the night when a great ugly beast had torn through the town, ravaging the streets and heading straight for the horse stall behind the inn that he was to stay in. Just his luck.

As a known demon hunter, Garren would generally be called to eradicate the monster and secure payment in advance, but this demon had left him little choice as it wreaked havoc throughout the village like a rampant storm of claws and fangs. It was unlike any beast Garren had faced before. It ravaged with a hunger that appeared only to grow the more it killed.

It was strange, but new demons had been cropping up at an alarming rate in recent months. His services were being requested throughout Svakland more than ever before. It was worrisome, but good for business.

As the demon had ripped into the inn, Garren groaned in annoyance. All he wanted was to eat a hot meal and sleep the rest of the day away. But unfortunately, the demon wouldn't simply kill itself. With a heavy sigh, he had reluctantly grabbed the old mare he had ridden in on, gained the beast's attention, and led it straight out of town on the Daylight Road.

And now here he was, a little over thirty miles outside the small village of Randier, and his horse had gone lame. He had known the mare wouldn't last long, that this particular horse was far past its prime. He had already ridden it to its limits before arriving in Randier. He had chosen it for that very reason, leading a lamb to the slaughter. One life to save two hundred.

He dismounted, gently stroked the horse's mane, and whispered sweet words, consoling the hurt and frightened animal before he drove his blade into its skull. It collapsed, instantly a better, quicker death than what would have been if he had waited only a few moments more for the monster to catch up to them.

Far down the road, Garren could hear the distant snarls of the beast steadily scrambling toward him. The demon's gait was peculiar. He had noticed its limbs bending in unnatural ways, making it much slower than the old mare and allowing him plenty of time to prepare a trap. The horse was part of his plan, and he was just glad the poor mare had lasted as long as it did, providing a significant distance from the town.

He looked out at his surroundings, having already formulated a plan in his mind. Twin blades were secured on his back, a dagger strapped to each thigh. To his right was a large field bordered by a dusting of sweeping hills. To his left was a thick forest spanning as far as he could see, a tall mountain range shrouded in a blanket of clouds–which could only be the White Giants–lined its northern edge.

He looked back at the towering trees of the forest. "The Phantom Wood," he mused as his eyes took in the dark and foreboding wood. It held an ancient silence, as if all life had left its gloomy depths long ago. He let his gaze survey its edge before resting on a large boulder peeking through the dense pines. The perfect spot to stay hidden and wait.

He knew nothing of this demon other than its taste for livestock. He hadn't missed how, even though the creature had destroyed everything in its path, it had gone straight for the horses rather than the people enjoying a meal at the inn.

Garren grabbed the hind legs of the dead mare, dragged it out into the center of the road, and pulled it along until it was perfectly in line with the boulder. He sliced the mare from its neck to its belly, spilling fresh blood and entrails onto the road as a tempting feast for the demon. Once he had set his trap, Garren headed for the boulder, climbing its rough-pebbled surface until he reached the top, ensuring he was hidden from view but still able to keep watch over the road and the gutted mare.

As Garren waited, he thought back to the first demon he had ever encountered, far different from the monstrous creature he was about to face. In fact, the first demon he had fought had been quite beautiful. Until that day, he had been led to believe that demons were only a thing of legend. Non-existent beings of death and darkness that supposedly resided in the underworld. Demon stories were told throughout Svakland to deter children from misbehaving, but that all changed many years ago.

He had only been ten years old at the time, and it wasn't until that day that he realized he was different. He had ignored it for years afterward–the things he had done that day. It couldn't be possible, not for a boy–hell, not even for a grown man.

The memory materialized before his eyes as if he were right there all those twenty-five years ago.

A strikingly beautiful woman walked into Garren's father's smithy, looking for someone to fix one of the wheel rims from her carriage, or so she said. From the first moment Garren laid eyes on her, he knew something was off. Her skin glowed with a slight golden hue, like the rays of the sun were trapped inside, desperately trying to break free. Her ears were strange, elongated at the tips so slightly that if Garren hadn't been studying her features so closely, he would have most assuredly missed it. But it was her eyes that gave her away. They were far too large, almost catlike. A shiver raked down his spine at the sight, and the hair on his arms raised in fear.

His father was almost transfixed by the woman, unable to keep his eyes from her. Garren watched while his father spoke to her, observing her odd movements. She walked as if she were floating on air, her arms and legs barely moving with each stride. It wasn't until she smiled that Garren took action. Her mouth spread wide upon her face—too wide—and every single tooth was long and pointed, curving like the fangs of a viper waiting to strike. He didn't think, only reacted, knowing that something was wrong, this woman was wrong, and instinct told him he needed to get rid of her before something bad happened.

Garren grabbed a hot fire poker from the burning embers and whirled, hands shaking with terror. He stumbled, dropping the burning metal rod to the sandy ground. Quickly, he recovered it and drove its scorching tip deep into her belly, flesh sizzling. The woman shrieked a terrible, otherworldly sound that shook him to his bones.

Her eyes turned black. She grabbed the poker sticking out from her gut and, pulling herself forward along its hilt, she brought Garren closer to her, all the while plunging the poker further inside of herself.

Garren watched in horror as the creature took one slow step after another in his direction. Something wet and warm traveled down his legs, evidence of his fear. He released the poker, ran backward, tripped, and landed hard on his backside. The woman turned away from him and toward his father, still dazzled by her. A heinous cackle came from her as she revealed her tremendous row of fangs again. That was all Garren needed to see for his courage to slam back into him. He wasn't about to let her get close enough to his father to cause any harm, so he sprang to his feet, grabbing the poker to pull her closer before kicking out hard. The woman went flying into the wooden doors of the smithy and crashed straight through as if she had been kicked in the chest by a mighty steed. But when he went outside, she had vanished.

He thought about that day for a long time afterward. It wasn't until almost a year later that he realized what she had truly been. A demon. After that day, demons became all too real, rapidly appearing throughout Svakland as if the gates of the underworld had opened, allowing them free reign of their world.

But that first encounter would haunt him until the end of his days. If only he had gone after the demon, he might have saved himself a considerable amount of heartache and self-loathing.

Garren shook the thought away, snapping back into focus. The sun was steadily beginning its descent behind the pines. He raked a hand through his unruly black curls.

"It's too quiet," he muttered, eyes narrowing as they darted west from where he had come.

He listened closely for sounds of the approaching demon, but heard nothing. *Strange*, he thought, furrowing his brow. He had made sure the beast was following them, keeping a slow pace to ensure that he could hear its snarling at all times, that it was still on their tail. Something must have distracted it, veered it off the path. He sighed, shaking his head at his own stupidity. "Damn..."

A twig snapped behind him. He turned just in time to see a smudge of black against the emerald green of the forest. It was the beast gliding through the air, fangs bared, a set of catastrophic claws reaching for him. "Fuck!" was all he could say before the demon crashed into him.

3

ORIANA

1st day of the First Month, 1100

By the time the sun had fully ascended above the horizon, Oriana had gathered herself enough to venture into the nearby town, leaving her gore-spattered gown in a heap of shreds on the ground.

Not long after, she began sneaking her way through the back alleys and streets of the town—cloaked in shadow, as she was completely nude—a crowd started to gather in the square. Anguished cries of outrage and sorrow rang out as townsfolk carried the bodies from the field. Oriana sank into the shadows further, unable to look at the faces of the people.

Pulling her legs into her chest, she wrapped her arms around them and squeezed her eyes tight, shutting out the remembrance of her actions, of the blood. There had been so much blood. But behind her closed eyes, a flash of memory pushed to the surface of a knife materialized through the darkness, a ruby glinting on its end, buried to the hilt in a broad chest she knew so achingly well. Oriana flung her eyes open as the beating organ in her own chest constricted painfully, leaving her unable to catch her breath.

Oriana clutched at her bare skin in agony and attempted to slow her breathing, forcing the images from her mind. They were too painful.

A yell from the town square cleared her mind, her heart seizing from its torment. The citizens were growing angrier. She needed to clean herself and figure out how to blend in.

Oriana stalked further through the back alleys of the town. She crept on silent feet behind the wooden homes like a thief in the night, where she stumbled upon a wash bucket behind a house. Oriana sank to her knees before it, using the fresh cool water to wash away the evidence of the horror she had committed. After thoroughly washing away the blood and filth, she grabbed a simple chemise and gown left to dry on a low-hung wire.

The town was exceptionally small. She had made her way from one end to the other in a matter of minutes. On the south end of town was a road that ran east to west. Beyond that was the field she had come from, and to the north, a meager forest of pines curved in a crescent shape around the town. Even farther north, beyond the small forest, were magnificent white-capped mountains stretching as far as the eye could see.

Oriana donned her stolen garments, plaiting her snow-white locks into a single braid and tying it off with a piece of string she had yanked from the chemise. She stopped to close her eyes and take a long, deep breath. Her hands trembled uncontrollably.

So much had happened. Her nightmares had come to life; Anthes had committed the most inexplicable evil upon her. Clenching her fists, she shook the thoughts from her head. Now was not the time. She needed to blend in—to not seem like an outsider—while attempting to figure out where exactly she was. That was the only thing her mind seemed to glaze right over. She had no idea what town she was in, for she had never been here before. The last she could recall before the field, she'd still been in Elscar with...tears welled in her eyes as she thought of his name. She swallowed her emotions and breathed out her sorrow in one drawn-out breath before blinking away any lingering tears and walking into the town square.

The townsfolk gathered around the bodies, some openly mourning their loved ones and others yelling about finding the monster who did it. Oriana hovered on the outskirts of the square, listening for any information to glean her whereabouts. That was until her eyes landed on the screaming woman from the field. The woman's eyes locked directly onto Oriana's. But before she had a chance to alert anyone, Oriana reached within herself, pulling on her glamour magic and casting an enchantment over her features.

Her hair darkened from snowy white to the same auburn locks adorning many of the villagers gathered in the square. Then came her eyes, transforming from their intense glowing green to a muted icy blue. Her willowy frame was at odds with the women around her–much taller and less curvy–so she created a new version of herself that was petite yet well-endowed. Her enchantment complete, Oriana watched as the woman shook her head before turning away, eyebrows furrowed in bemusement. Oriana let out a sigh of relief.

Her gaze caught on an oval wooden sign, squeaking on its hinges as it waved in the biting winter wind. Golden letters glinted in the sunlight that read, *The White Fox Inn & Tavern*. Oriana headed along the packed dirt streets toward the clay building. Ivy climbed up the facade, spreading out like the tentacles of a great octopus.

She pulled open the heavy wooden door and was instantly assaulted with the scent of ale mingling with something sweeter and something far more foul. She couldn't tell if it was pleasant or abhorrent. A little of both. The place was packed full of townsfolk, a few of whom turned their heads at her entrance, but quickly returned to their drinks, uninterested.

Oriana maneuvered through the throng of people, picking up bits and pieces of conversation as she went.

"What would have done something like this?"

"There hasn't been a snow lion come down from the white caps in years."

"Maybe wolves? Some of them had been ripped to pieces."

Oriana already knew she was in the north due to the aching chill in the air, but the "white caps" could only be referring to the White Giants. She was farther north than she had thought. Her mind wandered, attempting to remember the villages closest to the imposing mountain range, when one of the townsfolk yelled out, "Protect our town! Protect, Sardorf!"

A chorus of "Aye!" rose around her, ale sloshing onto the tavern's wooden floorboards as tankards raised into the air.

Sardorf. Oriana had heard of the town. It was small, without a lot of natural crops or means of supplies to trade. She recalled a conversation she once overheard about how the small northern town nestled beneath the White Giants "wouldn't last another winter." If that were true, these people wouldn't go down without a fight, not after what she had just heard.

Oriana kept her head down and headed straight for the elderly man stationed behind the bar, motioning for a tankard of ale.

As she watched the bustling scene around her, Oriana couldn't help but notice that the lonely barkeep was practically sprinting throughout the tavern to bring both food and drink to the patrons. The idea formed itself. She had no place to go, and her home was...there would be nothing to go back to. Even if she could.

When the barkeep made his way back to the bar, half-empty tankard in hand, she reached out, grasping his arm to gain his attention. "Might you be in need of some help?"

31st Day of the First Moon, 1100

Sardorf was a tiny village with little more than seventy townsfolk that sat just south of the large mountain range dividing the frozen northern plains from the rest of Svakland. Oriana had woven her enchantment all throughout the small town, integrating herself into the minds of the people and securing a room at a barley farm due east of the village. As her enchantment took root, she was instantly disguised and included as one of the townspeople. And now here she was an entire month later, and no one was the wiser of who she was or what she had done.

"Here's your first month's pay, lass." Kieran, the owner of *The White Fox*, handed her a small jingling pouch of coins. The sound of the clanking coppers was barely perceptible over the loud table of men singing the chorus of a bawdy tune, one too many in their cups.

"Thank you," she said with a soft smile.

"You're a hard worker, lassie. Hiring you is the best decision I've made. Why don't you take the rest of the evening off? Head out and do something fun before the sun sets." Kieran dried a freshly cleaned tankard with a ragged cloth. When she made no motion to move, he flicked the rag at her and yelled, "Get!"

Oriana turned, hanging her dirtied apron on a hook by the bar before heading out the door. She shielded her eyes from the bright sun, which had just reached the low point on the horizon so as to blind anyone who was looking straight ahead on their walk. Oriana shivered against the cold. It had only gotten brisker during the month she had lived in this town. No matter how warm the sun's rays were, there was always a chill in the north. Oriana pulled her cloak tighter around herself.

With a soft and weary sigh, her shoulders sagged in resignation. The visions of the night in the field sprang unbidden to the forefront of her mind. She shook them away almost instantly, feeling the sting of unshed tears hovering behind her eyes. Not a day went by that she didn't think of the events of that night, that her heart didn't constantly ache for the lives she had taken, along with the ones that had been taken from her. Oriana attempted to push it all into the dark recesses of her mind. Not the healthiest thing, she agreed, but she had done it in the past and could do it now.

She still didn't know exactly what Anthes had done to her, but she hadn't felt the urge to kill–that bloodlust–since that night, which was strange. No matter how deep the pit within herself she kept it locked in was, there was always an inkling of that darkness hovering just beneath her surface. Maybe she had finally succeeded in forcing it to such a depth inside herself that she could no longer feel its presence. But knowing Anthes and the specific nature of his words that night, there was more to it than that. Much more.

For now, she was content to meander through the streets of the quaint town she had nestled herself into. The air smelled of freshly baked bread and sweet almond pastries. Her mouth watered in response. She decided to celebrate her first month's pay and purchase a flaky pastry, nibbling on the treat as she headed to the barley farm.

Birds sang high above while distant chirping echoed from the depths of the wood, crickets, frogs, and rodents, creating a symphony of wildlife. She loved this peaceful walk from the village to her cottage, and it was all the better with a delicious almond pastry in hand. She breathed in the crisp fresh air, turning her face up toward the sun to feel the last inkling of its waning warmth before the night.

She let her eyes search their surroundings, finding herself wishing the forest was larger, thicker, and more whimsical. This far north, everything was colder and drearier. No greenery except for the sparse pines and scattered bush. Everything was the same shade of green and brown wherever you looked. Still pretty in its own way, but rather dull.

She ached for a bit of warmth, for flowers of every color, for crystal clear sprawling seas. Perhaps she would travel to a new part of the world once she had saved enough coin to do so. All she knew was Elscar. And although its beauty was fathomless, she knew there was more out there waiting for her.

She couldn't imagine going back to her home there, not now, possibly not ever, not after what Anthes had done. She could still recall his face looming over her, cold and pious, an expression of contempt forever locked upon his long, lean features. She could still feel his fierce, crimson gaze as it bore into her, dripping with disapproval. She blew out a shuddering breath, a cloud of steam rising above her.

By the time she finally made it to her lodgings, it had grown considerably colder. The sun's rays were just barely peeking through the frosted trees at her back. She thought about stopping by the main house to give the farm owner her first month's rent, but her fingers were already stiff and aching from the cold. She needed to thaw them by the fire. She would pay him in the morning.

She practically sprinted the last few steps to her small single-room cottage, slamming the wooden door behind her. Kneeling by the empty fireplace, she fumbled with the iron and flint, her frozen fingers shaking. Finally, a flame flicked to life. Oriana snatched the heavy woolen blanket from her straw bed on the cottage floor and wrapped it around herself, crouching as close to the fire as possible without bursting into flame.

She glanced out the window, watching as the final beams of sunlight descended into darkness. The night was clear. A speckling of stars twinkled amongst the midnight sky, and in its center, a full moon glowed brightly.

She sighed as her fingers and toes began to warm. It was then that a strange, dizzying sensation washed over her, the force of it nearly knocking her back. Every muscle in her body tensed. Her blood boiled. A feeling of pure rage that spread through her veins like wildfire. Her breathing quickened and her heart felt as if it might pound its way through her chest with each beat. She clenched and unclenched her fists from the rush of it.

"No..." A growl escaped her lips as her features shifted, the enchanted glamour she had set in place reversing on its own accord. She reached to tap her well deep within, but it was empty. Her magic was gone. "No!" she screamed. "What has he done?"

She ran to the looking glass that hung beside the window. All she could do was watch as her hair melted back into straight snow-white locks. Her eyes shifted to their natural vivid green, but then again to a glowing, monstrous yellow like that of a nocturnal creature, her vision suddenly sharper as if she were seeing in the beaming rays of daylight.

"You have control," she chanted. "Keep it separate, lock it down deep." But it was of little use. She witnessed in horror as her forehead morphed from its smooth and silky complexion to a grotesque, bumpy mass leading down to her nose—now in a sharp, menacing hook. And if that wasn't horrific enough, every tooth in her mouth began to elongate, grinding against one another and pushing out in a wave of pain until she had a mouth full of razor-sharp, jagged fangs. She stumbled backward, gasping in terror. The monster had broken free once again.

It was then that a knock sounded at her door. Her head whipped toward the wooden frame, alert. She could hear a steady thumping on the other side. A heartbeat. Oriana licked her lips instinctively.

"Oriana?" came a voice from the other side of the door along with another soft knock.

"Come in," she drawled, moving away from the moon's ghostly beams and blanketing herself in shadow.

The door creaked open, and Liam—the cottage owner—stepped inside, quickly shutting the door behind him against the biting cold. "I wanted to stop over to see whether you had the rent for this first month?"

"I do," she purred. "Come closer. I have it right here."

Liam slowly inched his way toward her. "Are you quite well? You sound strange."

"Oh, I am perfectly well, I assure you." She jangled the bag of coins in front of her. As Liam reached out for them, Oriana stepped into the light. Liam cried out in fright, jerking his hand away.

"Wh-what are you?" he stammered, backing away from her toward the door behind him, toward his only means of escape.

She graced him with a menacing smile, displaying her full set of masterful fangs. "Death," she hissed, and then pounced.

4

GARREN

30TH DAY OF THE TENTH MONTH, 1774

Garren braced himself for impact as both he and the demon plummeted off the boulder. The fall gave him barely enough time to snatch the dagger from his boot. Just before they crashed to the forest floor, he sliced. The demon snarled as the blade pierced its inky black flesh. Grotesque blood dripped from the wound, a grayish tan color like that of hot porridge. Garren landed on top of the creature and quickly rolled to the side, shooting up into a fighting stance and pulling a sword free from his back in the same movement. The demon growled, pushing itself up to its full height. Garren's eyes widened. This demon was at least twice his height, if not more. It was a terrifyingly ugly beast, unlike the one he had faced all those years ago in his father's smithy.

Its black, serpentine skin glistened in the dying sun's rays. Purple liquid dripped from its fangs and claws. Large, razor-like fins arched along its back, and two massive horns sprouted from either side of its head. Its long, feline snout huffed as it prepared to charge Garren once again. It clicked its claws together as it bent lower, digging hooved feet into the solid earth. Garren watched, assessing its stance.

The beast charged headfirst, horns poised to spear him against the boulder, but just before it reached him, Garren spun to the left, bringing his long sword with him and jabbing upward into the beast's middle. But before his weapon connected with the creature, an enormous black shape whipped toward him—the demon had a tail. It collided with Garren and sent him flying through the air and crashing into a tree ten feet away.

"You Gods damned fiend!" Garren roared. "That fucking hurt!" It growled in response, kicking back its hoofed feet and baring its fangs like a bull preparing for another charge.

The demon took off once more, charging with its horns angled straight for Garren at the base of the tree. Garren repeated his stance, rolling to the left just before the demon reached him. It rammed into the tree, one horn driving through to the other side, and roared as it attempted to yank itself free. Its long, reptilian tail whipped about in desperation. Garren leapt up, dodging the flailing tail, and thrust his sword into the demon's neck. It shrieked in pain as Garren twisted the blade before pulling it free. With one final tortured screech, the creature collapsed in front of him.

Garren wiped his blade on the forest floor, painting the grass with the demon's putrid blood. It smelled of sulfur and ash, like most other demons, though the color of the blood was always a surprise.

The first demon he ever killed had blood the color of the turquoise seas found along the southern coast of his home, Cirus. While the second one's blood had matched his blade so perfectly, he wouldn't have even known he cut the creature if it hadn't been dripping off the tip of his sword to form a puddle of liquified silver beside him.

It was peculiar, but Garren had never encountered the same type of demon twice. Each was its own horror, making it increasingly difficult to fight them. It was a matter of figuring out their strengths and weaknesses on the spot. But Garren had always emerged victorious. He had a keen ability to read the creatures' movements, to know their plan before they even began their attack. Every battle had always seemed to play in his favor. He didn't know how he was able to do it, but it was as if he could feel the very essence of the demons through the earth. A vibration that ebbed and flowed, alerting him to when and where they would strike.

This one had initially seemed to be a big dumb brute but had turned out to be cleverer than expected. He hadn't even felt its approach behind him. He would have assumed its sheer size would have shaken the ground or snapped branches as it approached. *Had he been too lost in thought?* This creature was indeed colossal, yet it wasn't the largest demon Garren had ever faced.

At only fourteen, he had taken up a spot on a trading ship, hoping to see more of the world around him. He loved the sea. Those had been some of the best days of his life.

At that point, he hadn't seen a demon in years, not since traveling to the Mines of Durial with his father. He had not been prepared for what he faced in those mines then, and he most certainly had not been prepared for the demon that met him on the sea.

They had been trading on the western coast of the Isle of Thray, their ship, the *Gilded Rose,* anchored out in the Sparkling Sea while the small boats ventured inland to trade their wares. Garren, being a boatswain, stayed on board the vessel when they were anchored for trade.

He had been on the main deck, looking over the port side of the *Gilded Rose,* when a shadow passed beneath the surface of the water and moved under the ship. The next thing he knew, the ship rocked hard to the left, as if something had rammed into it at full speed. The water drew closer as the vessel tipped on its side, and Garren was thrust into the crystal-clear waves as the *Gilded Rose* capsized.

He swam up through the sun-warmed sea, breaking through the surface, treading water as he looked out at the overturned ship and what he saw gave him nightmares to this day. A slimy-skinned creature had wrapped itself around the capsized vessel, coiling like a snake around its prey, squeezing until finally the entire ship gave out, splintering into pieces.

Debris littered the ocean, men flailed, grabbing onto floating pieces of the ship. But Garren wasn't worried about staying afloat. He was a deft swimmer who was always able to hold his breath for far longer than any of his friends growing up. He plunged under the surface, saltwater stinging his eyes, and searched for the creature.

He caught glimpses of shimmering white scales along a long, slim body. Bright yellow fins lined its sides in multiple rows, black and sharp at the tips like daggers. It resembled a giant water millipede.

The beast had been swift, slithering through the ocean with fluid ease. Garren followed it as best he could to get a full view of the water-like insect, and then, when it finally turned toward him, what he saw had him backing away, scrambling to swim as fast as he could in the opposite direction.

Four beady black eyes bore into him, its mouth a circle of layered sharp teeth spiraling down its throat, ready to shred whatever it engulfed. Jutting forth from its torturous mouth of death were four bug-like pincers prepared to pull its prey into the tunnel of endless fangs.

That water beast had been fearsome indeed, but exceedingly dumb. He had led it toward the wrecked ship, swimming for the mainmast which had wedged itself solidly between two enormous rocks on the ocean's floor. It was as if the rocks were caught in a joust, holding out the mast like a lance ready to spear its foe.

Garren had swum for the mast, and the water millipede darted after him at breakneck speed. Garren grabbed onto the mast with both hands, pulling his way down its length until he was at the fractured base on the seafloor. The creature had been traveling so fast, its mouth wide, ready to swallow him whole, that it swam directly into the ship's mast, impaling itself all the way through. Orange liquid spewed forth, bubbling as it rose to the surface of the turquoise water, and its body went limp. A perfect example of a big, dumb brute. He hoped to never come across a beast larger than that sea demon. He still broke out in a cold sweat just thinking about it.

Garren shook the memories aside as he turned to leave the forest, but as he took a step, he felt a sudden sharp pain. *Shit.* The wretched creature had sliced his side. As the adrenaline melted away, red blood welled, spilling down his torso onto his trousers. His wounds healed quicker than most, but this gash was deeper and larger.

Upon closer examination, he could quite literally see the unmistakable white of a rib bone peeking through the ripped flesh. It might actually require some stitching to help it along.

Garren observed his surroundings. The forest had grown preternaturally dark; he could barely see through its girth to where the Daylight road was. He looked up, but the foliage of the trees blocked his view of the darkening sky. Their branches fanned out like a shield above him, giving him a strange, unsettling feeling that they had grown that way to keep something in rather than out. He pushed the dark thought from his mind.

Garren assessed his options. He could head back the way he came, and with luck come across a traveler to hitch a ride with, but it was getting late. The sun would set in another two to three hours, and the chances of stumbling upon somebody were slim.

He was just inside the edge of the Phantom Wood, and he had been told, rather earnestly, that a small town called Sardorf lay somewhere within. However, a small part of him still wondered whether the outlandish story he was told held any truth. He had done his research, but the doubts still crept into his mind.

Garren glanced at the endless forest behind him, full of thick fog and monstrous evergreens, then back toward the road in front of him.

"The Phantom Wood," he mused for the second time this day, narrowing his eyes as he peered back into its gloomy depths. He felt oddly drawn to it, as if it had called out his name, beckoning him within.

This forest was the very reason he had traveled North. Its legends were ancient, each one dark and harrowing. It had all started a fortnight ago during an odd encounter with a man just south of the Red Dunes in Sangalia. Something about the man–his unique looks and the way he told his story–had Garren believing every word he said, so much so that he had ventured all the way north to the Phantom Wood itself.

After being hired to kill a rather remarkably small demon that had nestled itself deep in a mine of underground tunnels beneath Sangalia, digging its way directly into the homes of the city's residents for nightly feasts, the elderly man had pulled Garren aside. His eyes were a dark sapphire rimmed in violet. The strangeness of the desperation within them had drawn Garren's full attention.

"Deep in the Phantom Wood, far north of here, there is a small town. It is called Sardorf," the man had said, voice heavily accented in a garbled sort of way, running the words together until they formed a single word.

Garren had combed through his mind for anything he might know about the Phantom Wood, but had come up empty. He knew nothing of the forest, nor of the town within it.

"The town has been trapped within the forest for centuries, thought to have been long ago abandoned, forgotten through the centuries. No one knows it, but it is still there. Isolated, but there," the man continued.

"And how do you know of this town if, as you say, no one knows it still exists? I myself have not seen it marked on any map."

The man had reached out, gripping Garren's tunic with more strength than he would have expected the old man to have. "Because it is my home."

Garren had examined the man, noticing his unusual clothing, the reddish hue of his graying hair, and back again to those peculiar eyes. "Tell me more," was all he had said, and the man regaled him with a long tale of an age-old demon, full moons, all within the mysteriousness of the Phantom Wood.

What seemed like hours later, Garren had been thoroughly convinced to make the long trek north and attempt to find the lost village of Sardorf.

The man spoke of a bloodthirsty monster that attacked the town every seventy-five years, on the eve of every blood moon. The old man had entered the Phantom Wood, trying to find a way out, desperate to find a way to help his kin, unwilling to let them suffer on the eve as he had. He said that the beast moves swiftly, leaving no living creature in its path, that it would massacre half of his people when the red moon came.

"Where does this monster go between red moons?" Garren had asked.

"No one knows. It hibernates somewhere, possibly in the Phantom Wood, waiting until it can kill again."

The man went on to tell Garren of how he had been lost within the maze of mist and trees for days, his mind foggy and addled until he somehow finally stumbled out at the edge of a Loch. Weak and exhausted, the man had staggered his way along the edge of the Loch, making sure to never step foot back within the forest lest it take hold of him and he would be lost once again, possibly forever.

When he had finally spotted the telltale signs of a town, he wept in relief. He then began his hunt for a savor, for any form of help he could find for his people. The search had led him to Garren.

Garren winced at the aching pain in his side. Far to the east down the Daylight Road was Varian, the Sovereign City, but it was a much greater distance than he could go on foot, especially while wounded. Randier was closer, but still a considerable distance that he wasn't sure he could make. But all that set aside, would he even be able to find this town of Sardorf? What if it truly was a myth–an elaborate fantasy conjured up in the man's aged mind? As soon as that thought sprang forth, a feeling settled deep in his gut that said otherwise, and instinct had not failed him before.

Garren closed his eyes. "Shit," he cursed into the sea of mist and trees. "I guess it's now or never."

He clutched at the gash, blood still leaking through his fingers and down his side. "Right then. Just don't die," he said before walking straight into the Phantom Wood.

5

ORIANA

1st day of the Second Month, 1100

D usk had given way to dawn, and Oriana sat in a ring of flesh and blood.

The night had been a ravage of death. Unable to move, her eyes remained frozen on the shredded corpse of the last person she had devoured. She knew very well that any survivors would be cautiously making their way outside as the sun climbed its way into the cloudless sky. She couldn't be here when they did.

Her hair was matted with the gore of her victims. The gown she wore—once a vivid azure—was now soaked through with a rusty red. Blood. There was so much blood. Unlike the last time, when she remembered only bits and pieces about her night of bloodshed, tonight she remembered everything. Every face, every scream, every thought, and every taste.

It was as if she had been trapped in her own mind, watching the horrors unfold through her eyes, but her control had been severed like a head from its body. Watching her own curved, talon-like nails tear into flesh. She had tried miserably throughout the night of carnage to stop it, to take back her control. But when she finally realized the effort was hopeless, she did the only thing she could. Oriana cowered, forcing herself down into the cavernous pit of her soul, clinging to any good thought, any good deed she had done in the past, desperate to shut out the ravenous slaughter of her bloodlust as it continued to rage through the town.

Her magic had vanished like a breath in the wind, and her bloodlust's whims of death had held her prisoner. Every horrific detail of the night was now forever etched into the forefront of her mind, where she knew it would play over and over again on an endless loop.

Oriana stood, hands shaking and legs wobbling like that of a newborn foal. Anthes had thrust a ruthless curse upon her, and ruthless she had been.

She took a tentative step, checking the strength of her legs. Biting back a cry of harrowed outrage, she clenched her fists and turned toward the paltry forest where she belonged, away from those she would harm, away from whatever semblance of life was left.

And Oriana fled.

She wove through trees, over fallen limbs, and around boulders, never daring to stop even as her lungs grew dry and she wheezed from the exertion. The brush and branches of the forest grabbed at her, threatening to slice through her skin, but she pushed forward. She would have welcomed it, the sting and prick of her flesh being punctured, but it never came. The lack of it–the physical pain, the piercing of her flesh–made it all the more unbearable. She deserved to feel pain, to be stabbed through with a curved blade, ripping through organs and expelling sinew as it was torn free. She deserved the excruciating pain of a thousand terrible deaths, one for each life she had taken. But she could not.

The curse was the only explanation. Anthes didn't want her to be able to end or evade the curse through physical harm or even death. He was cruel indeed.

"Bastard!" she screamed, as if he could hear her.

Oriana didn't stop until she made it back to the barley farm, her legs finally giving out from under her. She fell to her knees in utter torment and came completely undone.

The tears flowed unbidden, streaking lines through the blood caked upon her cheeks; she was too weak to hold them in any longer. She was so exhausted, mentally drained, and no longer able to move.

Oriana lay there, a broken shell of who she once was, remembering her victim's faces and their terror with agonizing detail. She closed her eyes, wishing the images, the screams to go away, but they only grew clearer, louder. It was then that her belly roiled, and she vomited the contents of her stomach onto the cold hard earth until there was nothing left inside of her. She turned her head away from the sick, not wanting to know what had just come up.

Oriana lay there until she had no more tears to shed, every ounce of the salty liquid soaked into the dirt beneath her. Finally, she looked up, taking in the scene of the barley farm, the only place she had thought to go. A place she had begun to call home.

The farm around her was littered with limbs. Red glistened across every surface. It was like an artist had dipped their hand in blood and thrown it in every direction, creating an abstract work of slaughter. An arm rested on a bale of hay, two fingers missing from it. Bile rose in her throat at the thought of where those two fingers were. A decapitated body lay beside the barn, entrails ripped from its middle, pulled across the ground in an array of butchery. Oriana gagged and turned away from it.

She was a monster.

She could still feel the blood of these kills on her flesh. She could hear Liam and his wife's screams in her head and taste their lifeblood on her tongue. See their petrified faces.

Oriana curled herself into a ball in front of the barn, her back turned to what was left of Liam's wife. She shook as she began to dry heave uncontrollably. She had become that which she tried so desperately to suppress her entire life. That part of her that wanted death and destruction enjoyed the idea of torturing, of watching someone's life slowly leak away until there was nothing left but a sack of meat and bone. It was her darkness, her other self.

Ever since she was young, she had felt like two wholly different people, as if two complete and whole consciences were inhabiting the same body. Each one vying for the right to dwell on the surface. It was a constant internal battle, the two consciences forever warring with one another.

Until now, until this curse, she had successfully suppressed her darkness. Her other more prominent half, making up her light and her love, the part she wished to be always on the surface, had been winning. It was only now that the darker self, the true evil that lurked in the shadows of her mind and soul, finally seemed to be set free. It was her bloodlust, her demon, and now she knew that it would have complete control every thirty days on the eve of the full moon. Now truly a separate conscious form. The realization rocked her to her core, dizziness overtook her, and the world began to spin around her.

Anthes's voice came to life in her memories, *"In the cover of night's celestial glow, a lust for blood left hidden will grow."* The words now made perfect sense. How had she not realized it before? She had been in denial.

She had been a fool.

She would now become the part of herself that she wanted to rip from her very soul every single month and if she had only tried to understand, dove back into those agonizing memories to fully grasp the words of the curse, she might have prevented the bloodshed from rearing its ugly head this past night. She could have at least done something–anything–to lessen it.

Oriana wrapped her arms around her torso, rocking back and forth, shutting her eyes tight against the memory that had kept her from analyzing Anthes's words and trying to understand what he had done to her. It was the reminder of what he had done just before he issued the words of his curse that had her pushing the memories away like a plate of spoiled fish.

Chestnut eyes flashed in her vision, the pain and love in them had her choking on a sob as she recalled the moment her heart and soul–the love of her life–crumbled to the ground before her eyes. Darragh had been pure and good; he did not deserve the end he was dealt. The Gods were cruel and mirthless beings, and she wished to see them burn.

She couldn't live like this; she couldn't let this happen ever again. She needed to save the people of this town, prevent her monstrous self from picking off every last living thing in this world. The screams echoed in her mind once more. She shut her eyes against it, "Stop!" and pounded her bloodied hands against the soil beneath her, plumes of dust billowing around her.

Oriana replayed the words of the curse over again in her mind, trying to piece together a way out, a loophole, anything to stop it. The only thing Oriana would bring to anyone was death and despair. She was a bringer of death who deserved no tears and no pity, only an eternity of misery.

There was nothing. No piece of the curse presented a crack to chip away at, a way to navigate through it without harming anyone ever again. She found nothing, and desperation took over.

Something gleamed in the morning rays just outside the barn, a pitchfork leaning against the wooden panels. She crawled her way toward it. She had nothing and no one left. She was all alone.

Grabbing the pitchfork, she ventured into the barn. There, near the barrels of hay, was a small crack in the wooden flooring. She wedged the handle of the pitchfork between the crack in the flooring before climbing up the rickety ladder to the hayloft. At the loft's edge, she stood, staring down at the sharp spikes below.

A world could not exist with her in it. She would be its destruction.

Oriana could not bear the thought of becoming that thing, that monster, every month. The idea of no longer having control, of being fully one person and then the other, was too much. She needed to end it. *No more death* was the only thing going through her head as she fell onto the jutting spikes below. Praying that the Gods would allow her this reprieve, that they would allow the skewers to punch through her flesh, spear her heart, and spill her lifeblood onto the hay-covered floor of the barn. But nothing happened. The tool did not pierce her skin. Her body had just simply bent over the metal as if she was leaning over the wooden beam of a fence before collapsing beneath her weight. No piercing pain or splatter of blood–her skin remained perfectly intact. She shouted at the sky, "You cannot do this to me! Let me end it! Let me be free! Offer me this, I beg of you!"

Even as she said the words, even as she had tried to impale herself on the spikes, she knew it wouldn't work. That she would survive.

She rolled off the broken pitchfork, pushing herself up shakily, taking two unbalanced steps, and sank against the barrels of hay stacked along the side of the barn, weeping.

She sat in the barn until the morning breeze chilled to a bitter cold, and blackness began to take over the cerulean sky. Cold, autumn wind blew leaves the color of apricots and mulled wine across the worn floor as she replayed the events of the past two months in her mind. She needed to find a way out of the curse, to find a way to suppress her darkness once again. She needed to become whole–a single being–and eradicate the monster that had been her constant companion since the day she was born. She needed to venture back to where it had all begun on that fateful night two months prior.

She needed to go to Elscar, the City of Dreams.

Oriana rode through the night and into the late morning of the following day before she made it to Elscar, or what was left of it.

The first time she had ever stepped foot within the city, the splendor and magnitude of it had granted her utterly in awe. She hadn't been able to move from where she had stood just inside the city gates, completely enraptured by the sheer magnificence around her.

People bustled up and down each avenue and winding road. The streets sparkled as if paved with gemstones. Towering structures stretched through the city farther than the eye could see. A bell tolled in the distance, ringing out the time of day.

It had been a place of art and beauty. Everywhere she had looked, she had seen more happiness–pure happiness–than she had beheld in her lifetime. She remembered thinking that she had finally found it after all these years. Home.

Now, the town lay in ruins. The crumbling castle was gone, once a masterpiece of shimmering stone turrets and buttresses, a building of inexplicable grandeur. Now fallen into the craters that covered the land. Buildings had been swallowed whole and forever buried beneath the surface, looking like a graveyard. It was as if the sky had fallen atop it, stars dropping down from the cosmos to lay waste to the town she had started a life in. Her home was barely a whisper of what it once was. A pile of rock and sand. Anthes had wiped the city of Elscar from the face of the earth.

She dismounted from her steed, feet sinking into the soft, upturned sand. A stench of rot and ash hovered over the land. Smoke clouded above it like an angry spirit. People had lived here, wonderful people she had grown to know and love. Now they were gone because of her, turned to dust on the wind.

Oriana sank to her knees, digging pale fingers, still stained red, into the layers of dirt, sand, and ash beneath her. This was all her fault. She should never have come to this place. She had been foolish and naive to think that Anthes would never find her here.

The memories circled like a flock of hungry vultures. She remembered how the moon that night had been the color of a ripe red apple, as if she could pluck it from the sky and take a crisp bite from it. It was a beautiful phenomenon that only happened once every seventy-five years; the villagers had explained. It bathed the town in a mystical haze of oranges, reds, and pinks.

But that night had felt wrong. Something had caused the hairs at the back of her neck to rise, a feeling of apprehension sweeping through her. And then he was there, standing right in front of her as if he had appeared from thin air.

Anthes.

She had frozen where she stood on the glittering cobbled streets of the town's market square, which now lay buried beneath a gaping crater, swallowed whole.

She remembered a soft, warm hand entwining with hers. Turning her head, she had found the most breathtaking light brown eyes greeting her with the love of a thousand lives shining within them.

Tears threatened to spill free, but she held them back. She had wept enough.

Darragh was gone. It would never be the same—she would never be the same—and she would never get over what Anthes had done to her, to these people, and especially to Darragh, the only one who made her soul sing.

Time itself had stopped when she first met Darragh. The world around her had fallen away, leaving only her and him. He had a head of tousled golden chestnut hair and eyes that sparkled with life, framed by soft features and an easy, playful smile. He would carry his painting supplies in a sack upon his back wherever they went. "Ana, my love." he would say, "I wish to paint the evidence of your beauty wherever we are. For it should always be remembered throughout time. The woman who stole the heart of her people, of all of Elscar."

It felt as if her heart had been stabbed through a hundred times over, and she feared the pain of that loss would never leave. What happened here would forever be a stain upon her skin, buried deep.

Oriana closed her eyes as the scene unfolded like the pages of a storybook behind them.

"Hello, Oriana." Anthes's cold voice echoed between the buildings, an indignant smile plastered on his face. Her nostrils flared.

Anthes was a large man, nothing but lean muscle under pale flesh. He stood at least a head taller than everyone in Elscar, and probably all of Svakland. His long white hair was braided back into one thick plait and shorn down completely to his scalp along the sides and around the back. His white beard was clipped short around his angular face. A long sword was slung on his back, an axe gleamed in one hand, and a belt of blades was strapped around his torso.

But it was his eyes that were the very image of death incarnate, identical to the glowing crimson orb in the sky, as red as the blood of a fresh kill.

She had not a moment to process what was happening before Anthes tore a blade from his belt and threw it. The sound of the blade rang out in her ears, cutting through the air as she watched, unable to react fast enough to stop it.

And when she turned to Darragh, she saw his wide eyes full of confusion, fixed on her as he clutched at the hilt of the knife, the blade embedded into his heart. A wail so desperate, so full of heartache, burst from her as she grabbed him, catching him as he crumpled to the ground.

"No!" she shouted. "Darragh, stay with me! Don't go!" But it was too late; there was no life left in his eyes. Her soul mate, her true love, was gone in a scant instant.

She tried to hold it back, tried to stop it from bubbling to the surface like a pot of boiling water, but it was all Anthes needed to do to unleash the monster. Her bloodlust, her thirst for death and destruction, was at the helm, its fury locked on the one man who had leashed it like a pet dog.

She whirled on Anthes. "You will burn for this!" she yelled.

The townspeople around them ran, dispersing into their homes, shops, and buildings. They knew that there was something different about this warrior; probably knew there was something different about her, but they had accepted her, and she loved them for that. These people hadn't asked questions; they had only loved her as one of their own from the moment she set foot in Elscar.

The pain of it hit her all at once, coming to the surface in a wave of misery.

Anthes's words stung as they circled her like a swarm of hungry piranhas. "You sully yourself with the weakness of this place. How dare you taint your soul with their filth. You know it is forbidden; you know the consequences."

Those cruel words had her lunging for him. She attacked, lashing out with her magic and creating an enchantment that grew into a large, double-sided blade. She swung, but Anthes brought forth his axe, parrying her assault.

He laughed, an acrid, haunting sound. "You think you can best me? You are nothing compared to me."

Oriana manifested a flaming whip, flinging it out at him, but Anthes caught it just before it collided with his face, yanking it to tear it free of her grip. Oriana willed it out of existence.

She stabbed her blade forward once again, hoping to catch him off guard, but she should have known better. With a swing of his enormous axe, he shattered her enchanted blade and drove his weapon into the earth below. The ground around them caved in, cracks and fissures splintering out like a spider web in every direction. Buildings collapsed; large gaping holes swallowed entire sections of the town whole. People screamed in fear and all Oriana could do was watch as the City of Dreams crumbled around her. Listen as the screaming died to an eerie silence. Her magic fell useless against the destruction. She couldn't stop it.

They were gone. They were all gone. Darragh was gone. Something inside of her broke, something that could never be repaired.

"You will pay for that," Oriana whispered, low and lethal. She should have led him away from the town, somewhere they could talk in private and fight away from this place, away from these people she called family. But she didn't. She was too full of rage, and the bloodlust wanted revenge.

"Mere cattle to be slaughtered." His voice was calm–too calm. "You will come home, leave this place and continue your duty as overseer."

"No," she spat in response. She would not go with him, she would not live her life the way he wanted, the way the High Council commanded. There was so much more to it. These people had shown her what life could truly be. "No," she choked the words out. "I will not."

"You would defy the High Council for this place? It is your duty. You have no choice."

"You're a monster! You just destroyed this entire town, hundreds of people ruthlessly taken from this world without even a thought! They were living beings, and I loved them!" she howled, tears now freely flowing down her cheeks.

His laugh was cruel and without humor. "You loved them? You fool. You will never be one of us. You are nothing. You want to stay with these people so badly?"

She hadn't given him the pleasure of a response. She would not beg, nor grovel before him. She would rather die than go back and be one of them, the thing that she was destined to be.

"Fine!" he roared, the ground quaking beneath them. "You give me no choice."

She stilled, knowing what was to come. "No," she breathed. "Stop..." But he had already set the words into motion, the spell swirling its way around her.

"In the cover of night's celestial glow,
A lust for blood left hidden will grow.

Two halves at war, broken apart,
Each vying for command over the heart.

The weakness of man your only satiation,
A single choice made will be your salvation.

When the power of crimson reigns free ten times,
Only one can survive and take over the mind."

That was the very last thing she remembered before waking in the field outside of Sardorf. It must have been the first town she came across with life. So much death that night and so much more death to come. She finally felt the full weight of her grief; it felt as if her heart had been torn from her chest and trampled by a team of horses, leaving a gaping hole in its wake.

She remembered her sweet Darragh. The way he called her Ana in their most intimate moments. The feeling of him against her. It was too much. It was all too much! Not only had she lost everything she loved in the cosmos, but she was now stuck in a curse to hurt, to kill this world she loved so much. It was the worst punishment, the most horrid torture.

Orianna cried into the night air, letting her anguish out. She screamed for Darragh and the love they had shared, for Elscar and its people, for Sardorf and the bodies she had left like breadcrumbs in her wake, and finally, she screamed for those she had yet to devour but knew she inevitably would.

After a long while, when her voice diminished to nothing but a breath, she got back on her mare and began the long journey back to Sardorf.

Oriana avoided the town of Sardorf and made her way directly to the barley farm. She burned the bodies of the farm's owners–her friends. She cleaned the blood and filth from every surface.

And then she came to sit in the center of the farm, legs crossed, hands resting on her knees, eyes closed. She breathed in deeply, chest rising with the effort, shoulders relaxing as she took in her surroundings. A soft breeze whispered through the trees, sharing secrets of yesterday and thoughts of tomorrow. As her body and mind found peace, she reached down into the depths of her magic and brought forth the enchantment she had brewed in her mind during the ride back from Elscar. The world around her changed as if a giant wave of air had risen above everything only to come crashing down upon it, creating something new in its wake.

The small forest began to grow and spread around her. The once thin, leafless trees thickened into mountainous evergreens that reached farther and farther into the sky as her enchantment took root. Their branches lengthened into sharp, needle-like foliage that fanned out wide above and below. Mist descended, weaving its way through pine and bark like a snake, filling the forest with a murky white, hiding both light and sight within the newfound darkness of the woods.

When her enchantment was complete, a hush settled over the now vast forest. No birds sang, no rodents scurried over branch or through brush; not even the distant chirping of insects could be heard in its depths, only the soft rustle of pine and low creak of wood as the trees moved, shifting their maze of shadow and gloom. It was a dark wood, created to addle the mind. To trap those who entered, a prison for her dark passenger.

For she knew that when she transformed into the monster, the forest would be her bastille. A labyrinth of pine and mist, ever-changing. A cage to keep her inside. She just hoped that, on the eve of the next full moon, it would work.

6

ORIANA

30TH DAY OF THE NINTH MONTH, 1749

Oriana caressed her forest of enchantment.

She breathed it in, sending out tendrils of magic to prod the mist and tweak the trees, persistently altering their position, creating an unsolvable maze to keep her inside. She reached out feeling for any living creature within the gloom, ensuring that she was completely alone within her dark forest.

"Well, dearest sister, what a lovely little predicament you've gotten yourself into."

Oriana spun, annoyance sagging her shoulders at who stood before her. "Aren't you supposed to be locked in the pits of Morial?" she sighed.

"Oh, that boring place." Orrick waved his hand flippantly. "I got out of there ages ago. What dimwitted warlord Anthes seemed to forget is that the pits of Morial can't hold me, not truly, anyway."

"Why have you come here?" Oriana gritted her teeth, dreading her brother's reply.

"Well, to see my dearest sister, of course! Imagine my surprise to find out you had also been banished, and cursed at that! Bad luck indeed," Orrick drawled.

She rolled her eyes. "Well, now you've seen what's become of me. Time to leave."

"Oh no, you can't be rid of me that easily. I want to see you in action." His eyes were alight with mischief. "You have done a lovely job of terrifying the townspeople with this forbidding forest. They won't even come near it. I've been to the village you've trapped here and heard the horrid stories they tell their children." He glanced at her with an impressed smirk. "Supposedly whoever goes into the Phantom Wood on the full moon never comes out. Oh, and beware the eve of the blood moon, for the White Demon will steal you into the night and bathe in your blood to keep her youth. Such tales, sister. So, tell me, how long has it been since you've feasted on their blood?" A wicked grin spread across his lips.

She began walking away from him without a response. He moved swiftly in front of her, blocking her path.

"I'll take that as an exceptionally long time." Orrick placed a hand on her shoulder, spinning her around and wrapping his arm around her neck so that her back was flush with his chest.

She stiffened, every hair along her arms and neck raising in rapt attention and fear for what was about to come.

"Let's change that, shall we?" Orrick chided, tightening the arm he had locked around her quivering throat so that she could not move her head. She brought her hands up, pulling at his arm, but it wouldn't budge. He was too strong.

She looked upward through the treetops at the swiftly dimming sky. Tonight was the full moon, and he knew it. She brought an elbow into his stomach, desperate to be released from his hold, but he only pushed the attempts away with his other hand. "Orrick, let go." She squirmed, digging her nails into his flesh without making so much as a scratch on his skin.

"And miss all the fun? I think not, sister." He chuckled as the forest around them darkened; the night was quickly falling upon them and the full moon was not far behind.

Oriana thrashed in his grip until a yellow haze cut through the darkness and she froze, standing as still as a doe caught in a hunter's sight.

The change began, and Oriana moaned as she felt it. The feeling had become all too familiar. She hated how natural it felt, as if it was a daily occurrence. It honestly seemed like it was after all this time. She had lost count of how many years she had been inflicted with this malediction.

"Very interesting," Orrick mused behind her.

She growled, the need for blood like a tangible thing moving through her. It had been years since she had last fed, since she had torn skin from bone, ripped muscle from bodies, tasted fresh blood on her lips. She smiled broadly and maliciously at the thought, revealing her horrifying rows of pointed fangs prepared to shred any living thing in their path.

As if sensing this, Orrick forced her to walk, never lightening his hold around her. As they trod forward through the fog, a young man, just barely into adulthood, came into view.

"I found you a nice little snack, dear sister. It seems he unknowingly wandered into your forest on the eve of the full moon. How ill-advised." Oriana could feel Orrick's expression spread into a sinister smile behind her. She snarled, squirming against Orrick's hold.

The man's eyes widened in sheer terror as he beheld her. She bit down on her lip, drawing blood, and stilled, cocking her head to the side–a predator assessing its prey.

"Your dinner awaits, sister," Orrick whispered, and then released her. Like an arrow drawn back taught before being released from its bow, she took off for the youngling.

The man turned sharply, sprinting away, but the fog was too thick. The trees shifted with each step and he stopped, completely blind to the haze that surrounded him. Oriana had been close behind, following his every move, waiting for this moment, for his confusion to set in, for the forest to trap him just as it trapped her from breaking free, from ravaging Sardorf and the other Northern towns. The man spun in circles, distressed, unable to find a way through the mist.

She heard his blood pumping through his veins, his heartbeat quickening with panic. It was music to her ears. She dove for him, jagged teeth baring into his neck, nails tearing through flesh. She drank deeply, feasting on his warmth, delighting in the kill. Ripping her teeth from his neck, she tore a chunk of skin and muscle free. Dark red blood sputtered from his neck in streams as he sank to his knees, choking as his life slowly drained from him. Oriana placed both clawed hands in the gaping wound and pulled, ripping his head from his body. She closed her eyes and breathed in the scent of his blood, the smell of death, running her tongue along the torn flesh at the base of his decapitated head.

"My, my sister, that was very...enlightening." Orrick's eyes danced with mischief as if uncovering some masterful discovery. "If you run, you might just find a few more surprises in this brilliant maze of yours."

"Why are you doing this?" She ground out, desperately fighting against the monster.

Orrick's jade eyes grew dark as a storm-swept sea. "Because he chose you. He has always chosen you."

She growled, whirling in his direction and leaping for him, but he was already gone.

PART TWO

THE PHANTOM WOOD

7

GARREN

30TH DAY OF THE TENTH MONTH, 1774

G arren's side burned as he trekked through the forest. "Gods…" he groaned, grasping at the wound the blasted demon had inflicted upon him. His hand came away wet with blood. The gash wasn't clotting. His legs felt heavy as if his boots were made of iron.

The forest was unnervingly quiet, devoid of the usual sounds you would hear in the deep wood. No sound of small animals moving about, the call of a falcon, or the rustle of leaves on a swift gust of wind.

The trees were thick with rough-hewn emerald needles. They towered above him, nearly reaching higher than he could see. Their gnarled branches creaking on a non-existent breeze was the only sound that could be heard. The needles of the pines just brushed the top of his head as he limped beneath them.

For a moment, he could have sworn a branch trailed after him, reaching out for another fleeting touch of his hair. He turned sharply, but nothing followed. Garren narrowed his eyes, pushing forward through the seemingly endless wood.

The towering evergreens, although haunting, were quite majestic and beautiful, if he was being honest. He had not seen trees this colossal or spectacular in all of Svakland. They were near perfection, but their stillness created an otherworldly sensation that sent his skin crawling.

Specks of dust floated ahead of him and danced in the golden rays of the dying sun, turning them into shimmering flecks of gold that swam through the mist swirling around him. It was magical, yet so out of place in the dark and menacing forest.

It was called the Phantom Wood for those who had supposedly gotten lost in its tangled web of fog and trees. The old man had told Garren that the legend of the forest dated back centuries.

"When the moon grows full," the old man said as he gazed up at the clear desert night sky, *"the trees move on their own accord, and the mist grows thicker, trapping those who enter its lair, feeding on their souls until they are nothing but a ghost added to the haze."*

Garren was witnessing firsthand the way the forest seemed to shift as he moved through it, the mist hanging heavy in the air and clinging to him like an unwanted cloak as he trudged onward. But the full moon was still a day away. If the forest was this disorienting now, he couldn't imagine what it would be like on the night of a full moon. It was a wonder the man had made it out of this place at all.

But it wasn't the unnatural nature of it that urged him to venture within its depths. No, it was the much darker legend the man had regaled him with.

The legend of the White Demon.

As the elderly man had spun his tale of the creature, Garren had become more and more enraptured with each word.

"The legend of old speaks of a barbaric demon that comes from the Phantom Wood on the eve of the red moon to feed on the blood of the innocent." The old man wove his tale. *"It is only this night, once every seventy-five years, that the bloodthirsty demon appears. Where it lingers in between, no one knows. But the blood moon will show itself once again in just a few short months. I fear for my people. I fear for the devastation that is to come."*

Garren had spent the past weeks scouring texts and tomes wherever he could for mention of the beast. However macabre, the idea of the creature excited him. The mystery was far different from any other demon he had encountered in the past twenty years. None had disappeared, only to return at a specific point in time decades later. Where was it hiding in between? Where did it go for those seventy-five years?

Yes, this creature was something else entirely.

It was at least several centuries old if the man had his facts straight. It sounded like a tall tale. Something parents told their children to keep them from behaving poorly. Like the stories his mother had told him as a child of nymphs, djinns, and ghouls. Stories passed down through the generations with no concrete proof to back them up, the details altered with each retelling.

Garren had found no mention of this White Demon in any of the texts in Sangalia. However, he had found mention of the wood in a particularly ancient tome. Even so, it held nothing of significance. No actual knowledge of the forest or the creature. It had essentially been a long-winded warning to deter anyone from trying to enter the cursed place. But even if the demon didn't exist and was simply a figment of the elderly man's imagination, Garren felt called to investigate. He was a demon hunter, after all.

He had fought and defeated many demons over the years. It wasn't until three years after that first encounter in his father's smithy–in his fifteenth year–that he fully grasped the existence of demons and their detriment to Svakland.

He remembered it all too well. It was the night he vowed to hunt and kill the creatures, to rid the world of their pestilence.

The sharp sting in his side brought him back to the task at hand. He needed to find Sardorf.

That was another thing he had found no mention of in the texts, Sardorf. So his mission was truly based entirely on an old man's word. "Blasted skies..." he murmured, his voice uncannily loud in the ominous quiet.

His movements were becoming increasingly more difficult. Sweat ran down his face and into his eyes, blurring his vision. Without a breeze filtering through the trees to cool his overheated body, he was beginning to stumble, and black spots danced in his view. The fog didn't help as it continued to cling to him like a constant weight on his back. The air was thick enough to be considered something else entirely. It pulled the breath from his lungs.

What the hell is this place?

The hair on his nape prickled as a shiver raked down his spine. The trees stared down at him like looming stone giants watching his every move. The quiet of this place was overwhelming, somehow worse than the deafening sound of a horde of people. The harsh stagnant air masked even the sounds of his own movement through the forest. Garren stuck a finger in his ear, rubbing it back and forth to ensure he hadn't somehow lost his hearing.

The mythical place was playing tricks on him. As he progressed further, he could have sworn that a few of the trees flickered in the corner of his sight as if they were translucent, disappearing before reappearing in the blink of an eye. He turned sharply, wrinkling his brow when they stood solid before him. He shook his head, blinking rapidly to clear his vision. *Was he hallucinating?*

He didn't like it; the feel of this place was wrong. Garren attempted to quicken his pace, but it was as if he were walking through quicksand. He dragged his feet along, rubbing at his eyes as they blurred even more.

He looked up through the tops of the trees and squinted to find the moon peering down at him. *How long had he been in the Phantom Wood? Had it been hours already?*

It was an utter miracle that the old man had made it out of this place alive. Curse him. Had the man led him into some kind of hell on earth? There was no way he had made it through this place. He had to have been confused, pulling from a story he remembered in the back of his mind and melding it into truth until he believed it to have actually happened to him. Had Garren really traveled all this way on an elderly man's muddled remembrance? His mind continued to circle on that thought with each halting step. Well, it was too late now, and the way the man had spoken of it had sparked something within Garren, making him take it for truth.

Garren felt himself being pushed further into the forest floor with every stride. He hunched over, sluggish and slow as the pain in his side worsened, and he began to wheeze, unable to pull enough air into his lungs. *Was the fog getting thicker?*

With a glance back up at the canopy of the evergreens, he found that a shining morning sun was there, just barely peeking its way through the thick trees. *Hadn't it just been evening? Was it a new day already? What was happening?* He had to be hallucinating.

Garren's heart raced, and his entire body shook with trepidation as he grew more desperate for escape. He stumbled over root and stone with every step, vision narrowing and blackness closing in on all sides. A ceaseless ringing began in his ears. It felt as if the forest was sucking the very life from him.

Just as he thought he couldn't go any further, a bright light shone in the distance. He pulled himself toward it, grabbing onto branches and pushing against tree trunks until he finally saw what looked to be a small clearing up ahead. Brilliant golden light beckoned him forward.

With one last push, he stepped out of the darkness and into the light, adjusting his eyes to find the glowing outline of a woman standing before him. And then the world went black.

8

ORIANA

31ST DAY OF THE TENTH MONTH, 1774

Sunlight streamed through the canopy of trees, basking Oriana and the world around her in its golden warmth. She bent down to a lush purple flower, brushing her fingers across the delicate petals before breathing in its laden fragrance. Oriana closed her eyes. The scent reminded her of her mother. She had always smelled like violets.

Blowing out a heavy breath, she opened her eyes and headed into her cottage to perch herself upon the small bed in the corner. The woolen blankets dragged on the floor as she pulled them across her shoulders. Hugging her knees tight against her chest, Oriana rested her chin upon them as she let a weary sigh escape her.

It wasn't often she thought of her family. It had been many years since she had seen any of them. But that small memory of her mother had brought up thoughts of them, specifically of her brother, Orrick.

It had been twenty-five years since her bloodlust had killed. Twenty-five short years since her brother had visited, luring those poor innocent souls into her lair. *The fucking bastard,* she thought. Her nostrils flared as her lip turned up into a snarl.

Since Oriana had created her enchanted forest, the Phantom Wood, the townsfolk called it; she had learned several things about her curse.

For one, her dark proprium reared its ugly head every full moon, threatening to wreak havoc and taking complete unyielding control of her person. Once in her demon state, her magic could not be used. Not by the monster nor by the light locked within herself–a prisoner forced to watch the horrors unfold at her own hand.

The absence of her magic was jarring. It felt as if an arm had been severed from her body. A piece of her gone, leaving a raw gaping hole in its place.

Luckily, any enchantment already set into motion or solidified when not a creature of death held firm. Meaning her magic was only gone from her person, not the world around her. It also meant that her Phantom Wood did exactly what she had planned it to do. It locked the monster of bloodlust inside, leaving it to circle the forest labyrinth and seek the freedom to feast. Not once had her demon broken free of the forest during the full moon. The blood moon, however, was a different story.

Anthes had given the rise of the blood moon significance within the curse. Every seventy-five years, when that full glowing orb bathed the world in its ruby beams, her forest no longer held her. The monster would break free, heading straight for the closest thrum of life, Sardorf. There was nothing she could do. She had tried everything she could to break free and stop the bloodshed, pushing against the control that the bloodlust had, but it was too strong, and she was too weak. So, she was forced to give up and watch, trying to block out as much of the carnage as she could.

Oriana thought back to the lives she had stolen on the night of her brother's visit. Their faces forever etched in her mind, mingled with her countless other victims. The youngest of them, the man that she had savagely decapitated, had not been from Sardorf. His fair complexion and frosted blue eyes had her guessing he was from the frozen city of Frosborg, far north over the mountain pass. It didn't feel like twenty-five years since that night.

With only three short months until the next blood moon, her anxiety and trepidation were high, rising far above the clouds with each dire thought. Without the forest to hold her, how much damage would she cause on that one night? How many would lose their lives?

And there was one slice of understanding clawing at her, trapped in the back of her mind. She knew one thing for sure, one thing that the curse had made very clear. *When the power of crimson reigns free ten times, only one can survive and take over the mind.* Once the tenth blood moon rose, the monster would be all that was left.

Oriana forced the thoughts from her head, stamping them out as if they were pesky bugs that had snuck under the covers.

Centuries had passed with no change and no inclination as to how she could break free of the curse. She had spent decades trying to find a way out, but it was no use. She had come up short every time. Too many times, she believed she had figured it out–cracked the riddle–but her bloodlust would gain full control once again every full moon. After so many years of fighting, she had come to the tragic conclusion that it was pointless. She couldn't suppress it. The bloodlust was inevitable.

Tonight was another full moon, which only meant another month had come and gone. And she would spend another month wallowing in self-pity and misery. She was tired, so inexplicably tired.

And so she spent most of her time sequestered in the small cottage on the old barley farm, which had become overgrown with weeds and ivy that snaked its way through the entire farm, invading every corner with its twisting vines. On occasion, she ventured into Sardorf to help

Haldis, the village healer. It was her way of trying to give back and help save lives rather than take them. It was her only reprieve for what she had done, but it didn't truly cancel out the horrors she had committed. It only made her feel a bit better for a fleeting moment, and then the memories, the bloodied faces of her victims, would swim back into her vision like a school of fish swarming around a piece of discarded bread.

Oriana had only gone to help Haldis once in the past month. It was during an unfortunate outbreak of lung fever, a terrible illness that filled the lungs with fluid, effectively drowning a person from the inside. She remembered when the sickness had first come to Sardorf many decades ago. It had wiped out half the village. Some survived, but most died. It had been during the blood moon, fitting that an atrocious sickness would infect Sardorf during the only time when the Phantom Wood could no longer keep her trapped.

There were not many healthy lives to feast on that day. Her bloodlust turned away, revolted by the sickness that plagued the villagers. She remembered the smell of them, pungent and harsh like meat that had been left to rot in the sun for days. The repulsion had sent her traveling west to Bone Lake, to the town on the other side, to feast on healthy flesh.

With a huff of resignation, Oriana unfolded herself from her bed and ventured outside, looking back at her small cottage now covered in the most vivid array of colors, magnificent flowers that only grew in the southern region of Svakland. A lush, flowing bouquet of yellow, pink, purple, and orange sprouted from every crack and crevice. In a dark existence, one must find beauty where they can. And so, Oriana had used her magic to create it around her. Whereas the forest was dark and ominous, a maze of looming emerald pines and twisting branches that moved, fabricating a labyrinth of nature, her small corner of it was filled with babbling brooks, lush gardens and clear blue skies. It was a bubble of paradise, a utopia of her own making. A small piece of heaven in her own living hell. It mocked her.

Oriana closed her eyes and listened to the trickle of water over rocks, the singsong chirping of birds overhead, and the soft rustle of her gardens as a fresh autumn breeze moved over them. But above the peaceful sounds of her enchantment was one that did not belong. One that was not hers.

Her eyes shot open at the sound of something stumbling its way through her forest. It sounded as if it was coming right for her and would soon invade her ring of bliss, but that couldn't happen—it wasn't possible. The enchantment was meant to deter any trespassers from her sanctuary. To lead them far away.

Suddenly, a large form came into view, pushing its way through the darkness of her forest. Her eyes widened and her heart picked up speed. What was it? She thought of only one person–Anthes. She took a shaking step back toward her cottage, but then a thick, tanned arm shot through into the light and an unrecognizable figure stumbled forward not long after, collapsing face down directly in front of her.

"What in the name of the Gods..." She bent down and gingerly poked his shoulder. He moaned in response. Kneeling, she placed two hands on his shoulder and pushed to roll him onto his back. He was large, with skin deeply tanned and covered in hard muscle. A thick beard stubbled his square face, his features lean and sharp. His dark hair was slick and dripping with sweat, curling down just below his ears in a shaggy mess of waves. Small wisps of silver mingled with what almost looked like blue-tinted locks. *Curious*, she thought, squinting her eyes to distinguish its true color.

He was young, possibly in his late twenties or early thirties. A large scar carved a jagged line along the side of his face, from his forehead down through his temple and toward the curved top of his ear, which looked to have a small chunk ripped from it. His breathing was shallow, chest rising and falling in an uneven rhythm. And he was covered in blood.

Oriana examined the wound at his side. She breathed in sharply at the sight of black tendrils snaking their way outward from the deep gash. The bleeding had stopped, but the entire wound was now black and swollen. It was hot to the touch.

"Poison," she murmured. If not treated soon, he would surely die. As if sensing her thought, the man groaned and his eyes fluttered open, peering into hers. She pushed herself away from him. When in this place, she held no enchantment over her features but instead left her true self unmasked. Her white, flowing hair cascaded down her back in loose waves, as her green eyes glowed bright in the light of her paradise, a stark contrast to her pale skin.

He gripped her wrist weakly, pulling her back toward him with a manic look in his silver eyes.

"You've been poisoned," she said, yanking her wrist from his grasp before bringing the back of her hand to rest on his forehead. He was burning with fever.

"You need a healer." She pushed herself away from him once again.

"Could you bring one?" his voice rasped in return. "I don't think I can stand."

Oriana turned her head sharply, avoiding his intense gaze.

"I...I can't go into the village," she sputtered. The full moon was only a few hours away. But this man was poisoned. She knew he likely wouldn't survive beyond the early hours of the morning, not without help. She glanced at the sky, assessing how long she had before sunset. She would most certainly not bring Haldis into the wood, especially not tonight. "I will get you as close as I can, but you will need to do the rest from there."

He gave a barely perceptible nod. "Thank you."

She crept her way closer, still wary, and reached to grab his outstretched arm. She gripped his forearm, his grasp already feeling considerably weaker than just moments before, and yanked to pull him upward. He growled, barely moving an inch. "Sorry," he muttered.

She said nothing, only bent down to wrap her arms around him and pull him into a sitting position. "Sodded demon," he grumbled. "What has it fucking done to me? I can't feel my right arm."

"Demon?" she asked, grabbing both arms and pulling hard, finally bringing him into a hunched standing position.

"I'm a demon hunter." He gritted his teeth as his wound stretched, oozing putrid black liquid. "I killed one just before coming into the wood, but it wounded me."

Oriana furrowed her brow. What sort of creatures was this man speaking of? As far as she was concerned, she was the only demon in this world. She didn't question him further, only draped his arm over her shoulder and began to help him back into the forest from which he came.

She practically dragged him through her Phantom Wood, his legs barely moving in assistance. The gash on his side looked worse with each passing moment. They were almost to the clearing, and she could see the soft light of the village filtering through the trees up ahead.

Oriana stiffened, biting her lip anxiously as the evening only grew dimmer. She needed to be far away from Sardorf–before the full moon rose–far away from her people, her town.

In the past centuries, her demon had only escaped the Phantom Wood and fed on the innocent nine times–the same number of blood moons that had passed since the curse.

On the blood moon, the forest did nothing to imprison her in its maze. Instead, it somehow froze in time, the magic stuck as if iced over. A condition of the curse she knew Anthes had deliberately put in place, weaving it into his words masterfully. For he knew of her power of enchantment, knew she would attempt to bypass the effects of the curse any way she could.

"Bastard," Oriana said through clenched teeth.

The man only groaned in response.

She remembered back to the first blood moon, when she realized its significance. She had secured herself within the forest per usual, making sure the beast would be locked within its cage of trees.

She had been far north when the moon rose, near the Mountain Pass that led to Frosborg. She remembered crossing the pass, seeing the sparkling spires of gold with tips of blue, green and purple that blossomed outward, giving the appearance of candied gum drops. As she drew closer to the snow-covered city, she could hear the beating of a thousand hearts which had only caused her bloodlust to pick up speed. With each step the beating grew louder until she was there, catching them unawares. The massacre that ensued far surpassed that of Sardorf.

The city of Frosborg had been celebrating the new year coming in the morning. It was a festival that went from dusk till dawn. But that eve when the snow turned red, not only from the moon shining high above, but from the blood of so many souls torn to shreds, it was the last eve that Frosborg had ever celebrated the coming of the new year.

The few survivors took it as an omen that the Gods were angry with their celebration because it was of the new year and not in honor of the Gods.

That was a night she wished to forget, but the visions swam behind her eyes every time she shut them.

Oriana could not shake the memories loose, could never stop the remembrance of her killing from remaining at the forefront of her mind. She brought herself back to the present and continued pulling the large man along to what she could only hope would be his salvation.

By the time Oriana and the wounded man stumbled their way out of the forest, the sun had almost completely retreated behind the White Giants.

Standing at the edge of the tree line, Oriana could see that lanterns were being lit, illuminating the town of Sardorf as the impending darkness of the evening crept in around them.

"There's the town. See that gray building there?" She pointed. The man's gaze moved slowly, a fog hovered over his eyes. "That's where the village healer is. Go there and she will help you. This is as far as I can take you."

She let go of him and he instantly crumpled to the ground. Oriana cursed and crouched over him, shaking his shoulder. "You have to stay awake. Open your eyes. You have to walk the rest of the way on your own." He didn't respond; the delirium of fever had fully overtaken him. She cursed again, frantically looking at the sky; it was only moments before the full moon and she needed to get far inside the forest before it was too late. But this man wouldn't make it that long.

She snarled, huffing at the stupidity of what she was about to do. Throwing an enchantment back over her features, she wrapped her arms around the man's torso and began dragging him to the healer's cottage.

9

GARREN

2ND DAY OF THE ELEVENTH MONTH, 1774

*G*arren wiggled his toes as they sank into the soft orange sand of his homeland, Cirus. The vast desert spread out farther than the eye could see, nothing but dunes for miles. He spun, looking for his parents' home, but each way he turned there was nothing but more sand. The blazing sun beating down upon his back urged him forward. With each step, his feet sank further into the velvety sand, slowing his progression. He grunted with each step as he was only dragged further beneath its soft surface until he was waist deep, struggling to move within the sand's firm grip.

Garren grabbed for purchase to break free, but with each movement, the sand continued to swallow him. He frantically dug with his hands, but those, too, were sucked beneath the surface. He writhed and cried out for help as *the sand crested his head. Closing his eyes and holding his breath, he awaited his impending doom, but it never came.*

Garren opened his eyes to discover that he was standing in a room, one he knew well. As he scanned the living room of his childhood home, his eyes landed on the kitchen table, and he cried out, falling to his knees and vomiting up the contents of his stomach.

Before him sat his mother and father, their skin tinged with the pale gray hue of death. He looked into their lifeless eyes, terror still frozen in their milky depths. As his eyes traveled down further, Garren vomited once again. Their chests revealed what had killed them in the form of large gaping holes where their hearts should have been. He let his gaze travel even further to the table they sat at, where their hands sat, an eating utensil still held in each of their grasps, but what lay on their dinner plates was not a meal. It was their missing hearts. Blood oozed from the no longer beating organs.

Suddenly, his father's hand moved limp and lifeless, like a puppet on a string, toward the plated heart. His eyes shot up to his father's face and, to his utter horror, he spoke. "You could have saved us." His father's voice was heavy and garbled as thick, dark blood leaked from his lips. "You should have saved us."

And then his mother's head turned to him, lolling like a rag doll's as she spoke one small word, "Why?" But Garren hadn't the time to respond to either of his parents before the ground beneath his feet turned to sand and he was sinking once again. "No!" he yelled, struggling to pull his feet out from the sinking sand, but it only dragged him down faster. "No!" he cried out once more, catching a final glimpse of his parents' butchered bodies before he stood on solid ground again, this time in complete darkness.

An arm wrapped around his neck from behind, cutting off his air supply. He choked, gripping the arm. It was cold as ice, skin slick as glass. Hot breath steamed at the nape of his neck as something wet licked behind his ear. A fleeting sideways glance revealed a wide mouth of pointed teeth ready to puncture his throat and a large set of feline eyes, alight with exhilaration.

It was her. The demon from his father's smithy all those years ago, and it wanted revenge. Garren ripped the demon's arm free of its hold around his neck, yanking the creature over his back as he bent forward. It hit the floor with a crack, letting out in a shrill, high-pitched wail that sent his ears ringing. He stalked toward it, but suddenly it vanished and in its place were his parents' bodies. They writhed on the floor as if possessed, and he stumbled backward.

"Mother? Father?" he called, his voice echoing around him.

Finally, they stopped moving. He walked tentatively toward them. "Mother? Father?" he said once again, kneeling between their inert forms and reaching a hand out toward his mother. Her hand shot out, gripping his wrist as

she sat up. It was not his mother who stared back at him, but
the demon who had killed her. "Hello, Garren."

Garren gasped for breath, bolting upright, ripping
himself from the horrific dream. Sweat trickled down his
forehead and chest as he breathed in a heaving lungful
of air. His head was pounding. The ceiling above moved
in circles, making him feel nauseated. It had been many,
many years since dreams of his parents' deaths had plagued
him. Yet even twenty years later, he still couldn't get that
horrifying scene from his mind. It was on that fateful day
that he swore to dedicate his life to fighting the demon filth
tormenting Svakland.

Garren blinked the sleep from his eyes, rubbing them
until he could see properly. *Where am I?*

Garren groaned and attempted to push himself up, but
a small, wrinkled hand shoved him back down. An elderly
woman leaned over him. "You need to rest," she clicked.
"You've had a nasty little accident."

"How long have I been here?" he croaked. His throat felt
as if he had swallowed hot coals.

The old woman offered him a cup of water, and he took
it gratefully. "You've been here two days. Your fever has
finally broken, but your wound has not healed enough.
Although," she said, "it seems to be healing much quicker
than I would have thought."

"Where am I?" he questioned, eyes searching the small
room around him. By the door was a wooden chair, along

the opposite wall was a worktable, and above that a small window, the only source of light in the compact space. "How did I get here?"

"You're in Sardorf. My young helper, Oriana, brought you here. She's come back each day to see how you are faring." The woman took the cup of water from him and walked over to the workspace. "She found you on the edge of the Phantom Wood. What were you doing in that place on the eve of the full moon? Bad things happen in that forest during the full moon. It is a cursed place," she mused, concocting an ointment at the table, which was covered in dried herbs and various jars of colorful liquids.

Garren didn't respond. It hadn't been the night of the full moon when he'd gone into the Phantom Wood. He had heard the legend, knew the lore of the place, and knew that to go into that forest on the night of the full moon was a death sentence. Had he really been in the forest for almost two whole days?

His trek through the forest was a massive blur. He remembered very little aside from a pair of stunning bright eyes the color of fresh spring leaves.

A soft knock interrupted the thought, and the door creaked open just a hair. "Haldis?" came a soft, disembodied voice from behind it.

"Come," the woman beckoned, still fixed on her work.

A petite woman with thick auburn hair, soft features, and eyes like a clear morning sky stepped into the room.

She wore a white linen blouse with a dark blue overskirt and a black belt. Garren found himself thinking how perfectly ordinary she was. Yet, he instantly lost the thought as her subtle, lyrical voice rang out again. "You're awake?" she said, cautiously coming to his bedside.

"Ah, yes," Haldis cut in, bringing whatever salve she had just made with her as she joined them. "Oriana is the one that found you in the field and brought you here." Her face fell into a frown momentarily as her eyes darted to the young woman so quickly he almost didn't catch it. "Oh my! I just realized we don't know your name."

"Garren," his voice came out gruffer than intended, hoarse from disuse.

"Well, Garren, it's very nice to officially make your acquaintance. You gave us quite a scare for a while. We weren't sure you would ever wake. But yesterday, your wound made exceptional progress. If I didn't know better, I would say the Gods looked kindly on you." Haldis dipped two fingers into the paste she had just prepared and rubbed it onto Garren's side. "Quite extraordinary."

"Thank you," Garren interrupted, turning to look at Oriana. "For bringing me here." He took a moment to assess her stature. How had this girl brought him here? She looked to weigh about as much as his right thigh. She couldn't be any taller than his shoulder.

She smiled meekly in response, looking down at her interlaced fingers held tightly in front of her.

"Lucky she found you when she did." Haldis began as if she had never stopped talking. "If you had still been in the wood once the full moon rose...well you would have been lost forever, merely a whisper among that dreadful place. How did you make it through the forest?"

Garren observed as Oriana furrowed her brows ever so slightly at Haldis's words. He shifted his focus back to the older woman to see her weary shoulders shrug upward at her reaction, which only seemed to make Oriana frown further.

"I honestly don't remember." He could remember bits and pieces, but it felt fuzzy in his mind, and his head hurt trying to bring it back into focus.

A silence fell between them at his words before Haldis said, "I've a few books I need to look through downstairs. Don't go anywhere."

He only nodded in response as she slowly took her leave.

Another, far more awkward silence filled the room as Garren glanced at the auburn-haired woman, narrowing his eyes at her twig-like arms.

Oriana's voice was gentle–almost harmonic–when she finally spoke. "I'm glad to see you're awake and faring well after your injury. What sort of blade cut you? Your wound was full of a gruesome black poison."

He looked away from her, furrowing his brow in contemplation. "It was not a blade," he murmured.

It was rare for a demon to succeed in injuring Garren. In fact, he could only recall two instances beforehand. It wasn't that he couldn't be hurt or sliced; it just took a lot of force to do so. Neither of those wounds had carried a poison or venom, and none had knocked him down this hard. But this demon had been far different than any he had faced before. Each one he came across seemed more menacing than the last. They were getting stronger.

"Then what cut you?" Oriana questioned. Her face had grown somber and her eyes intense, almost glowing with curiosity.

"A monster," Garren said, watching as an indiscernible flash of emotion passed across Oriana's face.

She opened her mouth to speak but was cut off as Haldis walked back into the room, setting a book onto the table. "You need your rest if that wound is to continue its healing. Come, Oriana, let's leave him be. We'll come back with your supper in a few hours."

He watched as Haldis shooed Oriana out of the room, shutting the door behind them.

Alone, Garren stood up, his head pounding for a few moments from the sudden rush of blood. His side pulled tightly where the newly healed skin had created an angry, puckered scar. *That's different*, he thought.

Garren sighed solemnly, closing his eyes and rolling his shoulders back, stretching the tightened muscles. How had he been out for two days? Nothing had ever kept him down that long–or at all, now that he really thought about it. He raked a hand through his hair in consternation. Every wound a demon had inflicted upon him had healed within minutes, never a few days or even a few hours. It was unsettling. And the fact that he had stumbled around that forest for almost two days unawares and then been comatose for another two days was more than unsettling. It was downright terrifying. What did it mean?

Had it been the forest that had somehow slowed down his healing, making the wound worse than it actually was. He understood why Haldis had called it cursed, something about it had felt unnatural, but he couldn't quite place his finger on why. There was no place in Svakland that even compared.

He touched the swollen skin on his side and wrinkled his brows as the unease continued to sweep its way over him. He searched the small room for his sword, which was leaning up against the far wall. Walking over to it, he snatched the blade from its resting place before releasing it from its sheath and slashing it against his palm. Red blood welled, but the wound healed within seconds as if it had never been there.

The young woman said the wound was poisoned, which undoubtedly hadn't helped, but the uneasy feeling in his gut lingered, telling him that the forest had done something to him. In its depths, secrets lay hidden, and he would uncover each and every one of them.

10

ORIANA

2ND DAY OF THE ELEVENTH MONTH, 1774

Oriana stood outside Garren's door, a bowl of stew in her hand. She'd told Haldis that she'd bring him his supper, eager to question him more about the monster he had spoken of. The demon—that's what he had called it when she found him in the forest. But that couldn't be. There weren't any other demons, only her. And if more dark creatures were roaming around this world, then that would mean...she pushed away the thought forming in her mind. *No, it can't be that.* More likely they truly were monstrous beasts that had somehow evolved in the centuries that she had sequestered herself to this small section of the continent.

Her heart pounded in her chest. The night Garren had stumbled upon her had been more terrifying than any night she had faced in countless years. She'd been sure that she wouldn't be able to make it back in time, that she would change just beforehand and feast on the unsuspecting folk of Sardorf. Haldis had been her savior that night. She was the only reason Oriana had made it back to the forest before it was too late, for Haldis was the only person who knew who Oriana truly was.

That night, Oriana had dragged Garren, as he lay motionless, all the way across the field to Hadis's door. When she'd burst inside, the old woman had jumped up from her chair like a spooked rabbit. Oriana didn't blame her; it was minutes until the full moon and there she was flinging open Haldis's door. "Hurry!" Oriana had yelled. "He's injured badly. Help me get him upstairs!"

Oriana had taken the brunt of his weight, while Haldis had carried his legs so that they didn't clop against the steps, causing him more pain or damage. Oriana had just about thrown Garren onto the bed before rushing out the door. She knew she wouldn't make it, but then Haldis had yelled down from the upstairs window, "Take my horse! Take Keely!"

"But..." Oriana had gasped.

"I know, child, but what is the life of one mare to that of six hundred people?"

Oriana had looked up at Haldis, tears glistening her eyes from taking any more than she already had from Haldis. Why the woman had taken Oriana in as her own was far beyond her thought capabilities, it just showed the true forgiving nature of Haldis, of all who lived in Sardorf.

"Go!" Haldis yelled.

It was all Oriana needed to hear. She sprinted to the stable behind Haldis's home, jumped onto Keely's back, and rode like lightning into the Phantom Wood. She had barely made it past the threshold of the forest when the change occurred. Poor Keely–what was left of her–was now buried next to Oriana's cottage at the old barley farm.

But Sardorf had been spared, and Garren had survived. She had saved him.

Oriana took a deep breath before tentatively knocking on the wooden door in front of her. He granted her access with a low "Come in," from the other side.

She pulled the door latch, cringing as it squeaked on its hinge while she pushed it open and then turned to close it behind her. As she swiveled back around to face him, she quickly averted her eyes. Garren stood at the window on the far side of the room and looked out at the forest beyond, torso bare, wearing only a thin pair of linen braies that fell to his knees.

"I-I've brought you some stew," she stuttered, silently cursing herself as heat flushed to her cheeks.

He spun, seemingly undeterred at the fact that she was seeing him in such an intimate thing as his underclothes. It wasn't as if she hadn't seen a shirtless man before. It was just that the only time she had since Darragh, was while helping Haldis with an injured or wounded man. And none of them were as...well sculpted as this man was, Garren. The fact that he was perfectly well, no longer bleeding or hovering on the edge of death's door, changed the intimacy of it. And it had been an exceptionally long time since she had been intimate with anyone.

Far too long.

He took a few steps toward her and she watched as his muscles tightened and moved with each step. He stopped to stand a mere foot away from her, and she looked up to see him smiling down at her. She averted her gaze, looking back down, but quickly realized that the smooth, solid muscles of his chest met her at eye level. She forced her gaze down lower, noticing that his wound was nearly completely healed. Her eyes narrowed.

"Thank you," he offered, taking the bowl from her grasp. She instantly spun on her heel, gripping the door latch before she could make a fool out of herself any further, but his gruff voice filled the room once again. "Won't you join me? I've a few questions I would like to ask you."

She stood frozen. She had questions for him as well. It was the reason she had come to his room in the first place. Releasing the door latch, she nodded and sat in the small wooden chair that rested against the wall beside the door. She felt a bit more comfortable being on the opposite side of the room from where Garren took a seat on the stool Haldis used when mixing her poultices.

She watched, awestruck, as he inhaled the bowl of broth and meat in just four gulping bites. Satisfied, he set the bowl aside and relaxed, resting his elbows on the table behind him in a carefree manner. Blast him for being so casual—cocky even, from the knowing smirk plastered upon his full lips. He knew exactly how uncomfortable she felt being here with him dressed as he was.

Her eyes drifted down momentarily to his bare torso and the taut flex of strength from his movements before flitting back up to his face, where she noticed a section of puckered flesh that traveled in a jagged line from his forehead down through his temple and toward his ear. She wondered what had given him that nasty scar. It looked as if someone had attempted to scalp him.

"So," He gave her a quick wink, that cocky smile still pulling at the corners of his mouth as his voice broke her from her trance. She turned her head to the side, hiding the humiliation that tightened her cheeks. "Haldis says you found me lying just outside of the Phantom Wood."

"Yes," she said quickly, clearing her throat and adjusting her position in the wooden chair that suddenly felt far more uncomfortable with him staring at her like that.

"And you brought me here by yourself?" he questioned, raising a brow.

She looked him in the eye. "Yes. I did," she replied curtly.

His eyes narrowed. "Hmmm," he grumbled so low she felt it in her bones.

She huffed, crossing her arms atop her chest, more annoyed at the warm feeling his voice coursed through her than the assumption that she couldn't have possibly brought him here by herself.

"Well, thank you," he offered, nodding his head toward her, face softening into an appreciative smile. "I think you may have saved my life."

"Think?" she scoffed. "You were delirious with fever. The poison had turned your skin black and you had collapsed, basically dead to the world already. I *did* save your life."

He laughed then, a rich and thunderous sound that had her toes curling. "Well then, Oriana." His toothy smile was large and genuine. "Thank you for saving my life."

She was moderately taken aback by his laughter. "You're welcome," she managed after a short, stunned silence.

She fidgeted with her skirts, smoothing the creases until there were none left. When she looked back up at him, he had leaned forward, resting his elbows on his knees, head cocked to the side, studying her. His hair had fallen across his face, the light of the setting sun turning it the most extraordinary midnight blue. He brought a hand up to brush the locks away, his bicep flexing at the movement The size of it made her gape slightly. *Fuck.*

"What sort of monster–as you called it–gave you that wound?" She blurted. "What did it look like exactly?"

He gave her an assessing look. "It was a demon."

Her spine stiffened at his words, nostrils flaring. That was exactly what he had said in the forest, but it wasn't possible. "A demon? I don't understand. Demons don't exist."

"Have you been living under a rock?" His eyebrows rose, and he sat upright, crossing his arms over his broad chest, snorting in stunned amusement. "Demons have been roaming these lands since I was a boy."

Oriana looked down at her hands resting in her lap. She was gripping them together so tightly her knuckles turned white. "How long?" she whispered, her gaze fixed on her bloodless knuckles. She loosened her grip and fidgeted her thumbs, twirling them around one another as she waited for his reply.

"How long? Are you telling me you truly don't know of the demons? Do you not have history books?" His silver eyes glowed with curiosity as he got up, moving closer to her to sit on the edge of the bed.

"Rarely do we get a visitor here in Sardorf. Have you not noticed the assembly of townspeople beneath your window? They are all hoping for a glimpse of the stranger that made it through the forest. And not many people leave. If they do, they never come back. The forest has a way of keeping people in and out if you don't know how to maneuver through it."

She watched as Garren rose and took two steps to the window, glancing down at the street below where she knew the flock of people was undoubtedly still standing. He chuckled, coming back to sit on the bed and propping himself against the wall behind it as he stretched his legs out in front of him and laced his hands behind his head. "So, you really have never heard of the demons roaming through Svakland?"

She shook her head. "We only know of the age-old demon that was first written in our history books centuries ago."

"But if no one comes or goes, how do you trade and get the supplies you need?" he pried further.

"Centuries of isolation have made our town incredibly self-reliant. We have everything we could need. No one has the need to leave." His head tilted at her words, and he brought his hands down to rest on his lap. She could tell he wanted to ask more about the town and her forest. But she needed to know exactly when these demons he spoke of began to appear, and what they looked like, for the suspicion evolving in her mind couldn't possibly be true. "Can you tell me what these demons look like?"

"Why are you so interested in such things?"

"I haven't seen much of this world. It's been many years since I ventured outside of Sardorf. I'm curious to know what has changed."

"So, you have traveled through the Phantom Wood and back again?" One of his dark brows arched.

Oriana inwardly cursed herself. "The Phantom Wood surrounds Sardorf and the only way in or out is through it. I have successfully maneuvered my way through it before, yes. It is possible." She chose her next words carefully. "I mean, you made it through, didn't you? I wouldn't advise it to anyone, or try again myself. Like I said, the people feel safe here. They have no reason to leave and don't want to." She was babbling now. She stopped, clamping her lips shut before saying anything else that his discerning ears might pick up on.

"Hmmm." He grumbled again. And that one sound, the one she again felt deep in her bones, had her jumping up from her seat and reaching for the door latch. "I should go. Let you rest."

"Leaving so soon?" He chuckled in the same deep tenor.

"It's getting late. I must head home before dark." The words rushed from her mouth. "I'm glad you're feeling better," she added before swiftly opening the door and leaving.

Gods, she needed to find out more about these demons, but it would have to be another night. She hadn't gotten anything out of him tonight, and she could barely even concentrate on the task at hand while he was so casual, so relaxed, so unclothed. It had been far too intimate. He might as well have been naked with what he was wearing and the way he had laid in that bed. She shivered at the thought. And that deep rumbling voice. Why did it have such an effect on her? She squeezed her thighs together. *Fuck.* A soft blush spread through her cheeks. Maybe her body was telling her it was finally time to move on and find someone new.

She sighed, leaning against the wall opposite his door, her palms flush against the cool surface. She would try again in the morning at breakfast, hopefully when he was fully dressed.

II

GARREN

3RD DAY OF THE ELEVENTH MONTH, 1774

The golden glow of sunlight streamed through the windows in Garren's room. The rays casting shadows from the great oak tree just outside across the wooden walls of the room. They danced and swayed on the worn floorboards as the morning breeze brushed by the oak's branches.

It had been a long time since Garren had slept past sunrise. He pushed himself up from the bed, stretching his arms above his head. He felt good—rejuvenated from such a restful night's sleep.

The aroma of freshly baked bread and lemon peel filled the room. A steaming pot of tea sat on the bedside table alongside a bowl of the most beautifully ripe strawberries, and a loaf of bread. Garren's stomach rumbled. He dove into the strawberries and almost groaned from the sheer bliss they caused him. The last time he had strawberries this good was...he couldn't even remember. Life on the road didn't always bring the most appetizing meals.

As he plucked another from the bowl, he wondered how this secluded town with no means of trade managed a strawberry harvest in such a late month. It was winter, and he was quite certain strawberries didn't grow in these temperatures, especially this far north. He stored the curiosity in the far reaches of his mind, letting it sit until he could investigate it further.

After he finished his meal, he promptly dressed and headed for the door. Just as he was about to open it, a knock sounded on the other side. Pulling it open, he found Haldis standing at the entrance.

She glanced at the empty tray by his bedside. "Good," she said. "You've eaten. Now come let me take a look at how you're healing."

"Oh, that's not..." he began, but she held up a bony finger and pointed toward the bed.

"Sit," she commanded.

"Honestly, I feel better than I have in ages. I don't think there is anything more to be done."

"I'll be the judge of that, thank you. Now sit." She pushed him down onto the edge of the bed and lifted his shirt to inspect his side. "Extraordinary," she mused. "Just two days ago you were at death's door, and now there isn't...well it is as if the wound was never there. You don't even have a scar." She brushed her fingers against the perfectly smooth skin in amazement.

"You are a very good healer." Garren yanked down his linen shirt. "I thought I might explore the village today."

Haldis scurried back to her table of herbs and potions, blankly staring at the vials. But she waved a hand at him nonetheless, silver braid swaying along her back as her head from side to side, and she began grabbing different bottles, "Yes, yes. Go on your way."

Garren hurried out the door before she could insist that he stay for her to inspect his wound–or lack thereof–further. He knew she was pondering his speedy recovery, wondering what poultice she had created to improve his predicament so quickly.

The town of Sardorf bustled with life. The sun hung high overhead doing little to warm him as a swift breeze whipped around buildings chasing any of the heated sun's rays away. Garren was greeted with the delightful scent of smoked meat and something sweeter that had his mouth watering even though he had just eaten. The townspeople filled the streets, going about their daily tasks, selling wares from carts. Children played, chasing each other down the road, laughing and shouting. A smile played upon his lips as he took it all in.

As he continued to survey the town, his eyes caught specific details, such as the strange clothing the people wore, the lack of a single horse or carriage in sight, and the build of the architecture throughout.

Men wore long tunics that hung just above the knee, with tight stockings of varying greens and browns to cover their legs. Heavy, woolen capes lay across their shoulders, and upon their feet were odd, pointed shoes that looked little more than rags crudely sewn together. Their garb was outdated by many years and paltry compared to the rest of Svakland. Garren looked down at his own clothing: his thick black breeches to his black leather boots laced to the knee, his gray linen shirt tucked into his trousers, and his padded woolen overcoat lined with coarse bone buttons down the left side. He cocked his head to the side as he continued to study the town.

The buildings were constructed entirely of wood. At the base of each structure was a cellar of stacked, interlocking logs that formed the shape of an anvil, narrow at the base and fanning outward at the top. A small door had been cut out of the structures, just big enough for a single person to fit through head or feet first.

Atop the sturdy, cellar bases were great square structures that looked like homes and businesses. Each one had its own ornate carvings etched into the wood above the doors and windows. Some were as bare as the rustic wood they were originally built with, while others had been smeared over with an off-white clay in order to trap in heat.

Garren looked up to the tops of the buildings and nearly gasped. A garden grew atop each roof, full of grass and vegetation spreading along the shallow wooden peaks. He felt as if he had been transported into an entirely new world.

He watched in awe as a small boy climbed a rickety old ladder up to one of the rooftops and began plucking ripe red tomatoes and cucumbers of the deepest green from the vines growing there.

The entire village was an amazing sight of weathered buildings with vivid rooftops overflowing with flourishing greenery. It was incredible.

As Garren walked in the center of the street enraptured by the odd happenings in the town around him, his gaze lingered on a small woman with auburn curls cascading down her back, her hair much the same color as the other townsfolk, but somehow, he had picked her out from the crowd. Her movements were more graceful, more precise than any of those around her.

Her silken locks were tied back with a vibrant ribbon the color of new spring leaves. It brought an echo of memory to the forefront of his mind of brilliant eyes that twinkled like emeralds looking down at him. He blinked, and the vision was gone, carried away on the icy wind that had swept past him, sending a chill down his spine.

He tilted his head, studying the woman further as she moved to a cart full of dried meats. The brightness of the morning illuminated the paleness of her skin, giving the appearance of sparkling snow on a sun-kissed winter day.

The woman brought a hand up, flicking a stray strand of hair over her shoulder and, for the briefest moment, Garren could swear he saw a lock of white fly over her shoulder before it settled alongside the rest of her hair, the same auburn color he knew it had always been.

He shook his head. Maybe he wasn't fully over the delirium of the fever just yet.

Garren looked back to the woman just as she turned to face him. Her eyes connected with his. They were a startling green, almost a perfect match to the ribbon in her hair. The left side of her mouth quirked into a slight, magnificent smile, and he found himself wondering how he had ever thought her to be ordinary the night before. "Oriana?"

Oriana walked toward him, her smile slowly fading from her mouth as she took in the look of confusion he knew was plastered on his face.

The closer she came, the more he noticed that she really was as ordinary as he thought her to be the previous night. She had rather plain yet sweet features, and what he could now clearly see were blue eyes, not green. The light must have been playing tricks on his vision.

"Good morning, Garren. It looks as if you are faring well this morning," came her lyrical voice, cheerful yet timid.

"Good morning. Yes, I am very well. Thank you," he rasped, clearing his throat. His skin felt unbearably hot all of the sudden. *Strange,* he thought, tamping down the urge to adjust his overcoat.

"I was just on my way to the market square. Would you like to join me?" She squinted up at him.

He still couldn't comprehend how she had carried him all the way from the forest's edge. There was just no possible way. Garren wasn't only double her in height, but probably more than double her in weight as well.

"Yes," he offered in reply. "I would actually like to see more of the village."

Oriana nodded politely before spinning on her heel and leading him down the dirt road they were standing on. As they went, Garren noticed that the road curved rather than forming a straight line as most towns in Svakland had, creating a grid of intersecting pathways.

Garren looked to the line of buildings on his left that followed the circular path of the road; beyond them was a field of tall grass which seemed impossibly green for this time of year. His gaze traveled past the swaying verdant green field was the Phantom Wood.

In the clear light of day, the trees looked like great sentinels standing guard over the town. Yet, the forest still held a heavy darkness, a silence he remembered well but now, it seemed to almost bleed from it, creating a barrier, warning anyone from entering its bleak depths.

He remembered how it had called out his name before, beckoning him further inside, yet now it seemed to push him away, as if it wanted him to stay put right here in Sardorf.

"Garren," Oriana's voice pierced through his trance. "This way."

He smiled weakly, huffing out a quick, "Sorry." With one last glance back at the looming forest, he turned and followed Oriana farther into the town.

As they passed by villagers, Oriana waved and exchanged pleasantries with a few. Garren didn't miss how three of the townsfolk mentioned how long it had been since they had seen her and that they hoped she was well.

"Were you ill?" Garren finally questioned, curiosity getting the better of him.

"No," she said simply.

"You don't leave Haldis's often, then?" he countered.

She didn't respond at first, but when he opened his mouth to question her further, she said, "I'm not sure it's any concern of yours what I do in my day-to-day life. We quite literally just met one another."

He chuckled at that, noticing how she stiffened slightly. "Touché," he said, unperturbed. "Will you tell me what you do for Haldis at least?"

"I help her with whatever she needs, whether it be with a patient, making a salve. Today she needs me to pick up some fresh honey and herbs from the market."

"That is very nice of you," he said, attempting to ease the tension in her posture. "Tell me, how long have you been working with Haldis?"

She spun at that, pointing an irritated finger at him. "Look, I'm not sure what your game is or why exactly you are even here, but I'd rather not be interrogated about my life."

"Okay, okay," he said, raising his hands in defense. "I just wanted to get a sense for who you are, is all. Can I ask questions about the town then?"

She sighed, some of the tension melting away from her shoulders, "Sure."

He didn't hesitate before bounding right in with his first question. "Why does everyone here grow their gardens on their roofs? I've never before seen something so fascinating."

"There isn't any room for them in the ground. Look around. Sardorf is little more than wall to wall houses, plus the plants flourish more on the roof. Closer to the sun and plenty of water when it rains."

"Why not use the surrounding field to plant crops and things?" he countered.

"It–" She hesitated for a moment before answering. "It puts people too close to the forest."

Garren could understand that. The very sight of the forest sent a chill down his spine. He remembered how it felt as if the very life was being sucked out of him, but that had been during the full moon. Was it different during the weeks before?

"How often have you ventured within the wood?"

"That sounds like a question about me again," she huffed.

"Right, sorry." He tried not to roll his eyes; this woman was beginning to test his nerves. "How about this, is the forest always so–" he paused, searching for the right word. "–dangerous to walk through or only on the full moon?"

She stopped walking, shoulders rising and falling in rhythm with a deep breath. "The forest is a place of unknowns. It is not a place you or anyone else should ever go. The village knows that. The people here have no reason to go into the Phantom Wood. Everything they could ever need is right here in Sardorf."

It didn't exactly answer his question, but he supposed it was as good a response as he was going to get.

Oriana continued walking, and Garren followed, continuing to observe all he could of the peculiar town around him.

It was full of people, more people than he would have expected in a town of this size. The closer they got to the market square, the buildings grew taller and more clustered together. Sardorf certainly wasn't lacking in numbers. He felt as if he were walking through the Sovereign city or his home of Cirus as he forced his way through the throng of packed people. This town was much too small for this number of people. He feeling a bit constricted, unable to follow Oriana closely.

"Do all of these people truly live here? How do they all fit? The town doesn't seem large enough," Garren said to Oriana's back. "Why has the town not built out further?"

"There is nowhere to build but up." She gestured toward the towering wooden structures on either side of them.

Garren peered down either side of the wide road. The buildings truly were a feat of genius and master craftsmanship for the simple materials. Each home had been built in unison with the others beside it, creating what looked like a single structure that snaked its way along the curve of the road until it fell out of view.

More structures had been built atop the main buildings, tiered in layers like that of a great cake, each one slightly smaller than the one below. There were villagers on rooftops harvesting their crop, standing on balconies, looking out windows–everywhere.

How could there be even more people than what he was already seeing upon the streets? It was mind-boggling. "Why couldn't the town build out into the field?"

"It keeps the town away from the forest, providing a sort of barrier so their children or animals don't wander in, or can at least be caught before they do." She almost had to yell the words above the noise of the overcrowded street.

"Come on, hurry up! If we don't hurry, this week's supply of honey will be gone before we get there."

She was quick and small, easily navigating her way through the mob. Garren groaned, forcing his way through the horde after her and trying not to knock anyone over along the way.

Up ahead, he could make out a large fountain with a grand statue of a woman upon it. That had to be the market square.

When he finally pushed his way out into the opening of the square, he quickly realized it was going to be near impossible to maneuver his way through it. The town's center thrummed with life, pulsing like a beating heart, the streets simply the veins feeding it with the townsfolk. The sight only intensified his thoughts of Sardorf needing to build out further. The people were like weeds, growing and sprouting from every nook and cranny around him.

Villagers crammed around merchant carts overflowing with spices, tapestries, fabrics of every color, smoked meats, and fresh vegetables. For how far removed this town was, they certainly seemed to be thriving. No matter how far behind they were in advancements, architecture, or clothing, the village of Sardorf seemed far more alive and joyous than any place he had visited before.

The air in the town center was sweeter–a mingling of florals, rich mossy earth, and delicious treats. Garren looked down to say as much to Oriana, but she was gone.

"Well, shit," he sighed, looking out over the sea of varying red and auburn-colored heads. Garren raked a hand through his own dark locks scattered through with gray, so different from all those around him. "I guess now's as good a time as any to find some answers," he muttered and headed into the fray.

He made his way to the beautiful stone fountain in the very center of the square. It depicted the scene of a woman delicately etched with details of flowers wrapping around her like a silken cloth, one welcoming hand held out, and the other wrapped around a stalk of wheat. It could only be a depiction of Linea, the goddess of nature and the harvest.

A few young lads were at its base, playing with the water, giggling and splashing it at one another. Garren found that much could be learned from children; they were a wealth of information, always listening to the adult conversations around them and spilling secrets like an overturned bucket of milk.

Garren took a step closer and was suddenly hit in the face with a spray of icy cold water. The three boys froze, staring at Garren–the strange outsider–with looks of fear on their faces. But Garren only threw his head back and barked out a loud chorus of laughter. "Well, that's one way to wake a person up," he chuckled. "Thank you, lads."

The boys looked between one another, eyes wide, before joining in with Garren's laughter and coming round the fountain to stand beside him.

"Sorry mister," said a boy with large blue eyes and two missing front teeth.

"We were just having a bit of fun," the freckle-faced boy next to him added.

"Say, mister," ventured the third, whose bush of orange-red hair almost swallowed his head whole. "Where did you come from? You're not from around here."

"I'm from a city far south of here called Cirus. It's a land of sand and sparkling blue seas. Where the sun is hot and it never grows cold."

"What's a sea?" the freckle-faced boy asked.

Garren was taken aback slightly by the question until he realized these children had never seen the sea. He felt a sudden sadness for them, trapped within this small world by a dark, unnatural forest.

"Haven't you ever heard of or read about the sea?" Garren inquired. Surely, there were storybooks about pirates and creatures who lived in the ocean somewhere in this town.

"No," the boy with two missing teeth shook his head profusely. "We don't like to read."

"Blah, yuck!" the orange-haired boy chimed in.

The third nodded his head profusely in agreement.

"It's a large body of water," he said, composing himself. "Think of a million fountains put together."

Their faces took on a look of wonder, and Garren's heart ached at the sight. He loved the sea more than anything. All that vast, endless ocean, spread out past the horizon. It made him feel free and alive. It was the one place he could truly breathe away from the cloying world of demons. Most of them, anyway.

Long ago, before the death of his parents, he wished to sail across the ocean with dreams of discovering what else was out there. He had imagined grand new lands full of mystery, sights never before seen. New discoveries to share with the world broadening their horizons. And what a discovery he had made. An entire town lost to time, erased from history. It was extraordinary.

"What'd you come here for?" the orange-haired boy asked, pulling Garren from his wandering thoughts.

"Did you actually make it through the forest?" the toothless one added, mouth hanging slightly ajar.

"Yes, I did," he answered first before adding, "I came to learn more about your town and the forest."

"How did you make it through?" all three boys eagerly shouted in unison.

"Have any of you gone into the forest?" he countered.

"No way!"

"Never."

"Are you crazy?!"

"Do you know anyone who has gone into the forest?" Garren asked, trying a different tactic.

All three boys grew very quiet until the toothless one finally spoke up. "My older brother went in last year. His friends dared him to, but he never came back out again." He looked down at his feet, kicking a speck of dirt with a pointed shoe.

"I'm sorry," Garren offered, not knowing what else to say to the boy.

"How did you make it through, anyway? Everyone knows not to go into the forest. Only my Pa goes in to get wood, but he always stays half out into the field and only cuts the trees on the edge. All the townsfolk do," said the freckle-faced boy.

Garren thought about this for a long moment. "Do people cut down the trees often?" he finally asked, sifting through the mound of thoughts that had sprung to his mind at the boy's comment.

"Every day, I guess. Why do you ask?"

"I just wonder, if trees are cut down from the forest every day, why isn't the field surrounding your town bigger? With all the cutting over the years, I would think that the wood would begin to thin slightly, and your town could grow larger, spread out more."

The orange-haired boy laughed. "The trees always grow back."

"What?" Garren's brow furrowed in confusion.

"Once they come down, they go right back up as if they had never been cut at all."

"That–that's impossible," Garren breathed.

"Only one person ever goes in and comes out again," the toothless boy whispered, looking back up at Garren with those large, innocent blue eyes.

"Stop it, Sven." the orange-haired boy said, punching the other boy in the arm. "He only thinks he's seen her, mister. No one goes into the forest, ever. Not unless they got a death wish."

Sven's eyes remained on Garren, though, and Garren found himself asking, "Who?"

"Don't say it, Sven. You'll get in trouble spreading lies about Miss Oriana." The orange-haired boy clamped both hands over his mouth as soon as the name was out of his mouth.

"Is this true?" Garren asked sternly, raising a brow as he glared down at them, crossing his arms over his chest. "You've seen Oriana go into the forest? How many times?" She had mentioned making it through the forest and back again once, but he needed to know if that one time was what the boy had seen or if she often went into the wood.

The boy's eyes darted between his two friends before the freckle-faced one said, "We have to go now! Nice meeting you, mister. Sorry about getting you wet." And with that, the three boys took off through the crowd.

Garren groaned, turning from the fountain to look out over the endless sea of heads bobbing, like apples in a barrel. He scanned his way across for any glimpse of Oriana, but found nothing. It would be impossible to find her in this swarm, so instead, headed down one of the side streets in search of a less crowded area of the town, better familiarizing himself with this strange small borough locked in the center of a mysterious forest.

As he wandered, he found that the town had been built into a circle, with streets fanning out from the center to the outer edge and three circular roads intersecting them.

He understood the children's fear of the forest. The mystery of the unknown scared people, but there was a thrill to it as well—something that excited him more than it made him quake in fear. That very feeling of exhilaration had him walking toward the forest now. It was a sense of wonder and discovery. He wanted to know the forest, wanted to know the town, know their secrets and unlock all of their mysteries.

As he continued his trek, a thought sprung to his mind. He hadn't been able to find any text or passage about this town and the surrounding forest, but now he was here. He had made it through the wood and was in the very town that had somehow been erased from every history book in Svakland. What better way to learn about the Phantom Wood than through Sardorf's own texts and history books? There would be plenty of time to explore the forest, but first he needed to understand it, learn all he could about it.

It was then that he approached a young couple passing by. "Pardon, but I was wondering if you could help me. I'd like to know more about your town's history. Might there be a library nearby?"

12

ORIANA

3RD DAY OF THE ELEVENTH MONTH, 1774

Oriana left Garren to gawk in the village square while she headed to secure the supplies Haldis had sent her for. She studied him from afar, watching as he wove his way through the horde of townsfolk. He stood at least a head taller than everyone in the square, sticking out like a donkey in a herd of sheep. A giggle escaped her at the thought. He would most definitely not appreciate her likening him to a donkey.

She continued shopping, glancing over at him every so often to keep him in her sights. Her head whipped toward him when she heard a deep full-bellied laugh. Arching an eyebrow in curiosity, she observed him as he threw back his head and bellowed another loud laugh toward the sky. Pushing up onto her toes, she craned her neck to see what could have brought forth such a genuine and boisterous laugh, but no matter how much she danced on her toes, there were too many people making the task useless. She would have to go find out for herself.

Oriana hurried to finish her purchases, but when she finally turned back toward the fountain, Garren was gone. Scanning the crowd, she spotted his dark head of hair moving out of the market square and onto one of the roads leading in the opposite direction of Haldis's.

After finally winding her way through the market, Oriana made her way down the road she had seen Garren disappear onto. Glimpsing him far ahead, she quickened her pace until she was little more than ten feet away, where she found him in conversation with a young couple.

She inched closer, straining to hear their discussion. His head turned in her direction, and she darted behind a cart just before he could spot her.

"Could you direct me to the monastery?" She didn't fully hear his words but rather felt them rumble their way through the earth, just as they had sent vibrations through the floorboards the previous evening. She shivered, *curse his deep euphoric voice. How on earth did he do that?*

The gentleman mumbled something Oriana could not discern, pointing in the general direction of the monastery, his finger jabbing left then right and finally, forward to where she knew the obnoxiously large building would be.

She watched as Garren thanked the man, shook his hand, and down the road.

Why did he want to visit the monastery? Was he religious? She groaned loudly at the thought, eyes widening as Garren turned his head ever so slightly. Oriana pressed herself further against the house behind her, attempting to hide within the shadows behind the cart.

She waited for a few apprehensive heartbeats until she was sure he had gone before cautiously creeping out from her hiding place and hesitantly heading toward the monastery.

If Garren was just a religious man, hoping to make an offering to a god or offer his praises, then which of the Gods might she find him praying to? Considering his profession as some kind of warrior demon hunter, he would more than likely make his offerings to the god of war.

Oriana clenched her jaw as thoughts of the Gods crawled through her head like beetles in a rotting log. She held no respect for the Gods. Long ago, she had learned that the Gods were cruel and mirthless beings. She cursed their names daily, wanting nothing from them. Centuries of living with her curse had taught her all they cared for was themselves. They had not even a thought for humanity–or the cosmos they ruled over–aside from the power and glory they held over it.

By the time Oriana made it to the monastery, Garren was nowhere to be seen. She closed her eyes, shoulders rising as she inhaled a long breath, stress coiled through her as she looked up at the towering building. She silently coaxed herself to go inside. *It's fine. Just ignore where you are. It's just an ordinary building, like any other.* She opened her eyes and sagged her shoulders, tension still tightening through her muscles. The tall cylindrical stone steeple at the building's center peered down at her like a watchful eye, making her feel as if her every move was being observed. As if it were a living, breathing thing. It was the only building made of stone in the entire village. It had been constructed many years before she had even arrived in Sardorf. Supposedly, it had taken over twenty years to complete, as the villagers had trudged the stone up from the nearest cove. Hundreds had died during its construction, just to create a place that they felt was worthy of the Gods. It made her sick.

Goose flesh covered her skin as she continued to survey the imposing structure. It was comical how much just being near the building affected her. She knew very well that the monastery had no real connection to the Gods. It was a holy place only for those who resided in it, the monks, and for those they had coerced into believing the Gods cared for them.

She saw the monks as religious zealots, worshipping beings they knew nothing about. If only they could see the true nature of the Gods they praised so profusely, they would surely burn this odious building forged in the Gods' honor down to the ground, renouncing their names.

In her eyes, the monks were thieves. Claiming to know the will of the Gods, gathering tithes in their names, and evoking fear in the townspeople. The Gods did not talk to the monks or anyone in Svakland. Anyone who said they knew the will of the Gods or had heard them speak to them was a liar. And as if the townspeople hadn't already enough fear from the very thought of *her* lurking in the wood, biding her time until the next red moon appeared. Funny how the monks never accused the Gods of creating the monster that had terrorized their village for centuries. Somehow, they didn't believe it possible for the Gods to cause harm.

"Dimwitted fanatics," she huffed. Flicking her hair over one shoulder to rest on her back, she squared up against the ornately carved wooden doors, grabbed the brass rings, and yanked them open.

She stepped inside and was met with the strong scent of incense and something damp as if water had seeped in through the walls and never left. The arched corridor was dimly lit, sconces lined the walls, flames flickering from the sudden rush of air she had created upon entering. The doors groaned loudly as they swung shut behind her, the sound echoing all the way down the passage where she saw a brightly lit room at the end. She suspected it was the prayer temple located at the bottom of the steeple that had just been mocking her on the streets.

Her footsteps sounded all the way down the long stone hallway, the noise making her cringe. She didn't want to be here, hated everything about this place just because it made her think of the wretched beings that ruled over the cosmos. She attempted to quiet her steps with little success.

Woven tapestries hung along the walls of the corridor with vivid colors illustrating the story of the Gods as told by the monks.

It began with each of the six ruling Gods upon their thrones, surrounding a black orb. At the top of the orb, upon the largest throne, sat the god of life and death–king over the rest. On his right, circling down the curve of the black sphere depicting the world, was the goddess of nature and wisdom. Then came the god of storms and sea, beside him, the goddess of fertility and wealth. Next was the goddess of magic and beauty, until finally, there was the god of war and trickery, completing the circle.

With each step Oriana took, a new image emerged through the feeble light, sewn intricately into the tapestries. She observed the goddess of nature and wisdom creating the rich earth and the knowledge of good versus evil, then the god of storm and sea as he created the sprawling seas and endless skies of the world. The goddess of magic and beauty then wove her spells around it all, giving the world a dazzling appearance and spreading her love for all creation to the very core of the earth. Next came the god of life and death, creating the seasons that would cause nature to wither and die and then, in turn, create new life–a never-ending cycle of life and death–the very sustainability that the world would need to survive. Finally, the goddess of fertility and wealth and the god of war and trickery were depicted together, weaving their own godly powers through the world, showing the creation of humans and animals alike through the combined power of the two Gods. This is where the monks showed the downfall of humankind; their greed, pride, lust, envy, gluttony, sloth, and wrath. All things that lead to war.

Oriana laughed something cold and hollow, the grating sound echoing up and down the passage like an angry ghost. The god of war and trickery helping to create the life of mankind, it was altogether preposterous. She shook her head in incredulity before continuing on.

When she finally made it to the large prayer chamber at the end of the hallway, she saw Garren speaking in a hushed tone with one of the monks. She heard him say, "Thank you," before following the monk into the depths of the monastery.

Oriana, let her head fall back and groaned, cursing loudly. She would have to venture further into this damned place. When she brought her head back down to look straight ahead, she found a very displeased monk staring at her and pointing a finger rather forcefully toward where she had just come in through the front doors.

"I– I'm with them," she muttered before scurrying off after Garren and the monk he was following.

She sidled up alongside Garren, deciding it was useless to hide from him any longer, especially in this place. "What are you doing here?" she whispered.

"Are you following me?" he teased with a playful smirk.

Her heart skipped a beat as she looked up at him. He was absurdly handsome, which made looking at him without blushing exceptionally difficult. "No... well yes," she relented.

"I know. I saw you attempting to hide behind that small cart." He cast her a smug look that had her skin tingling. "I've come to look at their texts."

The monk brought them to the end of a corridor lined with rows of doors on either side. At the end was the opening to a spiral stairwell that led down into pitch darkness. Grabbing a lantern from a hook beside the doorway, the monk began his descent. Oriana shivered. Gods, why did this place have such an effect on her?

"Are you alright?" Garren placed a hand delicately on her back, concern furrowed on his brow.

She breathed in sharply from the heat that spread like wildfire from his palm, through her back, and down her legs.

"I'm fine!" she almost shouted before pushing him aside and hurrying down the steep staircase after the monk's fleeting light.

The bottom of the stairwell opened into a room full of countless shelves of texts and scrolls. Some, which she derived to be of the highest importance, were chained to the wall.

The monk lit the various lanterns, allowing light to filter through the room, and whispered something to Garren before heading back up the long spiral stairs.

"So, why do you want to look at these texts?" she asked. The place had the mingling smell of ink and cedar. The flames of the lanterns danced over the books making them look as if they were moving upon the shelves.

"I wish to learn about your town's history, of the Phantom Wood and the legends that I've heard surrounding this place," he said as he moved to the closest shelf and began thumbing through a few of the texts.

"What sort of legends have you heard?" Oriana wandered to the wall of chained books, glancing at the titles for anything intriguing.

"I was told of a centuries old beast that attacks your town on the eve of the blood moon. It is thought to live in the forest, hibernating until it is ready to feast again." Oriana felt the blood drain from her face.

"How did you hear of this? Who told you the story of the beast?"

Sardorf had been kept in isolation for hundreds of years. She had always assumed the outside world—the rest of Svakland—had forgotten it even existed, or even assumed it had been destroyed much like Elscar. It was better that way. Safer.

"I met a man who had lived here his whole life. He made it through the forest and told me of the demon. Do you know the legend?"

Oriana was glad he couldn't see her face. He had met a man from Sardorf? How had someone made it through her forest? Could it be that her enchantments were weakening? It was impossible, and yet here the possibility stood right in front of her, looking as if he fell straight from the cosmos—the perfect specimen of a man. It was disconcerting to say the least. She would have to reinforce her enchantment over the forest.

"Yes," she finally responded. "But that's just a tale that the townsfolk tell their children to keep them from going and getting lost in the forest."

"Hmm," Garren mumbled, continuing to search through the texts.

She turned and sauntered toward him. "Why are you so interested in demons?"

He chuckled in that low rumbling way that made her entire body shiver. "I could ask you the same question, you know."

"Well, I haven't seen any demons. I didn't even know they existed outside of Sardorf before you mentioned them." She instantly realized her mistake and snatched a book from the shelf beside her to hide her face from his view.

"So, you've encountered a demon in Sardorf, then?" He glanced at her, raising an eyebrow in that cocky way that was beginning to bother her.

"Well, no, but I did say I know of the legend. It's been a part of our town's history for a long time." Oriana flopped onto a small step stool next to the shelf she had been looking at, opening the tome on her lap. "Too long," she mumbled under her breath.

"And you believe it?" he prodded, a few books already in his hand, ready for his perusal.

"I... well, I..." she stammered before stopping and spearing him with her gaze. This man had a funny way of being able to make her say things she didn't want to. He could pry information from her with the snap of a finger. No one had been able to do that since...well since Haldis, she supposed. That woman knew everything about her—more than she wished her to know.

"What do these demons you have faced look like?" She needed to find out more about them. She needed to understand what exactly he meant by the word *demon*.

"The first demon I ever faced was actually quite beautiful." Garren's voice carried over the shelves. "It had black flowing hair, and pale sparkling skin. Anyone would have been taken with the creature, in fact my father was, but somehow, I saw past the beauty, to the demon that lingered beneath. I was just ten years old."

She scrunched her brows together trying to place his description. That hadn't been her. Could it have been another cursed being? But the black hair wouldn't have been...

"What exactly did it look like? Can you describe it in more detail?"

He didn't even hesitate or question her in return before saying, "Its eyes were large and feline, purple at first, but then they turned black, the entire eye, like a starless night. Its ears were slightly elongated, pointed at the tips. And its mouth..." He paused for a moment to gather his thoughts. "When it smiled, it spread open from ear to ear, revealing several rows of sharp, long curved teeth almost like a sharks."

Oriana sat very still, every hair on her body raised. He was describing a Phalik, a creature that should not be here.

"Can you describe any others that you have faced?" she called back to him, to wherever he was in the endless collection of books.

Garren's head jutted out from behind a shelf to look her in the eye. His body soon followed as he walked toward her, carrying a pile of books that was taller than he was.

"Yes, I can, but not until you tell me why you are so interested in them."

She grunted in vexation. "Does it matter?"

"Well, no, but I'm curious." He dropped the stack of withering books onto the circular table, dust billowing around them. Grabbing a chair, he pulled it in front of her, flipped it around so that the back of the chair faced her, and sat straddling it, leaning his forearms upon the chair's back rail. A mischievous smile spread across his face. "A seemingly innocent, quiet girl from a small town that has seen nothing of the world around her is obsessed with the thought of demons. It's quite odd. So, I ask again. Why are you so interested in demons?"

She narrowed her gaze at him, crossing her arms over her chest and trying not to roll her eyes. How cocky and frustrating this man was. He knew nothing of her. She had seen things; she had seen more things than he could even imagine. "Fine. If you must know, I do know of the legend of the White Demon, and I'm intrigued to find out if there are more demons in this world. I'm curious whether any of them resemble the White Demon from our legend."

His face held no emotion, no acknowledgement of what she just said. She had no idea what he was thinking. "So, it's called the White Demon?" he questioned, cupping his chin between his thumb and forefinger. "Why is it called that?"

"I don't know," she said. "Now, I've answered your question, it's your turn to answer mine."

He chuckled again and she cursed her body's response at the reverberations she could feel through the floorboards. Why could she always feel the depths of his voice vibrating through the ground? It was driving her mad, even worse she was getting used to the feeling, almost welcoming it each time he spoke.

"Well as it happens, I keep a log." He reached into the gray cloth bag he had been carrying with him and extracted a small leather journal tied around with sting. "You're welcome to look through it."

She snatched it from his hand like a greedy child offered a treat.

"Gods, you are much too excited about demons. Trust me, you never want to encounter one of them." He shook his head and got up, moving his chair back to the table in the center of the room and began looking through the texts he had discarded there.

Oriana left the book she had been reading discarded beside her and opened Garren's journal, rifling through the pages, eagerly reading his tightly scrawled descriptions of the demons he had encountered over the years.

Oriana broke the companionable silence that had settled between them with a sudden urge to tell him a piece of ancient lore. "Do you know where the word demon originated?" It had been ages since she'd been able to talk of such things with anyone. Aside from Haldis, she'd had little interaction with anyone these past few decades. She would go into the town for work, for food, for a small sense of company, but even that was fleeting. She had worked in every establishment possible throughout the centuries, purely for human companionship. The little fact of her not aging would have been a cause for concern in the town so her persona had constantly changed. She had taken up new work and made new friendships, however short-lived. Once the time came, she would simply disappear, emerging again as a whole new person and weaving a new story through the framework of the town just as she had before.

"No, I'm not sure I do. Seems like something a demon hunter should probably know though," he chuckled softly, turning his full attention to her. He closed the book he was reading, keeping one finger wedged between its brittle, crumbling pages to hold his place.

"It came before the legend of the White Demon. Centuries before, in fact, when a nameless man with hair of snow and eyes that changed color with his mood wandered the land. He would torture and mutilate people just for fun, moving from town to town. A being of pure evil thought to have sprung forth from the depths of the underworld, born in its fiery pits. The people thought the Gods had sent him to punish them for worshiping false Gods, made up Gods of their own making. They named the man *De* meaning evil in the old language and *mon* meaning spirit. Eventually the people began to worship the Gods of old, and the Demon just vanished." Despite telling it, she hated the story, hated anything that had to do with the Gods and their thirst for power and worship. Why would beings of unlimited power seek the praise and worship of mortal beings they created themselves? It made no sense to her.

"Hmm," Garren mumbled, leaning against the back of his chair. The wooden seat looked like it was made for a child with him sitting in it. "Well, I can agree that all demons are evil. I've not met one yet that hasn't greeted me with murder in its eyes."

She hmphed at that, diving back into Garren's journal of monsters. What he had described in its pages had her skin crawling and sent blood rushing to her head, feeling dizzy as she scanned through them. *Body like that of a human, extra set of arms, a single eye in the center of its head, and blood of silver.* A Murrir. He had even sketched a small rendering of it on the bottom of the page alongside the date he'd faced it. She read the next: *tail of a scorpion, body of a horse, serpent's tongue, fur red as a ripe tomato, blood of black.* "Skorfur," she breathed.

"What was that?" Garren asked, his attention shifting to her, silver eyes shining like a stalking nighttime creature in the dim lamplight.

"Oh, no it's nothing...just these demons, they don't seem real." *In that they shouldn't even be here*, she thought. They were in the wrong world; none of these creatures belonged in Svakland. It could only mean one thing.

She hunched in her seat, swallowing the hard lump that had formed in her throat, blood icing over in her veins.

"They are quite real. My imagination could not possibly come up with those creatures of death on its own." He shivered slightly at the thought, but then gave her a small smile that made her heart skip a beat.

"How many demons have you faced?" she inquired.

"Forty-seven."

"And did you best them all?" her eyes moved from the page to his face for a glimpse of his reaction to the question.

"Yes," his features hardened slightly, and she knew that look of pain, like a gaping wound that still spilt blood no matter how much time passed.

Oriana flipped through a few more pages, reading the descriptions there and naming each of them in her head. She needed to know the date of the first demon he faced and the exact year they began appearing.

Oriana examined each page thoroughly, each demon's description, their roughly drawn renderings, and the dates Garren had marked below them until she found her answer. The first encounter had been during the tenth month in the year seventeen forty-nine, twenty-five years prior.

She slammed the journal shut. This was bad, very bad. How Garren had bested all of them, she couldn't comprehend. Especially the Phalik: a cunning creature with extreme hypnotic power able to lure all into its grasp. An exceptionally powerful creature.

She studied his face, eyes catching on the long, jagged scar that ran down it.

"Which of these demons gave you that scar?" she questioned. Her bet would be on the Phalik.

His low chuckle rumbled through the room. "Surprisingly, this wasn't from a demon. I was born with it. My mother said I've always had it, ever since I was a babe."

Oriana hid her confusion from him. Sure, there were many different marks and deformities that could happen when a child developed in its mother's womb, but that scar had come from something else. It was the sort of mark that only came from forcefully cutting open the flesh.

"Do you have any other scars?" she asked, curiosity getting the better of her.

He hesitated a long moment before answering. "No."

"Not even from the one Haldis sewed up?"

His brows drew together as if the question had brought up something unpleasant in his mind.

"I'm sorry. I didn't mean to pry," she said, apologetically.

"No, it's alright. The wound on my side is completely healed. There is no scar."

Oriana didn't know what to say to that. She had seen the cut; it was one that would have unquestionably left a scar.

"I think I've found some promising texts," Garren changed the subject.

"These date back nearly seven centuries." He flipped to the page in the text he had been saving with his finger and pointed to a small section. "Here, it says that the forest was once sparse, that it didn't even reach to the White Giants in the north or to the Storm Sea in the east, but one day it grew out of nothing. It became thick, reaching across the continent from east to west."

Oriana shifted uneasily on her stool. "Strange," she muttered, opening Garren's book of demons once more, looking intently at the pages, concealing any reaction her face might give to indicate she knew more about the forest than she was letting on.

"Very strange," he accented, leaning back in his chair and crossing his arms over his chest, obviously trying to mull things over in his head. "If this text is to be believed, it seems there is some great mystery to the forest. I remember it feeling odd as I was making my way through it, as if it didn't quite belong." Oriana almost snorted. It most definitely didn't belong. "Will you help me search further? Take these texts and I'll look through these others."

Garren lifted a small stack of books from the table when a bizarre shriek suddenly escaped from him. His eyes widened, and he began violently smacking the books hard onto the table, over and over again, trapped in some sort of frenzy.

"Garren!" Oriana yelled, leaping from her stool. "What in the name of the Gods are you doing? You're going to ruin the texts."

His chest heaved with large, panicked breaths. "There was a spider."

Oriana just stared at him, blinking, her jaw hanging open. "A...a spider?"

"I hate spiders," he huffed, backing away from the table, eyes still wide.

"You're telling me that you have gone up against all the creatures in this book." She waved the journal at him. "Defeated each one, and you are afraid of a tiny little spider?"

"It wasn't tiny. Did you see that thing? It was practically the size of my hand." A shiver shook through his entire body as he sat back down. "They're unnatural. Little abominations."

Oriana simply shook her head. "You are a very peculiar man."

Garren ignored her comment, pushing the stack of books across the table to her. "I wonder if there is some sort of connection between the forest and the White Demon?"

Shit. Oriana's amused smirk dropped from her face. This man was much too clever. It was unsettling. She needed to do something. She needed somehow to deter him from his interest in the Phantom Wood.

A thought occurred to her in that moment, something that frightened her far more than the fact that he sensed the oddity of the forest. Garren had seen her in her natural state the night he had discovered her sanctuary. If these texts described the legendary White Demon, as the townspeople called her, in any great detail, he might discover more than she wanted him to. He might piece together that the demon and the woman he met that night were one and the same.

If he discovered that, he would venture into the forest and attempt to find the woman. She didn't want him going back into that forest for any reason, especially on the full moon. If he suspected that there was some connection between the woman he saw that night and her dark monstrous self, he would begin to pry and wouldn't leave until he found answers, until he uncovered her secret.

It was unlikely, but she'd known him for three days and could already tell that he was no fool. Most of the time, at least. She shook her head again at his irrational, outrageous fear of spiders. No, she couldn't take any chances, no matter how slim they might be.

With only a few more weeks until the next full moon, she needed to get rid of any texts that might describe her.

And more than anything, she needed to keep him away from the forest. If the legend was vague—if it didn't lead him anywhere—maybe he would leave.

"Okay," she agreed. "I'll help you."

13

GARREN

4TH DAY OF THE ELEVENTH MONTH, 1774

Oriana had fallen asleep, her head resting peacefully upon the opened tome in front of her. He tried not to stare as her breasts rose and fell in a steady rhythm.

He couldn't quite place it, but at certain moments, such as this very instant, Oriana seemed more radiant, looking absolutely divine, as if she were the most beautiful creature he had ever laid his eyes upon. It left him breathless and slightly weak at the knees, like nothing he had felt before. They were subtle moments where he again wondered how he could have ever called her ordinary, but in one slight movement–a change of the light, a trick of the eye–her features would transform again, back into the plain, ordinary girl she was when they first met. It was almost as if she were two different people.

He continued to study her sleeping form, adjusting his view of her to see if her features would alter, but she remained absolutely stunning at every angle. Her auburn hair shimmered in the dim light flickering from the wall sconces, shifting from the deepest red to a vibrant orange that cascaded in silken waves down her back.

Her breathing was soft, wisping out of full pink lips in a lulling flow. Her figure was petite yet offered gentle curves in all the right places. Garren shifted in his seat, his trousers becoming increasingly uncomfortable.

She had a rounded face with the most enticing dimples framed on either side of her mouth, which only amplified each time she bestowed him with even the slightest smile.

A small noise escaped her as she stirred, and Garren quickly looked back to the text in front of him so as not to be caught gazing at her while she slept.

She yawned, stretching as she slowly came out of her slumber, and it was the most charmingly delightful thing Garren had ever seen.

"I'm sorry, I must have fallen asleep," she sighed, rubbing her eyes. "How long was I asleep for?"

"Not long. A few hours at most." He didn't look at her for too long, worried she would change again, her features melting from the stunning creature she was, back into the unremarkable woman that didn't seem to suit her.

"What is the time of day?" she asked, looking around the room for what Garren assumed was a clock or window to the outside world, but there was no way to tell the time down in this dark dungeon of aging books.

Garren reached behind him to the jacket he had tossed over the back of his chair and pulled out a pocket watch from a small compartment inside his coat. "It's well into the early hours of morning."

"What is that?" She looked far more awake than she had a minute before, staring at the watch in his hand with wide eyes.

"This?" he said, unhooking the chain from his jacket and holding it out for her to take. "It's a watch, just a smaller version of any ordinary clock."

When her eyes still held a look of confusion and she continued to ogle at the brass watch in her hands, he questioned her, "How do you tell time?"

"There is a bell tower, which tolls from sunrise to sunset with each new hour, although it is often left forgotten, so we must rely on our candle clocks."

Garren was stunned. Relying on bells and candles to tell the time of day? They were ancient tools. This poor village had been so cut off from the rest of humanity for so many years; it hadn't the chance to develop along with the rest of Svakland. They were living in the past, completely unaware of how far behind the rest of the world they were. A sadness washed over Garren again for these people and the life that was stolen from them.

"Here, let me show you how it works." He came up behind Oriana's chair, leaning over her, his fingers brushing against the small part of exposed flesh at her nape as he placed a hand upon her chair, hovering over her shoulder.

"The numbers mark the twelve hours of each half day. This smaller hand here, shows the hour, while the longer hand here, marks the minute. It starts here at the twelve for midnight, once both hands get all the way back to the twelve, that would mark midday. Until they both continue all the way to midnight once more marking the start of a new day."

Oriana brushed her thumb over the glass face of the watch. "This is truly remarkable. Did you make it yourself?"

She turned her head to look at him and nearly collided with his chin. Neither of them moved away. A whisper away from one another, Oriana's eyes flicked to Garren's lips for a fleeting moment, then to his eyes, and then to the scar that marred the right side of his face.

She lifted her small hand and he sucked in a breath as she trailed a delicate finger lightly along the puckered flesh.

Garren closed his eyes as her touch sent a sudden heat coursing through his veins, igniting something primal within him—something that had laid dormant for far too long.

That was until she whispered, "This scar is not a mark from birth."

He pulled back. "What?"

Oriana's hand hovered in the empty air a moment longer before it finally fell to rest in her lap. The heat that had been building within him began to freeze over from the loss of her touch.

"That kind of scar is created by force, from cutting into the flesh, rather crudely, if I might add."

"Well, it wasn't," he said in a clipped tone. His mother would not have lied to him. She had no reason to. She never lied, not to anyone.

"We've been here too long. Daylight will soon break, and the monks will be waking," he said, changing the course of the conversation. Garren closed the tomes he had left open on the table and began returning some to their shelves, leaving the few he had yet to look through on the table for his next visit. "The monk said not to take anything from this room, but we were welcome to browse the shelves as long as we wanted."

"Did you find what you were looking for?" Oriana asked quietly, looking down toward her interlaced fingers.

"Not much." He rubbed his eyes with his thumb and forefinger. "I was able to find the Phantom Wood mentioned several more times, but there was nothing of note. The forest appeared sometime around the year two thousand. That is the best piece of information I found.

Other than that there was mention of all trade and travel stopping as the forest was too unpredictable, too hard to maneuver through. So all the roads and trade routes that once led to the surrounding villages and cities were left forgotten, hidden by the Phantom Wood."

Oriana simply nodded. "And what of the White Demon? Did you find any mention of her in the texts?"

Garren spun instantly to face Oriana. "Her?"

Oriana's gaze was firmly fixed on her fidgeting thumbs in her lap. She had done the same thing when visiting him the previous evening. It was a nervous habit, he could tell that much, but why was she doing it now? An ebbing suspicion grew that she was hiding something important from him, but what? For now, he would allow her to keep her secrets. It was late, after all, and they both needed rest.

"The demon has always been thought to be female," she said, pushing up to her feet and turning from him to shelve a few more of the books.

There was definitely something different about this woman. It was driving him crazy attempting to figure it out, piecing the puzzle together. Her outward demeanor and features just didn't seem to fit. It was as if she had placed some sort of spell over him, which only drew him in more. He thought back to how his mind oddly singled her out in the village streets. Somehow his gaze had locked on her in the sea of people, as if she had called out to him. He was quite certain that if he had fallen asleep in this dungeon and she had left him in peace, the absence of her presence would have awoken him instantly. But why?

"Why are you staring at me like that?" she said, and it was only then that he realized he had scrunched his brows together and narrowed his eyes at her.

"It's nothing," he said, clearing his throat. "I was thinking of another matter. Come, let's head back to Haldis's." He gestured for her to join him on the long climb back up the spiral staircase.

"Do you plan on coming back soon?" Oriana asked, as she looked down at the pile of texts and handful of scrolls he had left to rest on the table.

"I do." His voice echoed up the passage as he began his ascent back to the monastery. He heard Oriana's quick shuffle of footsteps behind him as she tried to catch up.

A soft milky glow illuminated the worship corridor as they continued in silence until finally, they reached the circular room, stepping underneath the skylight and into the light of the moon. In the center of the room was a stone font, carved to resemble a tree with its branches spread to hold the basin of water.

Oriana went straight to it, and Garren watched as she began splashing her face with the water and scrubbing at her skin.

Garren tried not to laugh. "I'm fairly certain that is holy water meant for use in prayer to the Gods."

Oriana, still leaning over the font with water dripping from her face, looked back at him with an unamused scowl.. "My mistake." She stood up, clasping her hands together and raising them toward the hole in the ceiling. "Oh, please Gods, let my hens lay two eggs instead of just one each day. Thank you ever so kindly." She went one step further by aiming a lewd gesture at them, spinning in a circle to make sure she bestowed it upon each and every one of the Gods' statues lined around the corridor before turning back to him. "How was that?"

"I take it you aren't religious then?" He raised both eyebrows at her.

"You could say that," she scoffed. "Are you?"

"No, not particularly," he said. "But I certainly don't think I would do what you just did."

She snorted. "Most wouldn't. Too afraid, I suppose, thinking the old bastards will kill them where they stand."

A ghost of a smile played on his lips. "How do you feel about leaving this place?"

He was graced with a small smile in return, dimples burrowing deeper into her cheeks. "That would be lovely."

They walked side by side down the passageway shrouded in darkness until finally reaching the front of the monastery.

Oriana practically threw the doors open, drawing in a deep breath. "Ahh, alas, fresh air." She closed her eyes, tilting her head up toward the night sky and spinning, her blue gown fanning out around her like a flower in bloom.

Garren couldn't hold in his amusement at her sudden change in demeanor. "You really don't like it in there, do you?"

She stopped and looked at him. "Is it really that obvious?"

He chuckled. "Tell me, why do you hold such animosity toward the gods?"

"I'm not sure we know each other well enough for that conversation just yet. It seems much too personal."

"Well, let us get to know each other better then." He wanted to find out all he could about her and the mysteriousness that followed her like a shadow. "Do you have family?"

"No," she said, almost too softly for him to hear. She suddenly looked as if her mind was miles away, lost in a past memory. Was it grief?

"I'm sorry," he consoled. "I lost my family, too. Many years ago, now."

Visions of his parents' brutal deaths shoved into the far reaches of his mind. The cloying memories haunted him wherever he went, like a heavy weight that sat on his chest, rendering him incapable of drawing a full breath. He had come to terms with their deaths long ago, but the heartache of their loss would never truly leave.

She looked up quickly, sorrow painted across her face. "I–I am so sorry for your loss." She grabbed his hand, squeezing gently before releasing it. "Mine are not...what I mean to say is–" she stopped mid-sentence, obviously searching for the right words. "My family is not dead. They are just gone."

Garren narrowed his eyes down at her. "Does that mean they made it through the Phantom Wood? Was that during the time you made it through? Did you all go together?"

He recalled what the young boy from the market square had said. *Only one person goes in and comes out again.*

Oriana. Who was this woman? His mind mulled over too many things–everything he had heard and learned in the past two days–but there was one thing that continued to stick out like black sheep in a herd of white. Oriana knew more about the forest than she was letting on.

Oriana's gaze was fixed pointedly on the ground in front of her, lost in thought.

"Yes," she finally said, quickening her pace until they had made it back to the market square, which Garren could now clearly see was actually a circle. The entire town was built out in the same circular pattern and the market was its bullseye. In the blue light of the approaching dawn, it was quaint and serene–empty of people and merchants.

Oriana took a seat on the edge of the fountain, looking out over the horizon. "We might as well watch the sunrise." She patted the spot next to her.

Garren obliged and took his place beside her on the fountain's edge. It was a beautiful evening. Garren placed his hands on the cool stone surface leaning back as he stared up at the stars. It was so peaceful as the early signs of morning made their way out of hibernation. He loved the stillness and quiet of this time of day.

"I can't imagine the pain of losing your family," Oriana swallowed. "That must have been an extremely hard time for you. How old were you when they passed?"

"Fifteen," he whispered.

She slid her slender hand into his once again, squeezing before pulling away just as before, but he held on tight, not wanting to feel the coldness he knew would come when the contact was broken.

"Many years before they died, I fought the demon that killed them. I wounded it, and it ran off. If I had only gone after it, finished it off that day, it wouldn't have come back. It wouldn't have..."

Oriana squeezed his hand once again. "It wasn't your fault. You know that, don't you? You couldn't have known it would come back. You were only a child."

He nodded, looking down at their clasped hands. "I know."

Her hand felt so fragile in his. He feared that if he gripped it too tightly, it would shatter in his grasp. But that touch, the small delicate contact of their interlaced fingers felt so damned good, as if they were two puzzle pieces that had finally found where they fit.

It made no sense. He had known this woman for a few days, yet being here with her in this moment felt right, as if it was destined to be.

It felt like home.

"What are you thinking of?" Oriana's angelic voice rang beside him.

"Of this place and of...you," the last word came out nearly breathless as he looked down into her glowing eyes. "I don't know what it is about you, but I feel something deep within my soul. I–I can't make sense of it. I feel like we have known one another for a very long time, but it has been merely two days."

A sudden warmth caressed his cheek as Oriana brought her free hand up to gently cup his face. He turned his head into it. Her eyes were alight with such a burning intensity that he couldn't look away. Garren brought his own hand up, placing it over hers and pressing his cheek further into her affectionate touch.

"There is something inexplicable about you," she said, rubbing a thumb tenderly along his jawline. As they continued gazing into each other's eyes, he saw hers begin to change, shifting into the most brilliant green.

Those eyes, so familiar. He recalled them peering down at him through a gloomy haze of mist and trees. He furrowed his brow, trying to see the memory clearer.

And then, her entire appearance began to melt into someone else, as if a veil had been lifted from her features. Her face and body thinned into exquisite, almost ethereal features. She was still the Oriana he had known the past few days, just altered somehow. But those enticing dimples stayed as if no ounce of will or fate could have ever changed them.

Was this her? Had she somehow been hidden from him, beneath a dull and ordinary outer shell, as if she were a flame that had been snuffed out and finally lit anew, shining bright for all to see.

The last piece of her to transform was her hair, the deep auburn fading away to reveal a magnificently exotic snowy white that stole the breath from his lungs. He had no idea if this was a dream or reality, if his mind was still playing tricks on him.

Her head tilted and she smiled up at him. And Gods help him, that small smile, so sweet and utterly brilliant, deepened those beguiling dimples notched on either side of her enchanting mouth, and it was as if the chain holding him back had broken free. His lips descended onto hers in an instant. Hands on either side of her face, he pulled her closer. She tasted of honey and something much sweeter.

He groaned against her mouth, reveling in the feel of his lips upon hers.

She remained frozen and stunned for a short second before conceding and fully sinking into the kiss. Oriana explored him just as desperately. His vision was suddenly marred as an image sharpened in his mind, as if a fog had been lifted, revealing what he had been unable to remember these past days. A paradise in the forest, a small cottage flowing with wildflowers of every color, a trickling stream, and golden rays of sunlight sparkling through the scene. And a pale, exquisite face with green eyes and flowing white hair.

Oriana, in the forest. In a utopia.

He pulled back abruptly. Oriana's lips remained parted, her eyes open in confusion. "Is everything alright?" she questioned hesitantly.

All was perfectly back as it had been, her rich auburn hair still tied back, her blue eyes sparkling, her petite, curved frame leaning toward him. Just an ordinary woman, sat upon an ordinary fountain, surrounded by an ordinary town within the most extraordinary of places. He shook his head, dropping his hands from her face. The lack of warmth was instant, and he found himself missing the smoothness of her skin.

"Yes," he finally managed. "We should get back to Haldis's before daylight, get some sleep."

"You no longer wish to stay and watch the sunrise with me?"

"Another time," was all he could muster before he rose and strode through the square, desperately trying to ignore the disappointment on Oriana's face as she trailed after him.

What just happened? His mind had somehow melded together dream and reality. It was late, he had been awake for far too long and his sleep-deprived subconscious had created a bizarre vision of Oriana as the woman from the forest. Possibly a hallucination as the poison finished working its way through his body.

What he did know was that whatever vision his mind had conjured was a true recollection. He distinctly recalled the feel of the place, the sound of the babbling brook, and the scent of something sweet and floral. It had all been real; that much he was sure of. There was some kind of paradise hidden in that dark and gloomy forest.

A hand brushed against his arm, pulling him from his thoughts. "Are you sure you are alright?" Oriana's soft voice drifted up beside him.

Garren stopped and turned, looking down into her sea blue eyes, a small ring of purple outlining the blue just like the eyes of the man who had sent him to this peculiar place. The question held within her gaze sobered his wandering mind. He offered her a small smile. "I am sorry, Oriana. I did not mean to..." He stopped searching for the right words. "I did not mean to break off our kiss in such a crude way. I–I think my mind is over tired and I keep seeing strange...visions."

Her brow furrowed ever so slightly, and she nodded gently before she said, "Of course. These past few days have been hard for you. Perhaps you aren't as fully healed as you thought."

"Perhaps." His head began to pound from the swarm of questions raging through it.

He held out an arm to her. "Come. Another good night's sleep should do the trick."

Oriana stared at him a moment longer; he could see the cogs of her mind turning like the inner workings of a clock. Finally, she conceded and looped her hand in the crook of his arm.

Linked together, they walked in silence all the way back to Haldis's, making it just as dawn had broken.

"I was beginning to think you had gone and gotten yourself lost in the forest." Haldis sat in a worn, high-backed chair, book in hand, fire blazing in the hearth beside her. He peeked a glance at the book's cover before she put it away, rising unsteadily from her chair. *Remedies and Rituals: The Healers Handbook.* She was no doubt still trying to piece together the miracle of his recovery. If he were being completely honest, he still didn't understand it himself after all these years.

"Forgive me, Haldis, I had hoped to secure a room at the inn, but the day has passed me by without even a thought. I will gather my things. I don't wish to intrude on your kindness any further." He moved toward the rickety old steps that led up to the two rooms that were upstairs, both meant as sick rooms for Haldis's patients.

"Nonsense." She stood and waved a hand through the air. "You must stay as long as you wish. You are not intruding in the slightest."

"I...I...thank you, Haldis," Garren stumbled on his words. "Your kindness will not be forgotten."

"Go on and get some rest. I want no more of your groveling," she said dismissively. "Oriana, won't you stay and keep me company by the fire?"

"Of course, Haldis," came Oriana's mild-mannered reply.

With that Garren took to the stairs, two steps at a time. He stepped into the room Haldis had so generously offered quickly, shutting the door behind him.

Garren leaned his back against the solid wood of the shut door, closing his eyes and releasing a weary sigh. He drifted back to the market square and to Oriana, her lips pressed against his, exploring and searching, desperate for more. It had felt...he had no words to explain it other than it had felt perfect, as if something extraordinary had fallen into place. What was she doing to him? Better yet, what was this place doing to him?

He had never, not once felt normal anywhere he had gone in Svakland, but Sardor was more mysterious than he was. It made him feel...normal for the first time in his life.

But the question was, why? What mystery was this town hiding? It was almost as if, with each new observation or piece of knowledge, he came across an entirely new puzzle that needed to be solved. Soon, he wouldn't be able to solve it all on his own.

He needed to figure out the jumbled mess in his mind, to focus on what had happened to him in the Phantom Wood and how the woman had played a part. He forced himself to push the thoughts of Oriana aside. She was a distraction that he could –hopefully– focus his full attention on later.

Tomorrow, he needed to lay everything out in front of him and begin to piece it all together.

Maybe he would even venture into the Phantom Wood in search of the strange utopia he remembered so vividly and the white-haired woman within it.

14

ORIANA

4TH DAY OF THE ELEVENTH MONTH, 1774

"Dearest child," Haldis cooed, taking her seat once again by the fire. "What ails you?"

Oriana smiled softly. "Haldis, I have lived for many years before you were even a thought in your parents' minds. You mustn't call me child. I am technically your elder." Her smile lingered as she took a seat on the floor beside Haldis, leaning her head on the armrest of Haldis's chair.

The old woman stroked Oriana's hair affectionately. "Yes, well, I don't see you looking like a wrinkled piece of flesh steps away from death's door. In that I best you, so I will call you whatever I like."

Oriana laughed outright at that. "I suppose I have aged well." She reached up and squeezed Haldis's hand as the woman who had been Oriana's constant companion these past years continued to stroke her hair.

"Yes, yes, now tell me, whatever is the matter? You look as if the weight of the cosmos is resting upon your shoulders."

"I'm not entirely sure," Oriana answered honestly. "Something happened tonight, and it made me..." Oriana paused, mulling over what she was about to say, surprised by her own thoughts. "It made me feel things I haven't felt before."

"Whatever happened, child?" Haldis continued to stroke Oriana's hair as she listened.

"Garren kissed me tonight," she confided, trying to understand the way she had felt in that moment. "I haven't been with a man since..."

"I know dearest, you don't have to tell me," Haldis soothed. "How did it make you feel?"

"It...it felt as if the very essence of my being had settled, finding contentment, finding that piece of itself that had been missing. I felt whole again for the first time in these six centuries with the curse." She stared into the dancing flames of the fire. "But how is that even possible? I've known him but three days. With Darragh it took time. It took getting to know one another intimately before I felt any sort of affection, and even that feeling, that...love. It was not the same. Maybe it was not true love at all."

Oriana thought back to the first time she had met Darragh. His eyes had sparkled like the Winter Sea, dark and captivating. She remembered thinking how attractive he was, but his body language had put off an heir of haughty arrogance that she had instantly despised. Eerily, It had reminded her of her brother. How incredibly wrong her first impression had been. He was the most loving, caring person she had ever met. A single tear escaped from the corner of her eye, and she flicked it away before it could roll down her cheek.

"With Garren, there is a connection of sorts between us, like a tangible thing that I can feel tugging at my core."

"He is different." Haldis began. "I felt it as soon as you brought him through these doors. That wound should have killed him. Anyone else would have perished within hours, but he endured the injury for days. I've been searching through my notes and texts, but nothing I did should have saved him. It helped, but his own body healed itself of that wound and the poison in his veins."

"He was lucky." Oriana offered, not wanting to think about it, not wanting to understand why he hadn't died or how he had made it through the Phantom Wood and into her utopia.

"He is different," Haldis said again. Oriana looked up into her tender clear-blue eyes and thought back to the first time she had met Haldis, many years ago.

Haldis had been only a child, barely in her tenth year; it had been on the eve of the last blood moon. When the monster attacked, she had been hiding beneath her family's home, peering through a small hole in the crawl space. She saw Oriana kill her entire family. Saw the slaughter of so many of the village people, and she saw as Oriana transformed from the hideous deformation of the demon and back into her true self.

When Haldis had ventured out of her hiding spot in the crawl space of the very home they sat in now, she had grabbed a discarded shovel on the ground and screamed, running for Oriana and bringing the sharp edge of the tool down upon Oriana's head and neck repeatedly. Oriana had sat motionless, letting her, welcoming it. How she had wished the little girl could have her revenge, could actually kill her and avenge not only her family, but all the others who had fallen victim to her bloodlust.

It had been many swings later when the young Haldis grew too tired. Adrenaline wearing off, she had dropped the shovel and stared at Oriana in confusion. "I'm sorry," Oriana had said, looking into Haldis' eyes, her own glistening with unshed tears. "I'm so sorry."

Haldis had stared at Oriana for a long time before hesitantly reaching a small, trembling hand out toward her. Oriana had looked up into her crestfallen face and downcast eyes, a look she knew mirrored her own, and took it.

The young Haldis had led her into this very home, and from that day forward, they had been inseparable, helping one another survive and form a new life together in Sardorf.

It never got easier the battle between her love for these people and the joy her dark self gained from ripping them apart.

Her only reprieve was that the two halves of herself had continued to stay wholly separate from one another all these years. In between turnings, she felt no darkness inside. Her desire to inflict pain, her thirst for blood, and her need for carnage no longer plagued her.

She had lived her entire life before the curse fighting off dark, menacing thoughts of death and destruction, thoughts that always crept to the surface, begging her to act upon them. But once tasted, a lust for blood cannot be quenched.

She would never go so far as to call the lack of those dark thoughts a blessing, for it was the same once the monster was set free. She no longer felt any goodness, no thoughts of love and peace, only bloodlust. It consumed her like a wave of malevolence that wished to tear through everything in its path. No matter which form she was in, she remembered everything from both consciousnesses, which meant she was still both, even if she couldn't feel the other side within her as she had always used to. It was confusing and disheartening because even though she couldn't feel the darkness, she knew the bloodlust was always lurking, watching her life with great interest.

The tenth blood moon loomed ever closer, and once it finally arrived and she became the bloodlust for the rest of eternity, she knew it would go for the people she cared for most. It would take its time savoring those kills, enjoying every moment. And in the end, it would destroy her home, Sardorf, and then, inevitably, all of Svakland until the continent was nothing but a blood-soaked world of death.

The wood in the hearth crackled and popped, sending sparks flying. Oriana blinked, returning to the present fireside moment with Haldis, leaving those intrusive, dark thoughts to simmer in the far corners of her mind. Soon, she would need to find a way to lock herself away, a way to keep the monster contained for eternity. Very soon.

Oriana coaxed the embers with a fresh log before tossing it upon the fire.

"How did Garren feel about the kiss?" Haldis asked as Oriana settled herself on the chair across from Haldis, on the other side of the hearth.

"He pulled away," she said softly. "He seemed almost agitated, and then insisted we come back here."

"Maybe he felt he was taking advantage of you?" Haldis reasoned.

"No. He looked at me like he had seen a ghost. Possibly the memory of someone else–a past lover, maybe–caused him to pull away." She remembered it well; he had pulled back so abruptly, startled, and his eyes had glimmered with confusion, as if he thought her to be someone else in that moment.

"It could be," Haldis agreed.

"Now that I think about it." Oriana pulled her legs up onto the chair she was now rocking in, hugging her knees to her chest. "He gave me a similar look yesterday morning just before I invited him to the market with me."

"Might you remind him of someone?" Haldis sipped on a cup of tea sitting beside her chair, on a small oval stool.

Oriana thought back again to when Garren had stumbled through the forest toward her old cottage. She had been in her natural state, no glamour masking her features.

Over the centuries, Oriana had changed her appearance, slightly altering the people's perception and memories of who she was. They thought her to be the daughter of deceased town's folk, and she would continue to change these glamours and perceptions of herself every twenty or so years, just when she began to get comments about how good she looked for her age. She had changed her features just enough to make herself look as if she could be related to the townspeople everyone remembered. Her current enchanted glamour was closer to her actual facial features than she had ever used, only really changing the shape of her face and the tilt of her eyes.

"The night I found Garren in the forest, he had somehow stumbled onto the barley farm, falling right through from darkness into light. I was in my natural state. Do you think..." Oriana placed her chin atop her knees. "What I mean to say is...this is the closest I've ever been to my natural facial features. Do you think he remembers?"

"You are letting your mind wander, dear one," Haldis assured her as she slowly pushed up from her seat. "Go get some rest. I'm sure he was just over-tired."

Haldis was right. She was letting her thoughts take hold of her, drawing conclusions and assumptions from thin air. There was no way Garren could connect her with the woman he had seen in the forest, even if he did remember her from that night in her natural state.

She shook away the thoughts, sighing wistfully. "You're probably right. Do you mind if I rest in your spare room?"

Haldis smiled. "You are always welcome in my home, dearest. You know that."

Oriana chuckled at that. "I know. Thank you, Haldis."

6th Day of the Eleventh Month, 1774

Oriana had slept well into the afternoon of the previous day and woke just in time to help Haldis make her early morning rounds to the houses, delivering the week's supply of medicines and ointments to the ill and elderly of Sardorf. By the time they were finished, it was dark and near time for supper. Garren had still been asleep when they started their rounds, but upon returning to Haldis's home, he was nowhere to be found. Oriana waited up for him, but finally gave up as sleep claimed her once again, electing to stay one more night at Haldis's.

She rarely stayed at Haldis's home, much preferring the blissful solitude of her wooded oasis. But she had been so inexplicably exhausted from the past few days that she couldn't seem to muster up the energy to go back to the place she called home. Part of her was also worried that Garren might spy her heading into the wood, and she most definitely couldn't allow that.

So now here she was, two days after her soul-shattering kiss with Garren, and they hadn't even seen one another, let alone spoken even one word after the event.

The next day, the full light of the morning shone in through the window, illuminating the room in an inviting warmth and waking Oriana from her slumber. She rose, collected herself, donning her favorite sapphire gown, and wandered out into the hall in the hopes of finding Garren still in his room, but his door was ajar and there was no sign of him. Oriana began to wonder if he had even come back to sleep the previous evening.

She descended the steps to find Haldis in her usual spot by the fire, scanning through one of her books on herbs and remedies. "Good morning. Did you see Garren leave this morning?"

"I did," Haldis acknowledged.

"Did he say where he was going?"

"He mentioned something about exploring the forest I believe." Haldis's eyes didn't even rise from her book. She simply flipped a page as Oriana stared at her, jaw hanging open.

"What!" Oriana yelled. "And you let him?"

"Well, why not? It's not as if you are there lurking in the bushes to rip out his throat. The full moon is many evenings away and something tells me he won't find himself lost within its maze as others seem to."

"Yes, but that is exactly why I don't want him going into the forest! You said so yourself that he is different. He found his way onto the farm, which should have been impossible. He somehow pushed his way through my enchantment, and he's obsessed with discovering more about the forest. About me! The demon!" Oriana threw her arms up, seething.

"Well, he isn't going to figure out it's you from a casual traipse through the forest, is he? Besides, he went in the opposite direction of the farm. I watched him go. Now

calm yourself, dear and come have a cup of tea by the fire."
Haldis reached out a hand, beckoning Oriana to join her.

"Haldis!" she groaned, shooting the elderly woman a
withering stare. "I don't wish for him to explore the forest
at all. He's clever and I won't chance him discovering
anything, no matter how small those chances are. I'm
going to find him." Without giving Haldis a chance to
argue, she quickly donned her cloak and rushed out the
front door, slamming it behind her.

She still didn't understand how he had made it so far
through the forest, especially mere moments before the
full moon, or how he had pushed his way into her paradise
at the barley farm, but she knew she didn't want him
to find it again. She had journals at the farm. Much like
Garren's book of monsters, only she wrote down victims
of the bloodlust. Their names, if she knew them, and
if not, the details of their features and everything she
remembered of them. She would never forget them. Could
never forget them.

Oriana stomped into the forest, pushing the fog aside
like a curtain so that she could see far into its depths. He
was nowhere in sight. She sprinted through the trees to
the barley farm. Looking across the stream, over the flower
beds and inside her cottage. He wasn't there, thank the
gods.

Where is he? Oriana closed her eyes, took a breath, and
reached out through the Phantom Wood; her enchanted

forest allowed her to see what was happening within. But the night he had stumbled upon her–half dead–she hadn't felt his presence at all. She hadn't even known he was in her forest.

She continued to reach out nonetheless, searching for the insufferable man. She not only wanted to prevent him from learning more about the forest, and her demon, but she wished to speak with him about their kiss.

Sleep had not come easy to her the previous two nights, her mind unable to settle from thoughts of the way his lips had felt upon hers. The warmth of his touch, the thrill of his body pressed against hers, and the tangible connection that tugged at her constantly. She couldn't push it away; it poked and prodded at every moment, almost as if it were pushing her toward him, and would only be satiated once they were together.

She shook the thoughts away.

Garren was not in the forest. She saw nothing.

Grumbling to herself, she chose a direction at random and headed out on her search.

Two steps and Oriana froze in place. "No," she breathed. The air around her suddenly grew uncomfortably hot, sucking the crisp winter breeze from the wood.

"Oriana," a voice sounded behind her, one that boiled her blood.

"Why are you here?" she said, back still turned to the voice.

"You know why I am here." His voice always sounded angry, as if he was on the verge of attack in the middle of war.

"You know my answer." She finally spun to look him in the eye.

Anthes was as menacing as always. The very picture of a ruthless warlord. His threatening red eyes bore into hers. She did not flinch nor falter from his gaze.

"You will regret it. When the curse fully consumes you, when you are trapped for eternity in this place and your enchantments leave you, you will regret it." His voice was low and lethal, grip tightening around the handle of the axe he always had in hand.

She did not give him the satisfaction of looking afraid, her emotions locked beneath the surface as she said, "What does it matter? Whether you run from it or not, destiny arrives all the same."

He stepped closer until he loomed over her. Anyone else would have fled in fear, but Oriana held her ground.

"You are a fool," he spat, and then he was gone. The air cooled once again into the harsh bite of winter.

Oriana exhaled the breath she had been holding, her entire body relaxing from its state of tension. She hated when he came to visit her. She would not change her mind. She would never go back, no matter the cost. In this place, she had found love and felt what it meant to be cared for.

She had lived.

Anthes had always been a stitch in her side, forcing her into battle and bloodshed against her will. She was almost as skilled in the art of war as he was. Maybe in another life, she could have been a great military leader, but Anthes would never have allowed that. He had always possessed an obsession for Oriana's unique gifts and used them for his own twisted purpose.

Every moment with him became an intense battle for her sanity. If only he had allowed her to hone her skill, to practice its use and ability, she might have gained complete control over the bloodlust. She might have been able to use it for good rather than evil, but Anthes never allowed her that chance. She was his own personal creature of death.

She would rather let the curse play out and be forced to trap herself in a prison of her own making for eternity than go back to serving as Anthes's weapon in war, annihilating masses of people for sport.

Her breathing quickened, blood boiling at the mere thought of returning to that life. It could never happen. Not ever.

Oriana screamed, conjuring a knife from thin air and hurling it at the spot where Anthes's head had just been. It embedded itself to the hilt within a pine tree before she closed her fist, and it disappeared, the smoking embers of her enchantment rising into the foliage above. She waited, slowing her breathing until her skin cooled.

With one final long exhalation, she pulled herself together and continued moving through the forest in search of Garren.

Oriana attempted to clear her mind, emptying it of all that had just happened and all that was still to come, until she finally heard something through the trees. Her head snapped in its direction as she peered through her forest of gloom.

There was the distinct sound of grunting and the soft rustle of movements through tall grass. She followed the sounds, realizing it was leading her toward the cliffs of Shipwreck Cove, where she often spent long hours sitting upon the cliffs, watching the swirling waters of the Storm Sea beyond.

As she came upon where the trees began to thin, giving way to the vibrant flowing grasses that stretched from the edge of the Phantom Wood to the rocky cliffs, Oriana was gifted with the view of Garren shirtless, sweat gleaming upon his torso.

He was moving through a combat sequence, his maneuvers held such precision, every chiseled feature taught with power. His lean body moved with more grace than she would have thought possible with his towering, brutish size. It was almost like a dance, the way he flowed through each sequence. He was magnificent.

She took a careful step forward, eyes still fixed on him, but a twig snapped beneath her foot, and she dove behind a tree.

Garren spun in her direction, muscles tensed and eyes narrowed on the spot she had just been standing in. He stalked closer. She shuffled round to the other side, back pressed against the coarse bark, but slammed face first into a warm, slick wall of corded strength. Oriana looked up into Garren's amused eyes and pushed herself away from his bare chest, heat rising to her cheeks and settling much deeper.

"Spying on me?" he said with a wicked grin.

"No," she parried quickly. "I came to find you. Are you crazy? You could have been lost in these woods for days."

"Well, it seems you found me easily enough. One might think you've been into this forest more than just a few times."

She couldn't discern the look on his face.

"It's still early in the month. The fog is not as bad. The trees seem to stay in their rightful place," Oriana said, but then chastised herself as she was giving herself away. Only someone that had been into the forest more than a few times would know that.

"Yet it took me hours to even get here, out of the forest. And I didn't even end up in the right place. I was trying to get back to Sardorf."

Only a few hours to get out? That would have taken anyone else days, weeks, eternity, she wanted to say to him, but held her tongue. He had still moved through the forest better than anyone else. The fact that he made it out at all was a testament to the fact there was something entirely different about him. She had known he wasn't any ordinary man since she met him–she had been in denial about it–but he was starting to show signs that he was more and more like her. But who was he?

"I had to get out," he said. "The forest it...it plays with the mind, muddles my senses." He looked out into the Phantom Wood behind her with a boyish wonder in his eyes, a deep curiosity that she didn't like.

"I had hoped to see you yesterday," she fluidly changed the conversation. "Where did you get off to?"

"I went back to the monastery to study the texts some more."

"Oh?" Her heart picked up in rhythm as she asked. "Did you find anything of interest?"

"Actually," he started, and Oriana thought her heart might jump straight through her chest as she anticipated his next words. "I've begun to form a sort of theory. I found an old scroll from the first attack of the White Demon. Then, they called it the Red Woman."

Oriana bit her lip to stop any sort of emotion from crossing over her features.

"It seems you were right about the demon possibly being female." He raised an eyebrow at her and she masked her features, remaining a blank wall as he looked down at her.

"So, what exactly is your theory?"

"Well, it seems the first time the demon attacked was on the blood moon some seven centuries ago, and then it came back the next full moon to attack again. That same evening after the second attack, it says that the Phantom Wood just...appeared. That is why it is called Phantom. They mentioned it like a shadow sweeping through the town and in its wake stood the strange wood. I believe the demon and the wood are connected in some way. It's the only logical explanation for the timing of the events. And it has stayed here ever since, the demon inside just biding its time until the next blood moon."

Oriana swallowed audibly. When they were in the monastery, she had spent most of her time placing enchantments over each mention of her within the texts. Anywhere she saw White Demon or Phantom Wood mentioned, she had enchanted the book to hide the pages. But she obviously should have gone back, scoured through each of the old books and scrolls to eradicate every mention there was of her.

This man was far too intelligent. *Damn it*. She needed to do something to stop his search. It was fruitless, after all. He could never defeat the demon, for she could not die. The curse prevented her skin from even being pierced, preventing any harm from coming to her. And in the end, she knew that if he went up against her, her bloodlust would destroy him, and she couldn't let that happen either.

Oriana was torn from her thoughts when Garren suddenly said. "I know you go into the forest."

"What?" The question came out like a harsh bite.

"A boy in the market told me. It sounded like he has seen you go into the forest on more than one occasion." His tone wasn't accusatory as much as it was curious.

"I–I," Oriana stammered, scrambling to come up with an excuse, some believable story as to why she would have been seen, but her mind was empty. "I do," she finally conceded.

The lies and secrets were becoming more daunting each time she spoke with this man. "I often like to come here, actually, to watch the water and storms swirling out in the sea."

"So, you are able to come here, and you haven't told anyone else?"

"What use would it be? These waters are impassable. It would be a death sentence for anyone to try."

Garren paused, looked out at the rough seas beyond, and said, "Those boys I spoke to in the market, they didn't even know what a sea was."

Oriana observed his shoulders sagging as a sadness settled over him, his body withering at the words.

"Garren," she said, placing a gentle touch on his arm and letting her fingers trail down to his large calloused hand. "The people here don't wish to leave. They like their lives here; they have no desire to travel outside of the forest."

"How do you know?" His voice was barely audible.

Because I have tried, she wanted to say, but couldn't. She had tried so many times over the years, but anyone she offered it to refused. Every single time, they all refused to go. They didn't want to go. And even if they all did, the monster would still need to kill. It craved carnage like a thirsty man craved water. It would just find its way to the next town as it had in the past when Sardorf was inflicted with the fever.

At least those in Sardorf knew she was coming. It was a part of their history; she was a part of their history. They had plans, ways of minimizing the death toll, and with each blood moon, there had been less bloodshed, less death.

"I wish to free them," he finally said, walking to where he had left his discarded shirt, leathers, and weapons, donning them all once again. "That is why I have decided to stay until the next blood moon. I am determined to rid this village and these people of the demon that plagues them once and for all. And just maybe, once I've killed it, this strange forest will fall away with it."

Oriana's eyes went wide. *You fool,* she screamed in her head. He didn't know what would happen. He would die if he stayed, and the forest would never come down. Even once the darkness consumed her, the enchantments would all remain. They had already been solidified, set into motion. They would not come down unless she brought them down herself. They would stay for eternity once this side of her was swallowed whole by the bloodlust, at least she hoped they would.

"Actually," he said, pulling free the longer of the two swords strapped across his back. The blade sang, vibrating through the air with a hum that she could almost physically feel wash over her. *Strange.* "I want to try something."

Garren swung his blade and hacked at the nearest tree.

"Garren!" she yelled. "What are you doing? You will shatter your blade." But in merely four powerful swings, he had cut the tree just enough, a large wedge of wood missing from its base, and all she could do was watch in amazement as Garren kicked the trunk and it toppled toward the cliffs.

Garren, however, was not watching the tree as it fell. His eyes were fixed intently upon the stump.

Too late, Oriana realized what he was doing. A brand new tree appeared in place of the felled one in a blink, as if he had never cut it down at all.

"The boy was right," Garren whispered to himself, brow scrunched.

"Garren, you should not have done that with your blade," she said, reaching for the sword hanging loosely in his hand, expecting to see cracked metal and chipped pieces along the edge, but the blade remained completely intact.

"Did you see that?" he said, still staring at where the new tree had materialized in confused awe.

She ignored him. Grabbing the sword from his grasp, she ran a thumb along the perfect, sharpened edge.

"Careful!" he yelled, moving to snatch it back from her.

"Ouch!" Oriana pulled her thumb quickly away from the sword, watching as red blood welled.

She froze, watching a drop traveled down the length of her thumb and dripped onto the grassy field. "Impossible," she breathed.

"Are you alright? Here, let me see." Garren took the blade from her and reached out for her injured hand, but the wound had already begun to heal, sealing just as he grabbed her.

"It's fine," she said, pulling her hand from his grip. "Just a scratch, it's already clotting."

Garren narrowed his eyes at her before wiping her blood from his blade and sheathing it once again.

"Wh–where did you get that sword?"

"I made it," he said simply.

"You made it?" Oriana heard herself say, but her mind had traveled elsewhere, trying to make sense of how a blade Garren himself created could have somehow broken through the limitations of her curse and sliced her finger.

"My father was the best blacksmith in Cirus, he taught me well."

"We should head back," Oriana blurted, turning and gliding into the forest.

"Wait." Garren grabbed her hand, spinning her around and yanking her until she was flush against his chest. "What just happened? Something has unsettled you. Tell me."

"N–nothing," her voice wavered as she peered into his eyes. They were like whirling pools of molten silver, eyes you could get lost in if you looked into them for too long.

There was something about the way he looked at her, as if she was the only thing he could see. As if all else had fallen away, and it was just the two of them in an endless void, blissfully alone, without the weight of the world sitting upon their shoulders. There was a power and passion hidden there that left her utterly enraptured. That tug, the palpable connection between them, pulled taut with an iron grip that refused to relinquish its hold.

"What is it about you?" he whispered, bringing his hand up to brush a stray lock of hair behind her ear. He lingered there, gently rubbing his thumb along the outer edge of her ear.

"What is it about you?" she mirrored back to him, desire lacing her words. This man was an unknown, something she had never encountered before. All she wished to do was to peel him back layer by layer, to know him more fully–not only intellectually, but intimately.

"Oriana, I–" Garren's words whispered over her neck, sending tendrils of excitement across her chest and down her back. He bent his head closer, and she pushed herself up to her toes, stopping just before their lips touched. "That night in the market square, I–" He couldn't seem to find the words.

She let a hand travel up to rest on his chest, as his thumb slid along her cheek, his hand cupping around the back of her neck.

"I took advantage, and I shouldn't have..."

"Yes, you should have," she breathed, closing the distance between them, unable to withstand the slow building heat coursing through her any longer.

She knew he had felt the same tidal wave of need wash over him because his arms instantly tightened around her, lifting her off the earth.

Oriana wrapped her legs around his torso, and he groaned into her mouth. She explored him with wanton desire, reveling in the pleasure of his kiss, his hard body pressed against her. He smelled of leather mixed with earth, lemon, and something sweet that had her desperately pulling him closer.

He growled at her desperation. "This is..." he whispered against her lips.

"Right," she finished, reaching a hand down to the laces of his pants, fumbling to untie them.

But then the unthinkable happened, and he stopped her, stilling her wandering hand and pulling away from their kiss. He set her back on the ground.. She looked up at him with a questioning gaze, finding that the silver pools of his eyes had turned to thunderous storm clouds.

"You found me in the forest." It was not a question, but a statement. She could see his mind working, attempting to uncover something from that night. "Where exactly?"

"Just on the edge of it, lying halfway between the field outside Sardorf and the trees," she had created this story days ago when he had first awoken after the incident.

His gaze held a look of doubt, freezing over as she visibly saw him retreat within himself, closing himself off from her.

"We should head back," he said woodenly. "I take it you know the way?"

She opened and closed her mouth, stunned at his sudden change of mood. Finally, she opted to turn on her heel and head into the forest.

It was going to be a long walk back.

15

ORIANA

31ST DAY OF THE ELEVENTH MONTH, 1774

It had been three long and agonizing weeks since the passionate and catastrophic kiss she had shared with Garren. She had thought of little else since it had happened, waking in the dead of night hot and flustered. It was pure madness.

Ever since that day, Garren had acted as if they were merely acquaintances, even though they took up residence in the same home. He would simply say a pleasant good morning, barely offering her a passing glance before heading out for the day, and she wouldn't see him again until the following morning. It was an excruciating and never-ending cycle.

Oriana had continued to stay at Haldis's for the past weeks, not wanting to chance Garren following her into the forest, only solidifying his questions and assumptions from the night of their kiss. He was getting too close to remembering what exactly had happened, and she didn't want him gleaning any more information, to piece it all together.

But the thing was, she wasn't the only one hiding something. He was too. They were both keeping secrets, so why did she feel so bad about it?

The list of odd occurrences surrounding him had only grown during the past month. A thousand questions swam through her mind whenever she thought of them, the first of them being how he had unknowingly gotten through her wards and into her utopia. She should have felt him, should have known he had been getting closer that night.

The second was why he hadn't died from his injuries that night. Oriana remembered it well, he had been balancing the fine line of life and death like a man walking a rope suspended high in the air. She hadn't thought he would actually make it, but she had tried to save him anyway. And to her astonishment, he *had* survived.

Third was the strange scar cut into his flesh that he insisted he had had since birth. But then, why did he not have any scar or section of pink healing flesh from the wound she had seen that night? It had been long and gapping, revealing the bone far beneath, yet she had seen the smooth, perfect skin that had replaced it with her own eyes. If something that gruesome could no longer be seen on his flesh, then what had given him that awful scar on his face?

One more oddity was that he was incredibly strong. She recalled him cutting down the grand evergreen tree in four swings, with a sword no less. And that brought her to the biggest mystery of all, the one that made her head spin and sent a chill—not the good kind—flooding through her. How did a man from the southern city of Cirus—a small, seaside fishing town—have a sword capable of piercing her skin, effectively surpassing the limitations of her curse? A sword he had supposedly made himself. It made no sense. The impossibility of it was insurmountable. What did it mean? Who exactly was Garren the demon slayer?

Oriana would think about all those things later, but tonight she didn't have time. Tonight was the full moon, which meant she needed to get into the forest soon. She sighed wearily as she finished dressing and combing through her tangled web of hair.

Usually, she would spend the week leading up to the full moon in the forest alone, clearing her mind, relaxing her body and soul, and preparing for the change that would take her. Often, she would look through her journals at the names of her victims, at the pictures she had crudely drawn of those whose names she did not know. This month she had not been given the opportunity of that ritual. Tension knotted her shoulders, her back stiff from a restless night of sleep.

Garren had practically lived at the monastery for the past three weeks. No doubt he was thumbing through page after page of every single work in that dungeon. He would never stop, not until he figured out the riddle of the Phantom Wood. He would search and fight until he was dead. Her chest ached at the thought.

Not a day had gone by that her mind hadn't been full of thoughts of Garren. He was like a parasite that had latched onto her brain. There was no denying that they were similar, both in mind and in spirit. It felt as if their lives had been written together since the beginning of time. She couldn't help but think they were supposed to have met–to be together–that their fates were entwined, like two branches of the same tree growing around one another.

Oriana sighed as she finished breaking her fast with Haldis. "I think I may head over to the forest now. I'd like to spend the rest of the day there, preparing before tonight."

Haldis smiled up at Oriana lovingly, like a mother to her daughter. "Very well, dearest. I'll see you in the morning."

"Yes." Oriana offered Haldis a warm smile in response. "See you in the morning." She tried not to think of the fact that she had so few mornings left with Haldis. The final blood moon of the curse hovered like a hunting snow lion on the horizon, waiting for its moment to pounce and tear her from herself. This woman had been her constant companion for so many years. It was strange how their relationship had evolved, considering how they had first met. Even at such a young, innocent age, Haldis had been wise beyond her years. Oriana's shoulders sagged as she headed out the door, the full weight of her looming fate resting upon them.

They had not seen Garren this morning, which probably meant he had either left well before dawn or never came home last night. It was infuriating not knowing. She wanted to know what he had been up to during his late-night escapades and daily excursions. He couldn't have been at the monastery the entire time, every day. She had attempted to follow him a few times, but the crafty brute had lost her in the crowd each time.

There was no avoiding it. She had to go into the forest today. She could worry about Garren and what he was up to later. Better yet, let Garren wonder where she was for a few days. Maybe it would get him to finally acknowledge her existence. She smiled vindictively at the thought of Garren feeling the way she had these past weeks.

As she headed into the forest, calmness spread over her. This place was hers—her forest, her creation. No matter what it was meant for, it felt like a part of her. It was the only true place she had called home for centuries.

The hairs on Oriana's nape prickled, raising with awareness. Someone was following her. There was a sudden shift in the forest–an imposing presence–and she knew exactly who it was.

That infuriating, conniving scoundrel. He had been waiting, watching her for who knows how long, just hoping to see her creep her way back into the forest. She knew it.

She sighed, frustrated, and rolled her eyes. He had picked the perfect time to finally show an interest in her again. It seemed she wouldn't be going to her cottage to spend some much-needed alone time before the evening after all. Well, if he wanted to ruin her day of solitude, she might as well have some fun with him.

Oriana pulled on the mist of the Phantom Wood, drawing it out, making it thicker and denser until one could hardly see their own hand held out in front of their face. She veered from the path, placing an enchantment of herself to remain on the trail, an illusion for him to follow through the forest.

She watched as he picked up speed, attempting to push aside the blanket of fog as it circled like a cocoon around him.

"Garren," she whispered, throwing her voice out so that he heard it just behind his left ear.

He whirled, searching the mist with an intensity that almost made her laugh out loud.

"Garren," she whispered again, pushing her voice so that this time it brushed against his other ear.

He turned, prodding the fog a bit more frantically.

"Garren," she whispered again.

He spun round to the other side, squinting through the haze and taking long strides toward the fading illusion of herself that she had enchanted to continue on through the forest.

This time, she crept her way behind him until she was so close he could surely feel her breath on his back, but just as she was about to whisper his name again, he spun with an arching fist and hit her square in the jaw.

She yelped and stumbled back. "Shit, Garren. I didn't realize you were so easily spooked." Oriana worked her jaw back and forth, rubbing at the soreness. It had actually hurt. She had felt the full force of the impact. She furrowed her brow. *What the hell?*

"How did you..." Garren looked behind him, where the fog had cleared and the enchantment of herself had disappeared, then back to her. "I could have sworn you were just..." but he trailed off, finally realizing what he had just done. "Oh, Gods, Oriana, are you okay? I thought you were...I didn't hold back on that swing, I..." he stopped again, hesitating, a sudden look of uneasiness crossing over his face. "I didn't hold back."

He said the last bit slowly, more to himself as if in question, trying to work out what had just happened.

"Why were you following me?" she asked, continuing to rub her throbbing jaw. He really hadn't held back. She had been hit countless times before, kicked by a horse, even fallen from the tops of trees in the Phantom Wood, yet none of those things had caused her even the slightest bit of pain. Yet, a single punch from this man and she felt as if he'd broken her jaw. First his sword, now this.

He didn't answer her question. His eyes were fixed intently on her as if he was attempting to solve a puzzle.

"Garren, I asked you a question. Why were you following me?"

He only continued to gaze at her, his eyes stroking over her, as his brow wrinkled.

"Where exactly did you say you were from again?" She tried once more, but when he still didn't respond, she slapped him hard across the face.

Gods, that felt good. She might have felt bad about it in any normal circumstance, but she had built up so much irritation and hurt toward how he had treated her these past weeks that it gave her just an inkling of joy to hit him like that.

"What the fuck!" he barked, grabbing her wrist before she had fully withdrawn it.

"You hit me first," she said with a shrug.

"Well, you shouldn't have snuck up on me." He took a step closer.

"You were following me."

"With good reason," Garren took another step toward her. The air between them shifted, their collective frustration sparking with a kinetic force that heated her to her core. "Hasn't everyone been telling me not to go into the forest, especially on the eve of a full moon? And what do I see you doing, but just that."

"What do you care? You haven't given me a passing glance or thought since that day on the cliffs." Her voice wavered, and she cursed herself for that small reveal of her emotions.

He growled an animalistic sound, yanked her to his chest, and wrapped a thick arm around her waist. "You–you are so incredibly infuriating. You are a mystery I can't seem to solve, and–" He swallowed, almost choking on the words. "You are a song my soul is constantly, hopelessly drawn to. You have not once left my mind, Oriana. Not since the day I met you."

Oriana breathed in his words, his scent and his entire being welcoming it like an embrace. She wanted nothing more than for him to kiss her again like he had that night. But it was that very thought that had her pushing him away, just as he had during each of the tender, passionate moments they had shared.

"Then why have you ignored me all these weeks? Casting me off as nothing more than a passing acquaintance?" She hated the way she sounded–like a jilted lover with a broken heart–but she would be lying if she said he hadn't hurt her.

"Oriana, I–" With each step he took toward her she retreated one step backward until he finally stopped, running a hand through his hair with a heavy sigh. "That night when you found me in the forest," he began. "I've been remembering things. I had been wandering through the forest for I don't know how long. Hours...maybe days? And just as my vision began to blur, and I thought I couldn't go on any longer, I saw a light. I followed it, pushing through the darkness, and when I finally made it, I was surrounded by the most mystifying place. It was overflowing with life and beauty. It almost feels like a dream, but I know it wasn't. I can clearly remember the feel and smell of the place." He paused, and it took great effort for Oriana not to react to his next words. "There was a woman. I can see her so perfectly in my mind. She had the most distinguishing features. When we kissed in the market square, it was as if you had transformed into her for a fleeting moment. It was disorienting, and I thought it to be some kind of hallucination, but then it happened again upon those cliffs all those weeks ago."

Oriana couldn't breathe.

"I didn't know what to think," he continued. "Two times it had happened and only with you. I thought it was me, that when I looked at other women in the town whose features might be similar, I would see her again, but it never happened. And then I recalled the morning when you invited me to the market square."

He was suddenly closer to her. *When had he moved?*

"As I watched you outside of Haldis's that morning, there was a sudden shift, just a flicker of your hair and eyes. I didn't think much of it at the time, but that had made it three times that you, and only you, had somehow changed before my eyes into that white-haired, emerald eyed woman from the forest. Too many times to pass as simply a coincidence."

Oriana didn't dare move; she just stared at him and kept her breathing steady and relaxed, a slow even rhythm. Her glamour must have faltered. She had been too overcome with emotion and need when she was around him. But even so the possibility of her enchantments breaking was slim indeed. It was not just a matter of them fading away over time. Her enchantments were tangible things set into motion and would continue until she willingly brought them down through her own power.

Had her subconscious somehow caused her magic to waver in his presence? Maybe a small piece of her had wanted him to know, to make the connection. But no–it could not be so. He had somehow seen through her glamour, just as he had found her small sliver of paradise in the woods.

Garren brought a hand to her chin, angling her head so he could look her directly in the eyes. The silver pools she had remembered as storm clouds all those weeks ago shimmered like bright stars on a clear winter night.

"There is something else," he said, and she felt a heavy weight settle in her stomach as she waited for his next words. "Last night, as I was looking through some texts in the monastery, I found something. It was a tomb I had already combed through many days before and yet this time, as I flipped through the pages, something peculiar happened. A new page appeared out of nowhere. It was not there at all, but then it was. And do you know what this page spoke of?"

Oriana didn't blink, didn't even move one muscle. Dread pooled in the pit of her stomach.

"It spoke of the Woman in White. A ghost with flowing white hair and glowing green eyes. She is said to be the White Demon's first victim, trapped within the forest, forever watching over the town of Sardorf. She has been spotted only a few times in recent years, but each time it was at the forest's edge where you found me, watching over the people like a guardian angel."

Oriana's head pounded as blood rushed through her at a racing speed. He was piecing it all together.

She had to stop this, had to stop him from digging even further into the histories. He couldn't find out who she really was. He couldn't come after the White Demon.

"Oriana." His voice was soft. "Are you the Woman in White?"

Her breathing grew shallow, her heart racing.

"You didn't find me on the edge of the forest that night, did you? You found me when I stumbled into that strange place filled with golden light."

"I–I." She had finally found her voice, but quickly turned from him. "I think we should go back to town."

Oriana took off toward Sardorf. It was too much. It was all too much. Garren would never stop. He would keep searching, keep uncovering secrets until he finally figured it all out. And it would be too late. She would devour him, and she couldn't let that happen.

Her mind conjured thoughts of Darragh. His death had been like a thousand shards of glass piercing her heart, but she knew that losing Garren would be far, far worse. Their connection ran deeper than anything she had experienced before. His loss would destroy her.

"Oriana!" he yelled after her, but she kept her pace and ignored him until they finally broke through the edge of the wall of evergreens.

"Oriana." He grabbed her wrist and forced her to a halt. "How?" was all he asked.

She knew what he wanted to know, knew that he was asking how she could possibly be the Woman in White, but there was only one thing in her mind, something she could not understand.

"Who are you?" she asked.

Garren only angled his head in question, but before he could offer any kind of response, the mid-morning air shifted around them. A cold bit through the warm rays of the sun, stealing the breath from her lungs. Garren must have felt it, too, because he went taut as a bowstring beside her.

A figure peeled itself from the town's shadowed edge, walking toward them.

"Well hello sister," Orrick's casual voice droned as he sauntered through the field between them like a cat coming to play with its favorite toy. "My, my. Who's your monstrous friend?"

Oriana watched as Orrick's gleaming white locks came into view before the rest of him. She glared into his glowing green eyes. Garren's head whipped up toward the voice, hand hovering over the dagger he had belted on his thigh.

Orrick only glanced at Garren's fingers inching toward his blade. "Oh, my dear boy, that won't be of any use to you."

Garren made no movement away from the blade, only remained as he was, eyes narrowing at the stranger.

"Sister," he chided. "Look at you, so very..." He flicked his hand back and forth through the air as if attempting to brush the word he was looking for from the air. "Common." He finally decided. "Blending in nicely, I see. Tell me, who is your new pet?"

She growled at that. "Orrick! Leave us. You are not wanted here."

He placed a long-fingered hand over his chest, stumbling as if he had been hit by a large blow. "You wound me, sister. It's been ages since our last visit. I've only come to see how you're faring. Exceptionally well, it seems." His eyes darted to Garren and then back to Oriana with an exaggerated wink. "Come now, where are your manners? Won't you introduce me to your new friend?"

"No," she snarled.

Orrick ignored her and slinked up beside Garren, cocking his head to the side as he looked him up and down, assessing. "Hmmm," he mused, left brow arching in interest as thin fingers rose to cup Garren's chin. "There is something about you."

Orrick frowned, taking a step away from Garren. "You are the one who killed my Martok."

"He killed what?" Oriana gaped, staring at Garren. There was no way in all the cosmos he could have killed one of those creatures.

Garren's brow furrowed, his body going rigid as Orrick stepped closer to him once again. Oriana looked between them, moving to interject, but she wasn't fast enough.

Orrick slashed a nail across Garren's cheek. Garren didn't so much as flinch, just continued staring at Orrick as if frozen to the spot. Blood welled on his cheekbone, but almost as soon as the wound opened it resealed itself, leaving only a single drop of blood that slid like a tear down his face.

Oriana's eyes widened. She knew many things were different about Garren, and she still couldn't figure them all out. There was a familiarity with him, something that she hadn't felt for a very long time. And the fact that he seemed almost to see through her enchantments, but this only solidified her suspicions. Garren was not mortal. So what was he?

Orrick licked Garren's blood from his nail, smacking his lips as he tasted the dark red liquid. He stopped abruptly, narrowing his eyes at his finger where his thin pink tongue had licked, before flicking them up to Garren's face, further furrowing his brow. "Impossible..." he whispered, but Oriana cut him off before he could do or say anything more. She didn't want to know what her brother was about to say, what he had sensed–or rather tasted–in Garren's blood. She could think on that later, question Garren later, but as much as she *did* want to know what and who Garren was, she wanted Orrick gone more, before he did something calamitous.

"I know what you've been doing these past years," she ventured. "Ever since your last visit, I'm guessing."

He whirled on her. "Oh Oriana, darling, try to lighten up. I'm just having a bit of fun. They're my creations, after all. What use are they if I can't play with them from time to time?" The smile he revealed in that moment could only be described as baleful.

She only gave her own minatory smile in return, "You've had your fun, now leave this place and take the beasts you've brought upon Svakland with you."

His hand was around her neck in an instant. "You don't tell me what I can and cannot do, sister," he snapped, motioning to the world around them. "All of this is mine to do with as I please. It's not my fault you fell in love with one of them. You should have never come here to begin with. It sickens me to even look at you." He pushed her away roughly. "Now, as much fun as this has been, I'm afraid I must take my leave." He looked at Garren then, tilting his head again in that same predatory way as before. "It has truly been...illuminating."

Oriana noticed the exaggeration Orrick had put on 'illuminating'. She looked at Garren with concern. What had Orrick seen in him? Orrick was far too pleased by the discovery for it to be anything unsubstantial, which frightened her even more.

"Dearest Oriana, I hope this evening finds you well." His laugh grated like two rocks striking together.

He turned to leave, but paused, looking back to say, "Oh my, what sort of brother would I be without leaving a parting gift?"

"Don't." Oriana breathed, fists clenching at her sides.

Orrick bestowed Garren with a wicked wink before he snapped his fingers and strolled into the Phantom Wood behind them.

16

GARREN

31ST DAY OF THE ELEVENTH MONTH, 1774

G arren could not move or form a single coherent thought.

Something had been seriously off about that man. A crisp energy had crackled around him, pooling at his feet like morning frost and following him with each step he had taken. The instant he had left, Garren felt the warmth of the afternoon sun beating down upon him once again. It was as if the man, Orrick, had drowned out all comfort with his very presence, sucking the light and heat from the world.

"Th-that was your brother?" Garren finally found his voice.

"Yes," she said, quietly, and he looked down to see her intently scanning their surroundings.

Her brother was almost the spitting image of the woman from the forest. Snow-white hair, pale green eyes, though admittedly, there was something sinister crouched behind them—as if he was a cobra poised to strike. Even their facial features were similar, elegant and beautiful.

"You are the Woman in White," he stated as fact.

Oriana stopped her perusal of the field and looked at him, the weight of the entire world in that one look.

"How?" he questioned. Suddenly, her entire body changed, as if she had stepped out of the shadows to reveal her true self. Garren was graced with the full force of her beauty, the very woman he had seen that night in the forest.

Her eyes sparkled brightly in the sun. She opened her mouth to say something, but he would never know what she was about to utter, for a scream sounded far off in the city, stunting her thoughts. Another quickly rang out, followed by a chorus of shouting.

Oriana instantly took off, sprinting through the field. She was unnaturally fast, possibly even faster than he was. He raced after her.

As the screaming grew louder, they only ran faster. Smoke swelled above the town. Villagers fled past them yelling for everyone to run. Something was burning. What greeted them in the town square was the most wretched, horrifying creature Garren had ever beheld.

Its head could only be compared to that of a majestic lion; its body resembled a great bear, only larger with claws that bore many inches into the ground. A tail whipped around its body and Garren gasped.

A serpent.

Its tail was a massive slithering black snake, lashing out and snapping its fangs at the fleeing villagers. And as if that wasn't enough to make a grown man cower in fear, its mighty lion head roared, breathing fire from deep in its lungs, setting several of the rooftop gardens aflame. *What in the name of the Gods is this beast?*

"Hurry!" Oriana bellowed. Garren watched in awe as she sprinted for the monstrous creature, sword in hand. Where the hell had she gotten a sword? Garren reached over his back and pulled his own longsword free, steel singing as it released from its sheath.

Oriana slashed at the beast's side, and it roared in pain. The snake head on its tail clamped its fangs around her torso, ripping her through the air in an upward arc before slamming her down onto the dusty dirt streets of the town.

"Fuck," Garren breathed before charging into the fray.

The creature's head turned to him, its lion's mane rippling in the breeze as it sucked in deeply. Garren picked up speed, but as the beast exhaled, opening its jaw wide, it spewed forth a stream of fire. "Shit!" Garren dove to the street, the flames singing the sleeve of his tunic. This creature was the most horrifying thing Garren had yet faced.

"We must lead it away from the village!" Oriana yelled, back on her feet. She stood with glowing locks blowing behind her, sword in hand once again, battle ready. Like a goddess come down from the heavens. She was breathtaking.

Garren watched in stunned panic as Oriana ran in front of the beast, waving her hands like a mad woman and screaming for its attention. To Garren's distressed annoyance, it worked. The creature roared. Oriana took off, and the beast took off after her, blowing fire as it went.

He groaned, pushing himself up to his feet. The town square was in ruins. Nearby buildings had crumbled, a few others were ablaze, and the heat of the flames flicked out toward other nearby homes and buildings. Garren's heartbeat quickened in his chest, adrenaline soaring through his veins. These poor people. Where had this beast come from? It was almost as if it had just appeared out of nowhere.

Orrick, he suddenly thought. This was his doing, his "parting gift" as he had put it. But how? What was going on? What sort of freakish world had he immersed himself into by coming here? There was far more to this town and forest's story than he or anyone knew.

Garren was thrown back into the present at the sound of more screams of terror, snarls, roars, and sparks coming from the direction in which Oriana had led the beast. He sprinted toward them.

Debris lined the way as Garren sped down the streets. Everywhere he looked, injured people lay in the road, others trying desperately to put out the flames that consumed their homes.

It was chaos.

One of the young boys Garren had spoken to in the market square stood covered in soot but unharmed amongst so many wounded, his eyes searching anxiously over the scene of destruction around him. Garren stopped and knelt beside the boy, placing a hand on his small shoulder. "Are you alright?" His words came out short and rushed.

The boy's large blue eyes held fear mingled with a trace of hope as he looked at Garren and nodded.

"Can you run?" he asked the child.

Another nod from the boy.

"Go then, quick as you can. Get the healer, Haldis. Help her get to these people. Help her save them."

A spark lit behind the lad's eyes as he took on the challenge and sprinted off toward Haldis's home in the opposite direction of the beast.

Beyond the chaos, Garren could make out Oriana locked in battle with the monstrous creature. It was a sight to behold. With each swing of the beast's snake head tail,

Oriana slashed and dodged. She was so small compared to the beast, it could surely swallow her in one giant gulp.

It roared in irritation, its serpent tail striking out, poison dripping from its fangs. He noticed that she was playing the defensive, more so than the offensive, dodging breaths of fire and swipes of the creature's lethal claws. She needed help.

As he snuck up behind the beast, its tail locked eyes on him, tongue flicking in and out of its mouth as it slithered through the air.

It coiled back and struck, snapping long shining fangs. He swung, cutting clean through its thin forked tongue. The lion head swiveled, growling at Garren and revealing a devastating set of monstrous sharp teeth.

Garren peeked a quick glance at Oriana. She had dropped her sword, her eyes were closed, and she stood completely still. *What is she doing?*

He turned his attention back to the monster, just in time to see its gigantic paw poised to shred him to pieces, but it stopped short, colliding with...a stone wall. Where the hell did that come from? It appeared out of thin air. "What in the name of the gods?" Garren marveled.

"Come and get me," Oriana bellowed. "You don't want him. It's me you want!"

The creature snarled, serpent tail hissing in her direction.

"Well come on then, you daft beast. Come get me!" She cast a fleeting glance at Garren before taking off into the forest. The beast barreled after her.

"For fuck's sake!" Garren huffed before he followed suit.

The beast crashed through the trees after Oriana. Garren trailed behind them, dodging and slashing as the serpent on its tail lunged and snapped at him. His eyes searched the beast. It was too strong, with mighty creatures at both its head and tail. One of them needed to be severed to make the beast easier to defeat.

Garren picked up speed until he was directly beneath the body of the beast. The serpent followed. Garren glanced over his shoulder, watching as the snake prepared to strike. Just as it did, he rolled out from underneath the beast until he was behind its hind leg. The serpent followed just as he had expected and clamped down on its own leg. Garren spun in an instant, slicing through the neck of the snake with one downward slash. The lion head roared in agony, tail thrashing as rancid green blood sprayed from its severed appendage.

The beast stopped its pursuit of Oriana and turned on him, but Garren was ready. He poised for an attack, but it never came.

The creature slowly rose into the air before him. "What..." he breathed, watching in bewilderment. It was the trees. The forest around them came alive. Branches wrapped around the body of the beast, around each of its limbs and its neck, lifting the creature higher into the air.

The monster squirmed, wrestling in the grip of the branches. It breathed fire on the trunks of the trees and, to Garren's astonishment, nothing happened. The fire disappeared from the trees as if it never was.

The branches pulled, splaying the great creature overhead, stretching it further and further. It was then that Garren looked to Oriana. She stared up at the display, pure death in her eyes, fists clenched so tightly her knuckles were white.

The beast squealed high above. It was her. She was doing this, but how?

Before Garren could think of it further, a torturous screech came from the creature, followed by the most horrid, sickening sound Garren had ever heard

The beast's bones splintered as each limb snapped in half. Its flesh ripped until each of its limbs was torn from its body, and with one final wail, the creature's head fell to the forest floor with a solid thud. The trees retracted their branches and gore rained down from the sky, falling in a circle around them.

Oriana sank to the ground, hugging her knees to her chest, head buried against them. He went to her, sitting beside her as she attempted to calm her breathing. So many questions flitted to the front of his mind, but he offered the one that wouldn't be an outright accusation against her.

"Wh-what just happened? What sort of demon was that?" he inquired. His mind was reeling with what he had just witnessed. The forest had been alive; it had literally ripped the creature into pieces before his very eyes.

"That wasn't a demon." Oriana wheezed, head finally moving from its hiding place within her knees. She looked at him with red-rimmed eyes. "None of the beasts you have been fighting are demons."

He furrowed his eyebrows. "What do you mean? What are they then?"

"They are beings from other worlds," she said. "You know demons to be creatures of death and darkness from the underworld. You have been taught that since you were a child, but there is no underworld, no hell as your people like to call it. There are only realms within the cosmos. Worlds created by the Gods. Well...by one god. The god of creation and chaos."

"How would you know these things? They cannot be true. There are only the six Gods of the High City. They rule over us and the levels of our existence, the Ether, the mortal world and the underworld. That is all there is." Garren's mind swayed. He felt as if he had been knocked in the head by a rock.

"Have you noticed that each demon you face is different? No two are alike. How each one you face is more vicious than the last?" Her tone was gentle.

"I...well, yes." he turned confused eyes on her. How did she know this? What was she saying?

"It took me some time to realize it, but tonight proved my theory. The creatures you have spent your life fighting, protecting Svakland from, shouldn't even be here. They don't exist in this world." She paused, a single tear rolling down her cheek. "It's Orrick. It's all my fault. He saw what I could do the first night he came to visit me all those years ago." She shook her head in disbelief. "When did the first demons begin to plague this world?"

"They...it was when..." He blinked, brows wrinkling as he tried and failed to answer her. His mind was far too confused. Too much had just happened. She wasn't making any sense. Nothing from this day made sense! How was she the Woman in White and Oriana? Where had her brother come from, and how was he responsible for the creatures he had fought his entire life? The questions were near bursting forth from his mind.

"What the hell is going on!?" He exclaimed. "How are you two people in one? How are you in the texts from hundreds of years ago? I don't understand any of this!"

Oriana opened her mouth to speak, but she gasped, her head snapping up to the sky peeking through the treetops, where the edge of a milky moon glowed. Night had snuck up on them. She scrambled away from him, rising from the ground and grasping her head, ripping at her scalp as if in great pain.

"Oriana?" He reached out a shaking hand toward her. What was happening? Was she in pain? He felt as if he had been thrust into a sick dream, full of secrets and lies.

She stopped suddenly and turned her head eerily slow until he could see her face, but what he saw was not Oriana. It wasn't even the Woman in White. It was a deformity of her features, twisted and pulled into something that he could only described as pure evil.

"Run," she hissed, in a voice that was so unlike hers, it sent chills down his spine.

"The White Demon," he murmured into the fog. Everything began to come into focus. All of his scattered thoughts became one. Oriana was the woman from the forest that night. She hadn't found him on its edge but within. He vaguely remembered her saying that she couldn't take him into town, that he had to go on his own, because...it had been the full moon. Oriana was the Woman in White was the White Demon. She was three people in one, but how and if this was all true, it meant she had been living in this forest for hundreds of years.

Garren could only watch in horror as Oriana's delicate features bubbled before his eyes, as if a million spiders were crawling beneath her skin. He winced as her face morphed into an unrecognizable distortion. Into a monster, like the very demons he had faced his entire life.

Grotesque pustules sprouted on her forehead and down the sides of her neck. Ridges molded down her nose, making her look more feline than human, her face permanently etched into a snarl. She smiled, revealing a row of horrifying teeth that could only be for shredding, along with the black, menacing claws that grew like thorns from her fingers.

Garren brought his gaze up to see a set of sickly yellow eyes staring back at him, filled with bloodlust.

"You should have run when I gave you the chance, boy," she sneered.

"I will not run." He held his ground, forcing himself to stare at her deformed, monstrous appearance, waiting for her to attack. He wouldn't kill her–couldn't–but he would fight her until the morning light. If the legends were true, the White Demon disappeared with the moon.

She growled, baring her set of needle-like fangs, sending a chill through his veins. They were eerily similar to his first encountered demon in his father's smithy, but far more terrifying. Larger, calamitously so.

Oriana had spoken of other worlds. She had said all the demons he had vanquished were not from this world, which could only mean that she wasn't either.

She charged; he stood firm. When she barreled into him, hands wrapping around his throat, he bore his toes into the ground, maintaining his upright position, and brought his arms up in a high arch, before bringing them down hard on hers, releasing her grip. She shrieked and he quickly fell to the ground, swinging a leg around in the same movement and effectively swiping her legs out from under her. He turned and watched as she fell, but then she stopped midair as if invisible hands had caught her and slowly pushed her upright once again.

"I'm not that easy to knock down," she hissed. Her feet never fully touched back on the solid earth; she remained suspended slightly above it.

"What are you?" he whispered.

A malevolent leer spread across her features. "I am the bloodlust."

"What does that mean?" he questioned, muscles tensed.

"Too many questions," she snarled, lunging so quickly that Garren had no time to react. Before he knew it, he was slammed down to the mossy earth, pushing the air from his lungs. The White Demon was atop him, holding him down, her nails digging through his leathers and tunic and into his shoulders beneath, drawing blood.

She cackled as her nails dug into him further. "I will enjoy ripping you apart, feasting on your blood." She sniffed the air above his bloodied shoulder, fangs lengthening and readied to puncture through him, but then she hissed, pushing herself away from him as if she had been burned.

"Filth!" she shrieked. "You are tainted by the gods."

Garren stared at her in disbelief, unable to speak. He rose, looking down at the punctures still bleeding on his shoulders. They should have healed within seconds, but somehow this place–the bizarre, mystical forest–did something to him, keeping the pierced flesh open to spill his blood. Garren wiped away the red trickling down his leathers. When he looked up to find her, the White Demon was gone.

"Oriana!" Garren's voice boomed, echoing through the forest and the mist.

17

ORIANA

1ST DAY OF THE TWELFTH MONTH, 1774

Oriana stood at the edge of cliffs overlooking Shipwreck Cove. The sea churned below, crashing into the sides of the rocky slope and spraying water in a mist that cooled her heated skin.

She was still reeling from the previous night, how Garren had watched as she changed into her horrid, bloodthirsty monster. And from what she had learned of him as well.

Haldis had known from the first day of being in his presence, but now Oriana truly believed it. Garren was not of this world. Even Orrick had sensed it, but it wasn't until now that she had fully realized it. Funny that it was her darkness that recognized it with such clarity. His blood had repulsed her. It smelled sweet, like honey and berries, not the salty iron taste that her bloodlust so desperately craved of those from this world.

Oriana listened to the symphony of the wind and sea as she watched the tempests form on the horizon, far out in the Storm Sea. Throughout Shipwreck Cove, splintered masts of great ships shot out of the waves like spears, ready to impale any who might enter these waters. A fleeting thought flitted through her mind of jumping off the cliff's edge into the deadly sea of stakes far below. She knew it would do nothing; she had attempted such feats more times than she could count, hoping that it would work just once and she could rid herself of this curse, of the guilt she constantly felt.

The Storm Sea beyond was impassable. Many had tried, but the wreckage that washed into this very cove was all that was left of them.

The sea breeze caressed her cheeks, sending her long wisps of hair dancing behind her. She wrapped her arms around herself, trying to keep warm from the cold wind. Over the centuries, she had stood at this very spot so many times. It helped to clear her mind, forget herself, forget the past and present.

The sun steadily rose from its slumber, painting streaks of pink and orange among the blue and purple of the sky. It was during this time, after every full moon, she recalled the faces of her victims. Each was permanently etched in her mind, inked behind her closed eyes. She saw them and their families. She saw their murdered, mutilated bodies. She remembered the taste and the feel of their delicate skin and bones ripping and cracking beneath her grip.

With each face, a new hot tear rolled down her cheek into the churning sea below. It was the only way she could pay tribute to them, through her tears and the agony she felt at what she had done to them.

Without turning around, she knew he was behind her. She could sense his presence, quietly observing her.

His soft steps ventured closer, and she felt his warmth beside her. Oriana knew he would ask questions and that she needed to tell him everything. She wanted to tell him everything. This connection, their unusual bond, had her yearning for him to know her true self, both the good and the bad.

He waited patiently until she had finished her silent recanting, her remembrance of all those she had ripped the life from too early.

When she finally finished, she opened her eyes to see Garren gazing down at her with a look that held concern and pain in its depths. She turned back to gaze out over the expanse of ocean that stretched before her. "There is nothing quite like the sea at first light." She smiled softly. "I'm sure you have many questions."

He nodded, following her gaze to the endless stretch of ocean, watching the same breathtaking swirls of wind and rain looming far out over the Storm Sea. "Who are you?" he finally asked.

"Will you sit?" she asked.

He simply nodded, and they sat together on the edge of the cliff, legs dangling off the side. They both remained silent until she mustered up the courage to speak.

"This is Shipwreck Cove," Oriana broke the quiet. "I come here to clear my head and think."

"Yes, I remember it well from my last journey into the forest. It's beautiful," he said, voice low and calm.

She smoothed out her skirts, blowing out a breath before looking up at him, her green eyes boring into his silver ones. "The cosmos is far more vast and complex than you know. This world and the people in it know only of the Six Eternal: Zanos, god of life and death, Linea, goddess of nature and harvest, Hylda, goddess of magic and beauty, Mathis, god of storms and wisdom, Petra, goddess of fertility and wealth, and finally..." She closed her eyes tight, almost choking on her next words. "Anthes, god of war and trickery."

A spray of sea water rained over them at that moment, as if Mathis understood her anger and wished to cool the heat rising within her, telling her he understood. Anthes was an enemy to many, friend to none.

She swallowed before continuing. "They are the six ruling Gods who reign over the cosmos and, as you well know, are worshipped and regarded as divine rulers in Svakland. But that is not only true here. It is true throughout the entirety of the universe. The Six Eternal have made it so. They want you and everything that exists to know of their almighty existence. They have invoked fear in the worlds, forcing praise and seeking glory. They drink it all in like fine wine, getting off on the worship they receive out of the people's fear. The cock sucking bastards," she added, pointing a lewd gesture up toward the heavens.

She watched as Garren's eyes widened at her insult. She knew that he did not worship the Gods, that he held no affinity for any of them as much of Svakland did. But during the past weeks in which she had known him, he had not once insulted nor spoken ill of them. She wasn't sure if he believed the Gods existed, but his expression showed her that he at least would never outright disrespect them as she had just done. Even so, he didn't say anything, just continued listening to her tale.

"There are not only the six Gods as the people of Svakland believe and worship, but an innumerable number of Gods," she continued. "Most are lesser Gods who follow the Six Eternal with the utmost fealty, allowing themselves to be used as puppets on the end of the Six Eternal's master strings. But there are also some Gods just as powerful, even beings more powerful than the six ruling Gods."

"How do you know that there are other Gods? What proof is there?" he questioned. "There isn't even definitive proof of the Six Eternal's existence."

"Because I am one. I am a goddess who has been cursed for eternity."

PART THREE

GODS AND CURSES

18

GARREN

1ST DAY OF THE TWELFTH MONTH, 1774

Garren's mind reeled. *A goddess?*

It couldn't be possible. There were no Gods; he never truly believed in their existence. The idea of powerful, otherworldly beings living in the sky was preposterous. But here he was, listening to this woman, this person he had come to care for so deeply over the past weeks, saying that the Gods were real, and she was one of them. A cursed one at that. It was all too much. He bent his head, digging his palms into his eyes as his head throbbed.

And yet the more he let the idea sink in, toying with the possibility that there were in fact Gods who existed and ruled over the world, everything that had happened in the past few days began to make more sense. It crept over him like a shadow in the night. It was as if a fog was being cleared from his vision, no longer clouded by ignorance. He was beginning to see things clearly for the first time.

"Your brother," he finally said. "He is a god also?"

"Yes," she said as she threaded her pale, slender fingers with his. "May I tell you my story? And the story of the Gods?"

He laughed a hollow humorless sound, pinching the bridge of his nose and shaking his head in disbelief. "Why not? Might as well uproot my entire world and everything I've ever believed in further."

She squeezed his hand, a sad smile pulling at the corners of her mouth. "I know it is a lot to take in, and not only hard, but life altering to believe when you have so firmly been against our existence, but I must tell you the story of the Gods. I must tell you *my* story."

He stared down into her sweeping green eyes, into their impossibly vivid glow and nodded for her to continue. Even though his head screamed that there was no way what she was about to say, what she had said already was true, he knew in his heart that she was telling the utter and complete truth. Just one look at her graceful features, flowing white hair, everything about her screamed goddess. A memory suddenly stirred of the first time he had seen her, when he had aimlessly followed the blinding light through the forest; he had thought her a goddess.

"How old are you?" he blurted.

She snorted, instantly bringing her hand up to her nose to hide her embarrassment at the crude noise. "That's what you want to know? Out of all the things you could ask me, and you want to know how old I am?"

He smirked, exhaling on a titter and shaking his head in comprehension of how dumb a question it was in the larger scheme of things. "I'm not sure I want to know the answer to any bigger questions just yet. I'm still trying to wrap my head around the fact that you are a..." He trailed off for a moment before whispering, "...goddess." The word felt strange on his tongue.

She huffed a small laugh. "Fair enough. I'm older than you, let's just leave it at that."

As the sun moved further above the horizon, the colors of dawn faded away and the light blue of the morning sky took their place.

Oriana sat quietly for a long moment with her eyes closed and her head tilted toward the heavens–toward her true home, Garren realized. It was strange, but the budding realization that Oriana was a powerful immortal being possibly thousands of years old didn't scare him. On the contrary, it felt almost like a relief. It meant that everything he could do wasn't all that odd. But that also brought up more thoughts of why he was so different. What did it mean?

He watched as Oriana inhaled deeply, her chest rising in a steady motion. She seemed to brace herself before releasing the breath, and her entire body relaxed before his eyes with that one outtake of air. He found himself wondering how she felt after a long day of fighting and changing into that...thing.

A curse. She said she was a goddess cursed. He had so many questions, needed so many answers, but now was not the time to seek them. He would let her begin the story of the Gods and hope all his questions would be answered.

"At the beginning of time, there were the Gods and the Zydells. While the Zydells wanted tranquility and peace—to just simply exist—the Gods craved more. They wanted power, yearning for glory. They wanted to rule. So, the Six Eternal declared themselves rulers over the cosmos, and the Zydells were left alone in their world to live in peace, forever separated from the Gods, and their rule. Neither could visit nor interfere with the other through cosmic law."

A swift breeze wrapped around Garren, sending a chill straight down to his bones.

"The Gods traveled far and wide across the cosmos, seeking out life to rule over, to show their power to and receive their glory, but there was nothing to fulfill their unquenchable need. So, for thousands of years, the Gods ruled over the seemingly empty cosmos, sat upon their thrones in the High City of Vanriel, and began multiplying their godly race into far greater numbers, coupling with one another until there were hundreds of lesser Gods for them to rule over. There were Gods of sun, Gods of sky, of darkness, peace, and justice. Gods of all things." Oriana stopped, looking up at him with questioning eyes. He noticed that they had faded from vibrant green to a dull, pale color as she spoke. Concern wafted over him; it was as if the light inside of her had been snuffed out, but he still nodded for her to continue.

"But there were two Gods that stood out as different from the rest. They were stronger, more powerful. Each possessing a power to rival that of the Six Eternal. One of these Gods was the god of creation and chaos. Whereas the Six Eternal could only create new life with one another, through their collective coupling, this god had the power to create entire worlds and civilizations at the snap of his fingers, all on his own."

Garren sighed deeply, and Oriana stopped her tale, examining his stature, sagging shoulders, and the distant look he knew his eyes had taken. "Are you alright? If you have questions I can–"

"No," he interrupted. "It's okay. I'm following, please continue." This was insane. Not only were there Gods, but there was an entirely different, all-powerful species of them called the Zydells? He would be lying if he said his mind fully comprehended her words, but he continued to listen, watching as the sun's rays sent shimmering ripples across the sea far below.

"The god of creation brought into being creatures of all shapes and sizes, some with great power, almost matching that of the lesser Gods and some beings with no power at all. As he created, the other lesser Gods grew curious, visiting these new worlds to see what the god of creation had built. The Gods mated with these beings, creating wholly new races of powerful half god creatures. The cosmos was growing at an alarming rate and the Six Eternal became agitated, unable to fully rule and oversee all that was going on in their cosmos.

Some of the half god creatures were good and just, but many were evil, corrupting the worlds. They became unruly, threatening the destruction of the universe. So Zanos, King of the Six Eternal, forbade the coupling of any god or goddess with a creature brought into existence by the god of creation, putting forth a decree that all halfling's throughout the cosmos be executed. This was a task eagerly taken on by the god of war and trickery. The god of creation and chaos was locked away in a place we call the Dark World, never to create again."

"This god of creation, he made Svakland? He made this world and me?" Garren's ears rang, pressure pounding along behind his eyes.

"Yes." Oriana looked down at the angry waves crashing against jagged rock far below. "That god is my twin brother, Orrick."

Garren stiffened. "Orrick? You mean to tell me...you're saying that Orrick is my creator?" That vile man–or god, rather–had created him? He had unknowingly come face to face with his creator; the thought made his stomach flip.

"Not only you and Svakland, Garren. The demons you have spent your life hunting–they are his, too. He has been messing with the worlds, bringing beings from other realms here to observe their destruction for his own amusement."

The ringing in his ears shifted to an unbearable chorus of clanging bells as bile rose in his throat. "I think I might be sick," he said just before the contents of his stomach forced themselves up his throat, and he spat them down into the ocean below.

Oriana placed a gentle hand on his back, rubbing soothing circles as his stomach settled.

"I–I don't understand. Why? And why only in the past twenty-five years? Demons were unheard of before then. What does all of this have to do with you being here and being cursed?"

Oriana dropped her hand from Garren's back, and a mask of sorrow fell over her features. An uneasiness overtook him at her silence and the pain he could so clearly see etched on her face. "The demons are my fault."

Garren drew his brows together. "How are they your fault? You're not the one who brought them here."

Oriana looked back at him, a tear rolling down her elegant cheek. He wiped it away with his thumb.

"Orrick escaped the Dark World many years ago and discovered that I was stuck here, cursed. He saw what I did when in my cursed state, what I had become. I believe he wanted to replicate that throughout Svakland and watch his creations fight one another. That was twenty-five years ago, and from what you have told me, he's been sending new and different species here to wreak havoc ever since."

Garren's nostrils flared, and he let a growl echo through his chest. "The bastard," he said, copying Oriana's lewd gesture from earlier and aiming it up at the bright blue sky. The Gods be damned, he didn't care anymore. His entire life had been ruined because of those demons. "I will kill him."

"You can't," Oriana said in response. "He would kill you before you could even lift your blade. A god cannot be killed by mortal weapons."

Garren's heart raced, threatening to break free of its confines. If it were possible, steam would be billowing from his ears from the fire that had been lit within his chest. But then he looked at Oriana, at the anguish palpable through the hunch of her shoulders and the curve in her back. She looked tired. As if the weight of a hundred corpses were slung upon her back. And they probably were, he realized.

"Will you tell me about you now? About the curse?" His voice was soft, heedful.

Oriana sighed, nodding. "Even with the halflings massacred, the cosmos remained expansive, far too boundless for the Six Eternal to rule on their own. So, a hierarchy of the Gods was created. The Six Eternal would remain at the top, with each of their own children below them. The children of the Gods were each given a world to rule over, to be overseer in the Six Eternals place. I was given the mortal realm, your world."

"So, you are our ruler? Why then do the people...why do *we* not know of your existence? Shouldn't all of Svakland be praising your name?"

She breathed out a short huff of air in a weak laugh. "It is as I said. The Six Eternal are power hungry, cruel, and mirthless beings. They think us beneath them, even if some of us are just as–if not more–powerful than they are."

Her eyes darted to him so quickly at that final comment that Garren wrinkled his brow, wondering if she was saying she was more powerful than the Six Eternal Gods. He didn't question her further on it, only locked that bit of knowledge away for another time.

"Besides, I was more an overseer than an omnipotent ruler. Our job as lesser Gods was to make sure the worlds didn't become threatening and unruly, remaining within the limits of the cosmic universe. I don't wish for the people's worship, anyway. I am not worthy of it."

At that moment, a cloud covered the sun from view, casting the cove in darkness as the wind picked up, bringing gooseflesh climbing up Garren's arms. He couldn't help but think it an omen for Oriana's next words.

"I remained the overseer of this world for centuries, observing the customs and ways of the mortals. I became enthralled by their simplistic way of life. These people who were mortal, their lifetimes cut so short, loved deeply and lived to their fullest. It was breathtaking. It *is* breathtaking. They hold such a beautiful outlook on life.

I found that I wanted to experience it for myself, to live among them as they did, as if at any moment life could be stolen from me. I wanted to discover love, to feel happiness. And so, I created a life for myself in Elscar."

Elscar? Garren knew that name. It was a town south of the Phantom Wood that bordered the Bay of Sorrows. He knew something catastrophic had happened there long ago and now it lay in ruin, forgotten amid the Bad Lands.

Craters the size of entire towns covered the land, the ground loose and erratic. Smoke still billowed from it, like a volcano on the verge of eruption. It could be seen all the way from the King's road. He had seen it with his own eyes as he traveled north. It was as if an eternal flame burned beneath it. Many explorers had been swallowed whole by the Bad Lands, lost beneath the shifting ash and sand, never to be seen again.

"You lived in the Ruined City, along the Bay of Sorrows?"

"Yes, but it was not ruined then, and the bay was called the Gulf of Wonders." Her eyes sparkled with an array of emotions. "It was a dazzling city full of wealth, light, and happiness. It was even more spectacular than the Sovereign City. But there is no one left alive today to tell of its beauty, of its people."

"Except for you," Garren cut in.

"What?" she questioned, caught off guard.

"You remember its beauty, its people."

A soft smile illuminated her face for a fleeting moment before darkening into sadness once more. "Yes, but they are all gone because of me. An entire civilization wiped out in a single day, all because I wanted to feel love like they did."

"And did you?" Garren's voice was a low rumble. Something in his chest tightened as he anticipated her response. He turned away from her, surprised by the sudden rush of feeling that his simple question had sparked.

"I did," she whispered.

Something shifted between them—an understanding at that moment. They had both lost so much. Garren took her hand in his, bringing it to his mouth and placing a gentle kiss upon it, letting his lips linger on the warmth of her skin, breathing in the scent of her.

"His name was Darragh," she finally said. "He was a grand painter, extraordinarily talented. He was the light to my darkness. Good and carefree, unlike me in so many ways."

"Did he know what you"–he cleared his throat–"who you are?"

Her smile was tender. "No. He thought me to be human, just like him. I think of him every day."

"How did you lose him?" Garren inquired.

"That is part of the rest of my story." Her grin fell into a frown. Garren squeezed the hand he was still holding, bringing it to rest in his lap and placing his other hand atop it.

"As I said before, it is forbidden for a god or goddess to be with a being created by my brother, Orrick. Anthes found me here and commanded me to leave and return to the High City as overseer of the mortal world under him, to be his right hand once again."

"Anthes?" Garren questioned. "The god of war and trickery."

"Yes." Oriana took a deep breath and her entire body went rigid before continuing. "I refused him, and so he took Darragh and the entire town of Elscar from me. Destroying everything I loved. When I still would not go with him, he cursed me for eternity. You see, I couldn't bear to leave this world. I fell so deeply and irrevocably in love with humanity that even though all those I had loved were gone, merely ash upon the wind, I couldn't leave. Mortals are a strange creation, something completely unexpected and surprising to come from my brother's hand. They know their lives are short and will eventually end in death, yet they love more fiercely and live life more fully than any other being in the cosmos. They are unapologetically human, and above all, they are grateful for the lives they have been given. They are everything the Gods and I are not, and with them I found my home."

Garren was at a loss for words. He opened his mouth several times, but nothing came out. It felt more appropriate to stay silent, letting her passionate words linger in the air around them, catching on the cool winter breeze and carried out over the stirring sea.

An unexpected calmness settled over him. Beside him sat a beautiful, powerful goddess, cursed to remain in this world as a monster, unable to protect those she was meant to look after. It was a story straight out of a fairytale, but his whole life had been full of impossibilities. He himself was like a walking storybook character. He could run faster than anyone in Svakland, jump higher, and hold his breath for an outrageously long time. He thought he might even be able to breathe underwater but was too apprehensive to try, out of fear of adding another unnatural ability to his arsenal. It would be just another unanswered question in his life, along with the fact that his skin was almost impenetrable. Any wound would heal within minutes, even sooner in some cases, and not even an ounce of pink raw flesh or puckered skin would be left in its wake.

Sickness was one more piece of the puzzle. Not once in his thirty-two years of life had he been sick. Not when the fever sickness threatened his hometown, killing hundreds, or when the pestilence spread like wildfire through every town in Svakland, taking countless lives. He had never even had a sniffle.

Oriana's story had only made him feel relief, a sense of peace washing over him. He had feared that his entire life would come and go without any answers to why he was different. Yet here was someone who was different too, who didn't even belong in this world. But that thought only brought up more questions. If he was more like Oriana than anyone in the mortal world, what exactly did that mean? Did he not belong here either? Was he just another of Orrick's experiments, brought here from another realm, ripped away from his true home and family?

An ache settled between his eyes. It was too much to think about, too much for his mind to handle right now. He angled his head at Oriana, letting his gaze linger on her stark white hair blowing in the breeze and her ethereal beauty. She looked every bit the goddess she was sitting on this ledge beside him, but who exactly was she? Which goddess?

"Oriana," he said, voice coming out breathier than he had intended. "Who are you?"

She turned, slipping her hand from his grasp and looking him squarely in the eye. "I am Oriana, goddess of enchantment and bloodlust, daughter of Hylda, goddess of magic and beauty, and Anthes, god of war and trickery."

19

ORIANA

1ST DAY OF THE TWELFTH MONTH, 1774

Oriana hated the look on Garren's face. Pity.

Yes, her father was a tyrant, but she wanted no pity. She had willingly agreed to her current situation in order to finally free herself from him.

Whereas Orrick embraced the part of their father that churned within him, Oriana suppressed it. And she had been successful at suppressing it for thousands of years, even since the decimation of the halflings. Where she and her father had single-handedly slaughtered each and every one of the half Gods. It was then that she realized the true hunger and power of her bloodlust. It was unstoppable; when it was unleashed, it left nothing in its wake but death and decay. So, she had locked it down until it was nothing more than a low rumbling growl, like a sleeping lion that, with one wrong move, would pounce, transforming into a beast of snapping fangs and shredding claws.

If it hadn't been for the wretched curse, she may have been able to keep the bloodlust at bay, slumbering contentedly for another millennia or two. But as soon as those words had spilled free of Anthes's lips, set into motion from the core of his power, her control was gone.

"I was born with my father's thirst for death," she began. "But my mother's love for life and beauty. As you can imagine, the two don't exactly mesh well together. My entire existence has been a struggle, a constant war battling deep within. I hated the bloodlust; it was like a stranger taking up residence in my body, constantly tearing through me for control. My father knew this. He resented that I did not embrace the bloodlust—the part of me that was him. He wanted me to destroy worlds, wipe out entire nations by his side. He wanted me to be his right hand, but I refused to let that part of me reign free. I didn't want any of it. I don't want to be a goddess, an eternal being with these powers of destruction. I wish to be mortal."

"So he cursed you," Garren whispered.

She nodded. "What you saw in the forest, that was my bloodlust. What you see now, this is the rest of me, the good of me. During the full moon, I completely transform. The curse has divided my two consciences into fully separate beings. When the bloodlust takes over, I am helpless, unable to stop it."

"How many years has it been?" he inquired, voice sullen from all that she had just dropped into his lap.

"Over six centuries."

"Will you tell me the curse? Do you remember the words of it?"

She almost laughed out loud. She had permanently etched those words into her mind centuries ago. Oriana recited it for him word for word.

> *"In the cover of night's celestial glow,*
> *A lust for blood left hidden will grow.*
>
> *Two halves at war, broken apart,*
> *Each vying for command over the heart.*
>
> *The weakness of man your only satiation,*
> *A single choice made will be your salvation.*
>
> *When the power of crimson reigns free ten times,*
> *Only one can survive and take over the mind."*

She watched as Garren mulled over the words. "And there is truly no way to break it? Nothing that your own power can do to stop it?"

"I have tried all I could think of. This"–she motioned to the Phantom Wood behind them–"is all I could do to help ease it. To keep the monster within me at bay."

"The forest is your doing, then?"

"Yes. When I was first cursed, I awoke just outside of Sardorf. My bloodlust had ravaged its way all the way to this town, and I woke up surrounded by bodies. At the time, I didn't understand what my father had done to me. Had no idea what it would cause me to do every month. Looking back, I think I was just in denial, trying to ignore what I knew would happen. So, I created a life for myself here in the town, hoping that I would be able to make it a new home and start over. But when the next full moon came and I turned into the bloodlust once again, I understood. It was right there in the words of the curse all along. *'In cover of night's celestial glow, a lust for blood left hidden will grow.'* I knew that it would happen every month and that my bloodlust would grow tired of the town, migrating through Svakland, feeding on every town until no one was left. I had to contain it."

"So you created the forest, enchanting it to be a cage for your demon?"

"Yes, and it worked. I realized that once I transformed into my bloodlust consciousness, I no longer had the ability to use my enchantment magic. It seems that by separating the two into their own bodily forms, Anthes separated the power of those consciences as well. So, on the next full moon, the monster couldn't find its way out of the forest. It roamed, enraged, through an ever-changing maze of mist and trees. Except, Anthes made it so I couldn't escape the curse, not truly, anyway. On the blood moon, my forest no longer worked, and the monster broke free to feed on the innocent lives of Sardorf, and it has continued to do so every seventy-five years until, '*the power of crimson reigns free ten times*'. On the tenth blood moon, I will be no more. The bloodlust will be all that is left."

When Garren said nothing in response, she added, "In a way, Anthes did me a favor by separating the two. I no longer have that internal battle. The struggle of right and wrong, good and evil warring between themselves in my mind. But it cost these people and me greatly and will continue to cost me for the rest of eternity."

Garren remained quiet for a long time until he released his hand from hers and pushed himself up without a word, heading into the forest.

"Garren?" Oriana scrambled to follow him. "Are you alright?"

He just continued to walk–faster than she could keep up with–until he came to an abrupt halt and looked around at the thick, menacing trees.

"Garren–" she began, but he held up a hand to silence her.

"Shh, listen."

Oriana frowned, furrowing her brow as utter silence surrounded them. It always did in the forest; she had made it that way. "I don't hear anything," she finally offered, trying to understand what he was doing.

"Exactly." He spun, taking a step toward her. "You created this place, this forest of moving trees and mist, with no sound, no life, no joy. You designed a place of fear and heartache for the people of that town, a place they don't understand and are too afraid of even stepping foot in, too terrified to travel through and find out that there is a whole big, beautiful world out there for them. Forests full of singing birds, chirping frogs, and scurrying rodents jumping from branch to branch. Vast oceans they have never even seen. A world that has so immeasurably surpassed them in advancements that they would be lost if they ever got the chance to see it." His nostrils flared, practically blowing steam.

"I–I did it for them, to protect them. To protect all of Svakland. It was the only way."

"By trapping them like caged dogs? You have stolen their lives, kept them hidden in this dark place, kept them scared. You are no better than the Gods you hate. You have been careless and selfish," he spat, the full extent of his ire dripping from every word. "And for what? Because you don't love your life? You can't handle taking ownership of what you are? You are weak Oriana, goddess of enchantment and bloodlust. You are not worthy of these people or this world. They would have been far better off without you and your kind. You should have stayed with the Gods where you belonged." Garren turned from her then and began stalking back toward Sardorf.

"Better off?" Oriana yelled to his retreating form with a scoff. "Tell that to the thousands of innocent lives spread far and wide throughout the cosmos. If my father had succeeded, if he had used me as a pawn in his schemes, this entire world would be gone, annihilated in the blink of an eye all because Anthes thinks it to be worthless in the grand cosmos. The next time you judge me for doing what I thought was right, think on that. You and all of these people would no longer exist, Garren, if not for me. You know nothing of the Gods or of me."

She watched as he paused and began to turn his head but stopped short, tensed his shoulders, and walked away from her. All she could do was stare at his retreating form, chest rising and falling with heavy breaths of both anger and of sadness, because as much as she hated to admit it, some of what he had said was true.

She *had* trapped these people, forcing them into a far different life than what they could have had if it were not for her. But the worst part was, she had never thought of another option, had never even tried to figure out another way and save these people from herself, from this life of solitude altogether.

But her bloodlust needed to be satiated. If she could have held it prisoner somewhere there was no life, no one to sate its hunger; she would have gladly done it. But it needed to feed, and it would have eventually made it out of whatever confines she had put it in, just as it did on the eve of every blood moon. The curse wouldn't allow for it to be trapped completely.

Would it have been better to let it roam wild throughout all of Svakland or stay trapped within one small town? And what Garren didn't know was that the town's people of Sardorf fought back. They had created traps and diversions to fool the monster, to slow its feast.

Secluding the demon in one town versus an entire continent was the lesser of two evils, was it not? The vastness of the forest she had built and the town within kept her bloodlust contained so that when it was able to break free, it returned to the closest forms of life it could find–in Sardorf.

Oriana didn't dare follow Garren back into town. He had made it abundantly clear how he felt about her and what she had done all these years.

She was far better off staying away from the town until the final blood moon came at the end of the month. Tomorrow, she would go to Haldis in the early morning and say goodbye to her dear old friend for the last time.

20

GARREN

1ST DAY OF THE TWELFTH MONTH, 1774

G arren was ablaze with feeling as his heart and mind warred with one another like charging beasts.

In the short time he had known Oriana, his connection with her had grown to insurmountable heights, reaching a point where he could scarcely imagine his life without her. The very thought of losing her had his palms sweating and his chest aching.

He had been harsh, possibly even cruel, with his words to her. But his mind was having a hard time accepting what she had done, the torment she had subjected these innocent lives to. Locking them away, keeping them from living fully, all because she didn't wish to be what she was, a goddess. He needed space. He needed time away from her to cool the fire burning through him, scorching the earth beneath him with each heavy step.

As Garren made his way through the Phantom Wood, he couldn't help but notice how clear it was. Oriana had no doubt made it so, allowing him to see the path in front that led back to the town.

He barked a mirthless laugh. She could have done this for the people of Sardorf all along. She could have given them free access in and out of the forest, bringing the enchantment back just for that one evening every month when the full moon reigned overhead.

But no, she hadn't allowed them an ounce of freedom. She had stolen their entire lives without even a thought for them, only for herself. He stood by what he had told her. She was no better than any of the Gods she hated so much. She was just like her brother and her father. None of them cared for anything other than themselves, and they would do whatever it took to achieve their own wishes.

Garren marched his way back to Haldis's, still seething with anger.

Upon entering the inviting place he had called home these past weeks, he was greeted with the scent of roasted meat and herbs. His stomach grumbled in response, reminding him that it had been an entire day since he last ate, a day full of draining pursuits—both physical and mental.

"I was beginning to think you hadn't made it out of your fight with that beast." Haldis was in her usual spot by the fire. "And then when the full moon came and still you had not come out of the forest...well, I feared the worst."

Garren's nostrils flared. "You've known. This entire time, I've been searching for answers, countless hours spent trying to understand this place, and you've known everything."

"They were not my stories to tell. Ultimately, she had to be the one to tell you, in her own time." Haldis set aside her knitting to look up at him. "Come sit by the fire and have yourself some stew."

Garren sighed, some of the tension in his neck and shoulders easing as he joined the elderly woman by the fire.

He served himself a bowl of the hearty meal, practically inhaling it before returning for another helping and settling into the chair beside her.

"How are you so calm about all this?" he finally asked.

"My dear, boy," Haldis began. "Life is a fickle thing. It takes us through countless journeys in an array of directions, some good and some bad. But all things happen just as they should. You can either choose to be defeated and angry by it, or try to understand the good that can come out of it. For all things have a good, no matter how dire or hopeless they might feel in the moment. Sometimes you just have to search harder for it."

"How is what Oriana has done been good for anyone but herself?"

"Oriana has a reason for the decisions she has made. None of them have come lightly, Garren. You would be wise not to judge someone so harshly before you have truly understood why they have done the things that you so greatly despise."

"I just can't fathom how she could have been so selfish as to imprison an entire village just to avoid her duty. I can't see any good in that. She has left these people to suffer so that she does not have to."

"Have you actually seen the people of Sardorf suffer?"

Garren shifted his gaze from Haldis for a moment. Every image that came to mind from his time in the town was one of happiness. Merchant carts overflowed with wares on market day, children gleefully running through the town without a care in the world, and he had not seen a single beggar on the streets like in his hometown or any other city in Svakland.

He thought about the gardens on the rooftops, every one of them overflowing with vegetation and crops to feed entire families. He hadn't seen an unhappy, underfed, or sickly face during his time here. Haldis was right; the people were not suffering. They were thriving.

When Garren looked back up at the elderly woman across from him, a knowing smile spread across her lips.

"She provides for them," he stated, realization blooming within him.

"The people want for nothing. Sardorf is a place of beauty and peace, of love and happiness. It was not so before Oriana. Yes, it is true that the curse is a terrible, terrible castigation that has been the cause of great grief for both the people here and Oriana, but this town was on the decline in those days. They were starving and had fallen into poverty.

Sardorf lies at the base of the White Giants. The winters used to be long and hard, providing little to no food source. They relied on trade with other more southern villages, but the long and endless snows made it nearly impossible for anyone to bring in food and wares. People were dying rapidly, sickness spread like wildfire, and the ground stayed frozen for long months, making the window for planting and harvesting exceedingly small. If Oriana had not come when she did, Sardorf would have perished and none of these people would even be here. Their ancestors would be long dead."

"But hasn't her...demon..." The word felt tainted on his lips when talking about Oriana. It wasn't right. "Hasn't it massacred just as many people? Would it really have been any different?"

"If Oriana had not created the Phantom Wood, locking herself away, and had left this town to face another harsh winter, they would have been long dead before she could have devoured them. What she gave them was time. She not only enchanted the forest, but the town itself. Oriana made it so that they could survive and flourish. The people know what will happen on the blood moon, they prepare for it, and each blood moon fewer and fewer of them die."

Garren didn't know what to say. His harsh words to Oriana rang loud in his ears. "Is there nothing that can be done about the curse? Some way to free her from it?"

"She tried for centuries, analyzing each word carefully–tried everything she could think of to break free–but nothing has worked. She always turns back into her bloodlust each full moon."

"There must be a way, something other than her returning to Anthes." *The god of war and trickery*, he thought. He was speaking of the Gods as if they were living and breathing beings as opposed to fantastical creatures written about in story-books. He still hadn't fully wrapped his head around it; maybe he never would.

Garren's head pounded as he stared into the blazing embers in the hearth. Was the curse really all that bad if Oriana had helped this town and these people survive? But then he remembered what she had said, that on the tenth blood moon, the bloodlust would be all that was left of her, and what would happen to the people then?

Garren's mind was suddenly sparked as he thought about the people of Sardorf. "How is the town and the townsfolk after last night when..."

"They are fine. A little shaken, but no casualties. Only a few bigger injuries and many minor ones. It was good of you to send the boy for me and lead that creature into the forest so quickly."

"That was Oriana," he said quietly, still hovering over what he had said to her. He had been so cruel.

Haldis only smiled at him. "Oriana protects all that she loves, asking nothing in return. She is a true goddess, our goddess."

"I said some unforgivable things to her, Haldis. I–I was so angry, and I didn't give her the chance to explain."

"In due time, child. Allow her time alone after her change and all she has revealed to you."

Garren sagged into his chair, letting his head fall back against it with a heavy sigh. No. He wouldn't allow it. He would break the curse. He had to. Garren sat up straighter and scowled at the flames flickering in the hearth.

"I will find a way, Haldis. I will break Oriana free of her curse if it's the last thing I do." Garren could have sworn he saw a spark of hope ignite behind the old woman's eyes.

2nd Day of the Twelfth Month, 1774

A large crash of shattering glass from downstairs tore Garren from his slumber. He was instantly on his feet, racing out the door and down the stairs.

Haldis was pushed up against the far wall in the kitchen, Oriana slowly walking toward her. The look in Haldis's eyes had him grabbing Oriana's arm.

Oriana snatched his wrist and twisted. Garren grunted in pain and released his grip.

"Haldis," a chilling voice hissed from Oriana. "I've long awaited this moment."

The demon. Garren paused for a split second. How? He didn't have time to think on it; he had to do something to get her away from Haldis.

Garren wrapped his arms around Oriana in a tight squeeze, lifting her off the ground in a giant bear hug. With her arms trapped in his embrace, she let out a screech that had Garren's ears ringing and Haldis covering hers in pain.

He could feel her breaking free of his hold. She was strong, stronger than him. Garren did the only thing he could think of and barreled through the front door of Haldis's home. The wood splintered, chunks flying out into the street.

The impact loosened Garren's grip enough that Oriana's arms came free. She brought one up, grabbing him behind the head and flinging him over her shoulder onto the dirt packed street. Pain seared through his spine.

Oriana growled down at him, but before she had the chance to race back towards Haldis, he swung a leg around, and caught her ankle. Oriana went crashing to the ground beside him. He rolled quickly atop her and held her wrists down above her head.

Oriana spat in his face, bringing a knee up in between his legs hard. Garren could no longer breathe. His strength left him momentarily as the pain between his legs grew to an excruciating crescendo. Oriana used the opportunity to throw him against the building next to them, wood cracking from the impact. Garren crumpled to the ground, sucking in heavy, agonizing gasps.

"Oriana," he rasped as his breath returned. "This isn't you. You need to take back control. Beat the demon."

She laughed at his words, narrowing her sickly yellow eyes at him. He gulped, finding it hard to look at her deformed face, but he didn't tear his gaze away for a moment.

"You know nothing of Oriana, boy. She is weak, just like you." The monster of bloodlust stalked toward him, stepping closer with each word until she was less than an arm's length away. Garren struck, his fist hitting her square in the center of her chest. The blow threw her backward so hard that she slammed into the side of Haldis's home, leaving an indentation in the building, cracks crawling outward from the spot.

Oriana slunk to the ground, unmoving.

Garren pushed himself away from where he leaned against the house across from Haldis's, wiping away the dribble of blood that had escaped from his mouth.

He stood over her and peered down at her face, covered by her pale, disheveled locks. Oriana jolted upright, staring straight up at Garren; her eyes had returned to their vivid green, her face no longer a monstrous deformity.

"Oriana?" he breathed, taking a tentative step toward her.

She stood, her eyes glazed over with a faraway look full of anguish and exhaustion. Taking a small step toward Garren, she reached her hand ever so slightly in his direction. And then she ran, bolting straight for the Phantom Wood.

"Oriana!" Garren bellowed, half sprinting, half limping after her, but she had already disappeared into the forest. By the time he got there, the trees wouldn't let him in. An invisible shield had been raised, pushing him back every time he tried to enter. He barreled into it repeatedly, desperate to force his way through the barrier.

"Oriana!" He slammed his fists on the enchantment once more before finally giving up and turning to limp his way back to Haldis's.

When he returned, Haldis was sweeping up the mess of wood chips that used to be her front door, but she dropped her broom upon seeing him. She came to grip his arm, leading him to her own chair by the hearth. He gladly sat.

"We have to find a way, Haldis. We have to break the curse." His voice held an emotion he hadn't felt in a long time. Haldis only nodded in response, brushing a loose strand of hair from his forehead like his mother used to. "I'm sorry about your door. I'll fix it before nightfall."

Haldis smiled tenderly at him before walking to her small bookshelf and pulling a book from the shelf. She dropped it into his lap. Garren looked down at the large tome reading the words *Gods and Curses* etched upon the cover.

"The Gods and their curses have been evident in this world since the beginning. I've looked through this book too many times to count. It has been passed down through my family for many generations. These stories are written by their own hand. My family has kept these stories secret, only passing them through our direct line of descendants." She handed it to him, placing a hand on his shoulder. "Many of these tales have been forgotten or twisted into something that no longer resembles the original history. I've not found much about breaking curses, only how they were inflicted or what they were. Maybe you will find something I could not. We start our research now."

Garren reached up and placed his hand over Haldis's, where it still rested on his shoulder, giving it a gentle squeeze. "We start after I fix your door."

21

ORIANA

2ND DAY OF THE TWELFTH MONTH, 1774

No, this isn't happening. It was all a dream. It had to be. It wasn't the full moon. But Oriana could not deny the scene laid out around her.

Garren stood in front of her, sweat dripping from his forehead, chest heaving with deep, exhausted breaths.

He took a single step toward her. She felt herself doing the same before she stopped, turned, and fled.

It was time. She had to leave. She had to set into motion the plan she only hoped would work to keep herself trapped for the rest of eternity. It was the only way, and it was something she should have done long ago. The plan had always been there in the back of her mind, but she'd always held hope that the day would never come when she had to use it. That she would miraculously break the curse or defeat the bloodlust on her own. But she hadn't, so the time had finally come for her to leave.

She could hear Garren's voice calling out for her. She ignored it, accepting the fact that this was the end. She would never see him again.

Smoke trailed after her through the wood, spreading out, and cloaking her as she fled. She didn't want anyone following her, especially not Garren.

A tear trailed down her face as she thought of Haldis. She hadn't had the chance to say goodbye. If she stayed any longer, she would surely hurt Garren or Haldis further, or worse, kill one of them.

Oriana fled to the only place she could, the only place she would be helplessly alone. To her utopia, to the old barley farm.

Oriana collapsed upon the silken, moss-covered earth at her farm, laying in her illusion of euphoria, and she hated it. Hated its beauty, its peacefulness, and the joy it was meant to bring her. She didn't deserve joy or happiness. She deserved only the cold misery of exile.

She couldn't look at it any longer, couldn't bear its beauty. Oriana lifted a hand, fingers splayed wide, before clenching them into a tight fist. The farm around her melted away into darkness. The enchantments shifted, floating into the sky like ash on the wind until no beauty remained. Shriveled, thorny vines replaced the lush, colorful flowers. The quaint cottage collapsed into a pile of stone and rotted wood. The farm finally returned to what it had been all those centuries ago when she first discovered the curse.

She looked at what was left of the old barley farm. There was nothing. It was just a ruin of rust and decay.

But something stark and white caught her eye. It was the edge of her journal sticking out through the rubble of her former rented cottage. She withdrew it from beneath the stone heap, blowing dust and dirt from the cover.

In this journal were the names of Liam and his lovely wife, Alma. The names of Haldis's family and all the others she had taken from this world. She hugged the book to her chest, letting the tears flow free.

For some time, she stood there, remembering her victims as she so often did, until finally making her way toward the cliffs that had become a comfort over the centuries. To Shipwreck Cove, the resting place of her final fleeting ounce of happiness in this world.

She was grateful then for the reality that she had found true love not once, but twice. For she could say with pure honesty that she loved Garren, and she would treasure their moments together for the rest of eternity.

Some were never lucky enough to find a Darragh or a Garren in their lifetime. It was quite magnificent that she somehow had, and both times in the mortal world. She did something then that she did not often do. Oriana looked up to the sky toward the place that she once called home and placed a hand over her heart. "Thank you, Hylda, mother, for the gift of love twice over. For that small happiness in a dark existence." She knew that her mother had blessed her with this, for Hylda could not interfere with the curse or her daughter's fate, but could offer small blessings in other ways.

She often wondered if her friendship with Haldis had also been her mother's doing, and so she thanked her mother for that as well. For the family, she had found in Haldis, for all the nights spent by the fire, for that human interaction that made the final years of the curse somewhat bearable.

As Oriana stepped to the edge of the cliffs, she lifted her journal into the fresh sea breeze, and she did something she had never done before. She prayed for her victims, for their souls. She apologized for taking their lives too soon, and she wished them peace in the afterlife, wherever it might take them.

The pages broke free on the wind, carrying over the churning waves of the cove, over the wooden spires of ships long forgotten, over the bones of the Storm Seas victims, until they disappeared into the horizon. Their souls set free among the cosmos.

A heavy weight was lifted from her shoulders. She closed her eyes and held her arms out on either side, letting the swift breeze caress her and envelop her in a welcoming embrace of comfort and relief. But all good things must come to an end as that heavy weight was slammed back down upon her shoulders with just one word uttered from a voice of pure evil.

"Daughter." Oriana spun at the call, her back now to the beauty of the swirling Storm Sea. Anthes stood just at the clearing of the forest, long, white plaited hair whipping around him in the breeze like an angry serpent. A look of rage forever chiseled into a face of stone. She watched as his muscles twitched in anticipation, always ready for a fight.

Oriana's skin sizzled with fury. She brought her arms back down to her sides, clenching her hands into white-knuckled fists. Steam spewed from her ears like a boiling kettle. This was his doing. He was the reason her bloodlust had reared its ugly head beyond the full moon's glow. "What have you done?" Oriana snarled.

"The Blood Moon is upon us. Your darkness knows. It strengthens. You have let it be free for centuries and it has tasted what it can have."

"No, you have let it be free. You cursed it to be so!"

"Did I, daughter?" He took a step toward her, red eyes narrowing on her. "Yes, I did indeed curse your bloodlust to be set free upon this world, but I did not curse you to be weak. If you wanted to, you could control it. That is your greatest flaw. It is why you will never be a true goddess. You are unable to let your gifts coexist. You know not how to balance them. Your hatred for your bloodlust consumes you. It blinds you and it will destroy you. You will stay cursed in this world for eternity."

"It is evil! It is you!" she spat. "I hate that most of all. You, Anthes, destroyer of worlds. That is all you do–you kill and destroy, wiping out entire races from existence. I wish to be nothing like you. I want no piece of you within me."

"You misunderstand what it is to be a god, daughter." His voice was full of contempt. "It is to rule. To ensure the survival of the cosmos. War is inevitable, it is necessary, *we* are necessary for all things to flow. Without us there would be no cosmos."

"I do not misunderstand, father. It is the way you rule–the way all the gods rule–that I do not understand. You only wish for glory and power. You have no care for the creatures you rule over. If you did, the cosmos would thrive. It would feel your love. It would not be afraid. It is your interference that causes destruction and war. You put the idea of war in their minds because you thirst for it. You are the cause of their pain and suffering. All of you!"

"You are no daughter of mine," Anthes growled. And then he was gone, leaving behind only a hot, scorching blast of wind that boiled her blood.

Oriana knew that whether she went back to her rightful place as the goddess overseer of the mortal world or stayed here to inevitably destroy it, Anthes would win.

If she returned, he would make her join him in the destruction of innocents. So, either way, innocents would die.

She had thought hard about this moment for the past centuries. A part of her had always worried that the curse would not end the way she thought. That her goodness would be killed off, and all of her enchantments would disappear with her. But Anthes had just unknowingly confirmed her theory.

He had not cursed her goodness. He had only cursed the bloodlust to rule. It had only required that side to feed. That was why her enchantments no longer worked during the blood moon. It was the curse's way of enacting its will. Her goodness could not die, not truly, and so her enchantments would hold firm.

With the curse ended, there would be nothing the monster could do to unleash itself from the grip of her magic. It would only have control over her body, and she would remain a powerless prisoner within her own mind forever, watching with pleasure as the bloodlust tried and failed to push through her enchantments.

Oriana looked out to the ever-present swirls of the Storm Sea, ready to shred to pieces anything that might draw near to the rocky shore. The sea was no longer traveled, for no ship had ever passed through it without meeting its doom below the cliffside. That made it the perfect place for a monster to be locked away for the rest of eternity.

She only wished she could say one final goodbye, but no, she couldn't. She shouldn't.

"Oriana," a voice called from behind her.

Garren.

It was as if their minds were one, as if she had conjured him from the fleeting thought of saying one final goodbye.

She spun, unshed tears glistening in her eyes as she saw him standing at the edge of her forest like a phantom in the night. She had been on the cliffs of Shipwreck Cove all day, until the stars filled the midnight sky, winking in and out as if to say *we see you, we are with you*.

"I had to see you," Garren's voice broke on the words, raw with emotion. "I thought you might be here."

She was at a loss for words, afraid that if she opened her mouth, only a strangled sob would come out. She hadn't thought she would see him again. She hadn't wanted to, for she knew it would be too painful.

"Are you alright?" His steps rustled through the grass as he came closer, edging from the gloom of the forest and into the shimmering beams of moonlight.

"No," was all she could muster, voice cracking.

He came before her then, grabbing both of her hands in his. "I am so sorry. I was an ass."

She smiled up at him, looking into his dark, breathtakingly exotic face, such a contrast to his cool gray eyes, noticing for the first time how truly different his features were from anyone she had seen before. "I could never stay mad at you," she finally offered. "I'm not sure anyone else would have acted any different after what I told you."

"But I'm not just anyone," he whispered, bringing one of her hands up to his lips and flipping it over to place a gentle kiss on her palm. The feel of his beard brushing against her skin and his warm lips pressed there sent a desperate, aching heat traveling through her.

"Garren, I..."

"Shh," he hushed, silencing her as his lips descended upon hers.

Oriana moved closer, melting into his embrace as he explored her with a gentle possessiveness that sent a tingling heat rushing through her. Their tongues mingled, teasing one another, each growing more ravenous as desperation built between them.

She explored him just as possessively, deepening the kiss as she unbuttoned his tunic, pushing it open to expose the hair-roughened, hard flesh beneath. Her hands traveled over him, feeling the taut muscle shifting beneath her fingers.

Garren's breath hitched and he left her mouth, trailing soft kisses down her neck that sent sensations of pleasure down to her most sensitive area.

Oriana moaned, moving against him, digging at his trousers, desperate to feel him, all of him.

Garren pushed her gown from her shoulders and yanked it down over her hips until it pooled at her feet, revealing her completely to him. He surveyed her fully. She bit her lip and squeezed her thighs together against the ache that throbbed between them at the look of pure lust on his face.

She looked down to the true evidence of his desire tenting his pants. He stepped closer, reaching out to cup a breast in each hand. His hands were rough, calloused from long hours of sword wielding. They glided over her erect nipples and she sucked in a breath at the swirls of ecstasy coursing through her.

"I need you," she rasped against him, pushing his trousers down so that his hardness sprung free for her to see. She grasped his length and he growled, moving his hands down over the smooth flesh of her belly and around her waist. One large hand migrated between her thighs, spreading her lips to feel the wetness of her anticipation.

"Fuck," he whispered into her neck, his cock twitching against her belly.

Garren tore off the rest of his unbuttoned tunic, stepping out of his pants before lifting Oriana from the ground with fluid grace and laying her down upon the soft grass beneath them.

"You're so wet," he groaned against her mouth.

His words only caused her need to grow, and she kissed him harder, placing her hands on his back and pressing him further against her, rocking her hips up to meet his.

He sucked in a ragged breath, sinking his full length deep inside her.

She almost cried out with pleasure. With each gliding thrust, she rose and met him with equal fervor, moaning against his lips.

Oriana clawed at his back, desperate to feel him closer, deeper.

Their bodies moved together, faster and faster, until their breathing grew hoarse. Ripples of intensity began spreading through her body in waves, building with each deep thrust until she shattered, gripping onto him and crying out in fiery pleasure, riding each euphoric wave of her release. Garren bit her lip before yelling out with his own release, collapsing atop her with a sweet sigh of rapture.

They lay there as their breathing slowed, their bodies still tangled together, her hand rubbing against his back in lazy circles.

Garren turned, pulling Oriana along with him, so that they were on their sides and he could observe her form more fully. His eyes were whirling storm clouds as he stroked them slowly over her physique. She openly did the same, letting her gaze wander down his sculpted, naked body before she smiled up at him.

"Like what you see?" he chuckled. A blush suffused her cheeks as swirling tingles of need began to course through her once again.

"I don't hate it," she said with a smirk, bringing a hand up to tangle in the dark hair dusted upon his muscled chest.

They were silent for a long while, indulging in the tender moment between them. It felt so final to Oriana. She knew that this is where she would say goodbye.

"How much time do you have?" Garren finally asked, pulling her closer so that their naked bodies were flush against one another.

"Until the thirty-first day of this moon cycle, when the tenth blood moon rises," a single tear rolled down the side of her face, swallowed by the ground beneath them. "That is why this is the last time we can meet. The bloodlust has grown stronger. You saw it just this morning. I could have killed Haldis. I would have," Oriana shivered at the very thought. "It isn't even near a full moon. It's gaining full control over me, and I cannot risk being in Sardorf and changing again. This is our final goodbye."

Garren cupped a hand behind the back of her head, rubbing a thumb along her jawline, and pulling her forehead to rest against his. "I will not give up on you. Anthes will not win."

She brought a hand up to hold onto his wrist, breathing him in—breathing the moment in—as she knew it would be their last together. "Don't you see, Garren? He has already won. He won when he cursed me all those centuries ago."

"No," Garren placed a gentle kiss upon her forehead, letting his lips linger before saying, "He has not won until the final crimson moon ascends."

22

GARREN

31ST DAY OF THE TWELFTH MONTH, 1774

G arren had granted Oriana her wish by not meeting with her again. In fact, he hadn't once seen her since the night she said goodbye. That night she had made it very clear that she was done, that she had accepted her fate and that there was no way to break her curse, but Garren could not accept it. He would not. He had not said goodbye because he refused to believe it was the last time he would see her. This was the beginning for him, not the end. He would go to the far reaches of the universe to save her, his goddess.

It had been an arduous and exhausting few weeks of combing through text after text to find anything that might spark something brilliant, that might answer everything. Haldis had helped him analyze each piece of the curse, inspecting it like a pair of scholars learning, poking, and prodding at a new species, attempting to understand its anatomy. She wished to save Oriana just as much as he did.

But it was all entirely pointless. Trying to learn about the Gods and their work was like learning how to sprout wings and fly. There were no records of anything of note, only scant suspicion and assumptions, tall tales of what the Gods were thought to be like. There was no concrete proof of anything, no knowledge of the Gods at all.

"I don't think our answer will be hidden within these old books, no matter how many times we read through them," Haldis finally said as Garren collapsed into a chair beside her, weariness gripping him from all sides.

He only grunted in response. They were fully out of options. Garren had suffered a headache for days now as the aching anticipation and realization of what was swiftly descending upon them–upon Oriana–came into focus.

The blood moon was only a day away. He would lose the one person who had set his heart aflame, who had completely stolen it, and refused to relinquish the grasp she held around it. His one true, unadulterated love.

Garren slammed a hand down hard onto the armrest of his chair. "There has to be a way!"

"The Gods leave little room for error in such things. They are not ones to be foiled, they don't take kindly to losing."

Haldis's words reminded him of an ancient tale he had read in the text written by her own family, *Gods and Curses.*

It was a particularly horrifying story of an entire civilization Anthes had cursed thousands of years ago. It hadn't helped in their search for answers, but had stuck out to him as he had heard it before when he was young. But the tale he'd been told was very different, a fantastical and upbeat rendering of the story, which certainly made no mention of a curse.

If Haldis's ancestors' tight looping scrawl depicting the story was to be believed, there had supposedly once been an island off the northeast coast of Svakland called Barinsia. It was surrounded by an ocean that the storyteller had called the Golden Sea.

The Barinsian people played with forces and power they had no right to, angering the god of war. The story went on to say that they had somehow found Anthes's battle axe and used its power to vanquish their enemies and gain full control over the mainland of Svakland. They sought to rule the world, and during the short time in which they held possession over the battle axe, they did just that, amounting to great power and wealth.

Haldis's ancestor wrote of a curse that Anthes had set upon the entire island and its people, effectively extinguishing their very existence. only to be replaced by swirling seas and endless storms, which was now known as the Storm Sea. According to rumor, the people were trapped beneath it, forever lost within the raging storms and churning sea. Many had died trying to navigate through the treacherous waters to find the great wealth the Barinsians had stolen, but the seas were unpassable. The island—and its people—became mere myth.

Garren couldn't help but think it a somewhat similar story to Sardorf, a town forgotten—hidden for centuries—due to a god's curse. He only hoped if the story were true and if the Barinsian people were still somehow surviving, that they had fared as well as Sardorf.

Oriana told Garren that Anthes had used her to wipe out entire nations and even worlds, but it seemed Anthes was fully capable of doing it on his own as well. These Barinsian people, Garren assumed, were just one of many Anthes had cursed in his eternal existence.

Garren clenched his jaw as ire rose to the surface, teeth aching from the pressure.

The only thing missing from the texts were the words of the curses themselves. Haldis's ancestors' book spoke of the Gods in great detail, describing their afflictions, but there was nothing about the exact words of the curse or any information on how to break them.

Oriana had spewed off word for word and her entire riddled curse. If Haldis and Garren could find others, they might have been able to analyze them and discover something, anything of use. But they were only left with the words of Oriana's curse.

Those words sat at the forefront of Garren's mind. He had recanted them forward and backward, left and right, and every which way he could, trying to distinguish something that would reveal the key to ridding Oriana of it.

He found nothing.

"If we could just figure out how to kill off the demon side of her, get rid of it, I know the curse would break. The entirety of it is centered around her bloodlust."

"It is not a matter of killing off a piece of her," Haldis began. "Each side of her is clutched within the grip of the other, fighting for dominance. The curse has heightened the hold they have over one another, to the point that Oriana believes them to be separate from one another. But they are not."

Garren narrowed his eyes at the elderly woman's words, trying to understand what she was saying.

"Together, good and evil war with one another, invoking a question of what is right versus what is wrong. It is the same with humanity. We are all half moral and half wicked. We each have a choice of which we will allow to reign; we listen to our own conscience to decide for ourselves what we will do. God or mortal, we are all two halves of a whole." She paused, thinking of her next words before continuing. "But Oriana is ruled by the fear of her bloodlust. She thinks it is stronger, but it is not. The curse has only made her fear a reality. Oriana is not truly gone when the monster emerges; she is just lying dormant, ruled by the curse." Haldis's eyes glazed over with memory for a moment. "I've seen it for myself, seen her within the monster, cowering behind its eyes. She is not fully gone during the full moon–she cannot be–for the two sides are still one and the same."

"So how do we bring her out? How do we break the curse?" Garren frowned, rubbing his eyes with the palms of his hands, wearier now than he had been during the entire past month of research.

"The key to breaking it is in the curse itself," Haldis mused. "The words are significant. They shape it. All words have meaning. But we could remain here, continuing to speak the words of the curse aloud and they would hold no more meaning to us than they did a week ago."

Garren's gaze lingered on the orange blaze of the fire as he mulled over Haldis's words. The words of the curse stated that under the full moon, her bloodlust would be set free to feed and would do so until the tenth crimson moon, unless she made the choice to return to Anthes's side. All of this they knew, but there had to be something they were missing, something *significant*, as Haldis had put it. She was right; they could keep going over it, but they weren't Gods, and didn't understand their world.

"What exactly are you suggesting, Haldis?"

"Answers will not be found in our world, Garren. We have exhausted our resources. It is now time to reach out to those outside it." Haldis's voice was calm, a soothing touch in the storm brewing in Garren's mind.

"A god," he breathed. "But how? We are running out of time. How would one even contact a god? And who would even answer the call if I tried?" Garren raked a hand through his hair. It was madness.

"Gods are creatures of power and revenge, Garren."

He looked at her then, to her face withered with age—wisdom shown on the plains of her features, in every line and spot. He was thankful that she had been in Oriana's life for the past decades—that Oriana hadn't been alone.

He knew what he had to do.

Garren walked to Haldis and bent, placing a gentle kiss upon the elderly woman's forehead. "Thank you, Haldis."

He moved to leave, but she grabbed his hand, holding on tight. "Save her, Garren. Bring her home safe."

"I will," he vowed and left the cottage, heading for the monastery to call on the god of chaos and creation.

As Garren stepped inside the monastery's dimly lit corridor, a sense of foreboding overtook him. The last time he had been in the presence of Orrick, he hadn't known he was a god. And now it wasn't the fact that he was a powerful, otherworldly being that sparked Garren's anxiety; it was the fact that Orrick had been funneling the beasts of death and darkness that he had spent his life destroying into this world. He was the very reason that Garren's parents were gone, along with so many innocent others. How was he to face the one who had caused so much grief? Orrick was vile, a being of pure, unadulterated evil. Garren feared that if the god came from his call, that he would do something dumb, like try to kill the immortal being of creation and chaos.

"Fuck, what am I doing?" Garren ran a hand through his dark curls, blowing out a breath of frustration. This was a horrendous idea, but like Haldis had said, they had exhausted all other resources. This was their only shot. And from that one moment of being in Orrick's presence, Garren knew without a doubt that the god was one that would revel in revenge.

Garren walked down the long-arched corridor, glancing at the intricately painted walls depicting the story of the Gods—as this world believed it to be—but he knew the drawings to be false. The real story was more than the people of Svakland could handle. Shit, it was almost more than he could handle.

Garren continued down the passage, attempting to settle his racing heart and cool the heated blood coursing through his body as he made it into the atrium. Streams of sunlight gleamed through the skylight in the center of the domed roof high above, illuminating the place of worship. Directly below it, a large basin sat on the marble floor to collect rainwater, a gift from Mathis. The water was used in religious ceremonies by those who had sworn fealty to the god of sea and storms.

Oriana would have hated it. He remembered her words; *the Gods don't care for anything but themselves and their own power and glory.*

He looked then to the towering statues that encircled the room. Each god and goddess stood looking down on the mere mortals below. Lit candles and other godly sacrifices lay at their feet.

He was glad to see that the room was mostly empty, probably due to the late hour. One monk lingered, having just stood up from the base of Hylda's statue–Oriana's mother, he realized, still in awe of that fact. It all seemed so unreal.

Garren approached the monk. "Excuse me, would you be able to help me? I am curious how one might call upon a god and talk to them directly."

The monk smiled at him, "One cannot speak directly with a god. You must pray to the god, offer them a sacrifice of great value to you. If they approve of your offering, they will show you. They will return your gift with one of their own."

"What do you mean?" he questioned.

"The Gods do not speak. They show you through their works. They will grant your desire, help someone in need. They show you through this," the monk said, pointing to his own heart.

Garren attempted not to roll his eyes. This was a pointless conversation. Orrick was not the type of god to speak to your heart. He was more likely to crush it in his palm. Oriana had told him that the Gods couldn't care less about this world. He didn't even know why he had asked the monk. Of course, the Gods didn't come here, nor did they speak to these people. He was on his own then.

"Thank you," he said to the monk. The man bowed before retreating, leaving Garren alone in a room surrounded by stone Gods.

Garren drew in a deep breath before kneeling on the cold stone floor. He raised his head up to the skylight and closed his eyes, trying to find the right words.

"Orrick, I call on you." Garren groaned as his voice echoed throughout the large room sending his words down each of the surrounding corridors. This was insane, idiotic. He looked around to see if anyone had entered or heard him. The atrium remained empty and eerily quiet.

Garren closed his eyes and sighed wearily, pinching the bridge of his nose between his thumb and forefinger. He could do this; it was the only way. He had no other options, and he was out of time.

"I summon thee, Orrick, mighty god of chaos and creation," he tried again, biting out the words as if they pained him to say. Garren cracked open one eye, peering around him, even though he knew no one would be there. If Oriana could see him now, she would laugh her ass off. Thoughts of her brought him back to the severity of his task.

"Orrick, omnipotent god of creation and chaos, I beg of you. Please, hear me. I need your help. I will do anything. Please, just hear me." He was met with silence. Garren let his shoulders sag beneath him in defeat. This was it. There was nothing else to be done. Oriana would be forever trapped.

A low cackle rang out, bouncing between the statues of the Six Eternal. Garren spun in every direction for the owner of the malicious laugh.

"Well, to say this is a surprise would be quite the understatement." Orrick slinked from the shadows of an alcove beside the statue of Anthes.

How fitting, Garren thought. "How long have you been there?"

"Long enough to hear your feeble attempt at paying me a compliment. Tell me, was it pure agony to speak forth the words '*Omnipotent god of chaos and creation?*'" He said the last part in a mocking tone. "I have to say, I was hoping I would see you again, but I wasn't entirely sure you would make it out alive from the battle with my little gift. Although, I suppose you of all people in this feeble world, would be the one to have vanquished that beast. Well, you and dearest Oriana, of course."

Garren's skin crawled. This was a bad idea. He itched to lash out at Orrick. To wrap his hands around his godly throat. "I need your help," Garren ground out through clenched teeth.

"My help? I didn't think you could surprise me twice, halfling, but I am baffled. Whatever could you need my help with?" Orrick knocked the candles and offerings from the base of Anthes's statue before sitting down, crossing one leg over the other and leaning back, casually resting his elbows upon Anthes's carved stone feet.

Garren only heard one word from Orrick's sarcastic retort. *Halfling.* "What did you call me?"

Orrick brought a hand to his chest, gasping in an exaggerated show of mortification. "Don't tell me you are unaware of your ancestry?"

Garren did not change the look he gave Orrick, only continued to stare at him with all the enmity he could muster.

"Well, this is just too good. A god living among mortals who doesn't know he's a god?" Orrick's laugh made Garren wince. It reminded him of a rusted hinge squeaking incessantly on a steady breeze.

Garren's breath hitched. He couldn't move, couldn't speak. *A god?*

"Demon got your tongue, Garren?" Orrick rose from his seated position and stalked toward him. "That's right. After our little encounter, you had me thoroughly intrigued. I did a bit of digging to find out who you really are. It seems that our High Ruler, King of the Six Eternals, Zanos, is your father. He, the very one who made it forbidden to lie with any being other than a god, who killed off all the halflings centuries ago, has been hiding a secret. A halfling of his own." Orrick looked at the statue of the god of life and death, bringing a hand up into the air and clenching his fist. With his nostrils flaring and his jaw clenched, the statue of Zanos crumbled into thousands of pebbled pieces, stones littering the ground around them.

Garren flinched at the god's destruction of the large statue. "I–I don't understand. My father was Bentos of Cirus, my mother Kira of Thengali. I grew up here, in Svakland. I...I am not a god."

"Oh, how wrong you are, halfling. Those people were not your parents. You have a far older and darker history than you know."

"Stop calling me that," Garren snapped.

Orrick only chuckled at his vehemence. "You are an entirely new creature I did not even know existed."

Garren remained utterly still. "What do you mean?"

"You, my dear strong friend, are half god, half Zydell."

Zydell? Oriana had told him of the Zydells. They were another kind of celestial beings, but he recalled her saying that through cosmic law, the Gods and Zydells were not allowed to visit one another. "How is that possible?" Garren questioned.

"Ah, I see my sister has told you of our cosmic law, prohibiting us Gods from going to the Zydell world. That is true. However, it seems that Zanos does not think the law applies to him." Orrick's eyes momentarily turned into a raging red flame before settling back to the same green as Oriana's. "The bastard. He's been secretly going to the Zydells' world for a millennium. You are living proof of that. He will understand the limits of my rage soon enough, both him and my father, for locking me away."

"You lie," Garren accused.

"If only I did, dearest Zydell. You are not the only one angered by this news." Orrick's eyes flickered yellow then orange before settling on red once again, matching his rigid stance and the snarl upon his lip. His eyes reminded Garren of a seahorse changing color along with his mood. "The Zydells are an entirely different race of immortal beings. They, too, were created by the cosmos just as the Gods were, and some would even say they are more powerful than the Gods, for a Zydell is a keeper of both time and space. They have not only the ability to alter the past, present, and future, but they can change one's reality completely."

Garren felt lightheaded.

Orrick began to circle Garren where he stood. "Our mighty King, Zanos, fell in love with the Zydell Queen Ada, continuing visits to the world, which ultimately resulted in your creation, the creation of an entirely new, powerful hybrid species.

For a millennium, you grew in your mother's womb, for such a power as yours takes time to develop. But it was not just you, no...Ada had triplets. Three children created with the power of both the Gods and the Zydells."

Garren studied the god intently as he spun his tale.

"The combination of both cosmic beings created a power that threatened to tear the cosmos apart. If left to fully understand and hone your skills, you and your siblings have the ability to end both immortal races and the cosmos itself."

The room began to spin in circles around Garren. He was lying; he had to be lying. Garren rested a hand against one of the statues and leaned heavily against it.

"Stand up straight, halfling, for that is not all," Orrick snapped. "You see, there are Gods that would have used your power for their own purposes, to gain control and fully rule the cosmos if they didn't accidentally destroy it instead."

"Anthes," Garren breathed.

"Anthes," Orrick confirmed. "He has always craved power, craved full control, and would have destroyed both

Gods and Zydells alike in the blink of an eye to get what he wanted. He discovered the existence of you and your siblings.

Zanos, the god of life and death that he is, wished to find a way to kill you all, but your mother, Allarina, hid each of you before he had the chance. She scattered you throughout the worlds I created. Rather clever of her to have chosen this particular world to hide you, really. It is one of the weakest I've ever made." Orrick barked out a loud, uncharacteristic laugh before adding, "I'm surprised you haven't yet killed them all, knowing what you are capable of. Have you even tapped into your abilities?"

Garren just stared at Orrick. "I–I..."

"You know, for one of the supposed most powerful beings in the universe, you're rather disappointing." Orrick came to stand before Garren then, smirking, said, "Maybe you just haven't been provoked enough."

Orrick's hand shot out quick as lightning, wrapping around Garren's throat and lifting him from the ground.

Garren sputtered and gripped Orrick's wrist with both hands, eyes wide as he felt the blood drain from his face.

"Come on, Garren, fight back. Show me what you are truly capable of." Orrick's eyes shuttered blue, frosting over with mirth, that amused smirk still spread upon his lips.

Garren flared his nostrils. He wanted nothing more than to see Orrick suffer just as much as the people of this world had suffered from his ruthlessness.

Garren could feel something rising inside of him, something cold and foreign. He welcomed it, allowing it to take over his body, his mind, every single fiber of his being, until a harrowing crack like the sound of breaking wood echoed around him. Then came the scream.

Garren blinked, and the cold that had frosted both his blood and bone melted. He looked down, realizing his feet were on solid ground once more, and saw Orrick collapsed, clutching what was left of his right arm.

The mangled flesh hung limply, bone splintered and poking through the skin in multiple directions. It looked as if a hammer had been taken to it, shattering it until it was barely recognizable as an arm.

"Fuck," Garren muttered. "D—did I do that?"

"Well, I didn't very well do it to myself!" Orrick lashed. "Put it back! Fix it!"

"I don't know how," Garren said, still staring at what he had somehow done. He looked down at his hands in disbelief, then bent closer to Orrick, reaching out his hands toward the mangled mess of bone and blood.

"Don't touch me again," Orrick growled, backing away.

"Do you want me to try to fix it or not?"

Orrick bared his shining white teeth at him before relenting. "I swear if you do something worse..."

"You'll kill me?" Garren finished, raising an eyebrow.

Orrick seethed, narrowing his eyes at Garren. "Just fix it."

Garren gingerly laid his hands back upon Orrick's arm, closing his eyes, attempting to pull on the power he had felt spread through him. Like a scared kitten hiding in a dark hole, Garren coaxed it back from where it had stayed dormant all these years. Icey tendrils climbed through him once again, and when he opened his eyes, Orrick's arm looked as if nothing had even happened to it.

The god only nodded at him in thanks, rubbing at his shoulder and bicep before pushing up to his feet. Orrick stared warily at Garren for a long moment before asking, "What is it you called me here for, halfling?"

Garren had almost forgotten the reason for this meeting. His mind and body were still reeling from all it had just discovered, but a single thought of Oriana brought him back to what was most important, saving her.

"I need your help."

"Yes, you've said that." Orrick crossed his arms and looked at Garren expectantly. "Well, are you going to tell me what you need help with, or should I go before you decide to practice your gifts on me again?"

"How would you like revenge?" Garren finally said. "How would you like to best your father?"

Orrick raised a single snow-white brow. "I like where your head is at, halfling. What do you have in mind?"

23

ORIANA

31ST DAY OF THE TWELFTH MONTH, 1774

The bloodlust had consumed Oriana ten times in the past weeks. It was just as Anthes had said–it was getting stronger. Her dark desires would soon be all that was left of her.

This being her final day, she wished to spend it where it had all begun.

Elscar.

She had left at dawn, only just arriving at the pockmarked, sandy earth that once was her home, right as the sun had completed its full arc into the cerulean sky.

These people–this place–could still be here. Would still be here if she had not... Thousands of souls that would have turned into millions.

Anthes had wanted her by his side to embark on an endless mission of destroying worlds that he believed could not be cured, that would inevitably cause their own demise. He thought himself a savior in his own demented way, but he never even gave them a chance. Didn't allow for them to figure out how to fix their worlds, to try. And that made him a monster in her eyes. He thrived on power. In his eyes, any world he considered weak wouldn't survive and thus weakened the cosmos.

By refusing to go with him and staying in the mortal world, had she not been as bad as Anthes? Had she not destroyed the people of Elscar? Had she not destroyed so many lives in Sardorf?

If she could turn back time and choose a different path, would all of this have happened anyway?

The questions endlessly circled her mind until her head pounded and her ears rang.

The "what if" no longer mattered. It had happened–all of it–and there was no going back to fix the wrongs.

Her existence had always been a struggle and no matter what happened, no matter the decisions she had made, that would have remained the same.

The Gods feared death above all else, for they were immortal, but Oriana had always been the one to fear life. Eternity was a long time to war with oneself. And oddly enough, now thanks to Anthes, she had found a way out.

A way to free her dark desires without harming anyone, without causing destruction.

If she had the chance to go back in time to change what had become of her, she would not.

Long ago freedom had been a word to laugh at, something always out of reach, a dream.

Now, it was so close she could almost reach out and touch it.

The city of Elscar was overgrown with brush and ivy. Centuries of abandonment had left the ruins exposed to the elements, further sinking them into the earth and allowing for new growth to cover the old city. Yet still smoke billowed from its destruction, a show of the powerful magic that destroyed it. Flames still flickered along the tops of the ruined buildings. With a wave of her hand, they were extinguished.

Oriana navigated her way through the tall grass and the craters marring the earth until she finally came to what was once the town square. This had been the main hub of activity within the city. Long ago, there had been a freshwater well in its center, where all the townspeople would visit daily to take water. It was now nothing more than a pile of dirt and rubble covered with mossy earth.

She sat there in the center and breathed in deep, closing her eyes as she let her enchantment magic roam free. It swelled from within her, pulsing out in waves. *With* each new wave, a new building pushed up through ash and sand, until Oriana had raised the town of Elscar and restored its original splendor, just as she remembered it.

A small, contented smile ghosted upon her lips at the site. Before, she hadn't wanted to remember the town for what it once was; she wanted to remember what had happened to it, what she had caused. But as the finality of her fate crept toward her, she wanted to remember. She needed to see the town standing once again.

Once the blood moon rose in the sky, she would be forever transformed into her dark self, but these enchantments would remain. Forever etched upon this beautiful world.

Godly creations were as immortal as the Gods and goddesses themselves.

She hoped that people would come here, and that they would create a new civilization from her gifts. For the first time since her final night with Garren, she was happy.

It was a long way back to Sardorf and she couldn't dally any longer. She had done what she had come to do.

As Oriana rode back to the Phantom Wood toward Shipwreck Cove, she thought of Haldis and of Garren. It had been agony these past weeks staying away from them, especially after her last meeting with Garren. She wished things could be different, that she could go back to him, and that they could somehow find a way together, but they couldn't. She had been stupid and too damn afraid to let him in, and now that she finally had, they were out of time.

Her heart ached at the thought of never seeing him again, of losing love for a second time. She wished she could say one last goodbye, spend one more beautiful moment with him, but she couldn't risk it. It was a sacrifice she had to make in order to save the entirety of Svakland. The clock of her curse was ticking, and she had stayed far too long in Elscar. The crimson moon was mere hours from replacing the sun in the sky. In the end, it didn't matter. They would be better off forgetting about her. It was easier this way. She would disappear, never to be heard from again.

Oriana had developed an idea over the centuries, having always feared that this time would come.

Far into the Storm Sea, where the water was the roughest and the storms mingled among one another, she would create an enchanted cage. She would venture out into the hub of tempests where no mortal had survived, and she would lock herself in the cage.

It was as good a plan as any. It would work; it had to work. There was no alternative. She would throw all her magic into the prison, creating an orb of swirling waters and endless streaks of lightning within the storms. Once the curse was fulfilled, once the sun of the first day in the new year rose in all its glorious splendor, she would be forever trapped within that cage of her own making. It would be an impenetrable force, unbreakable by the bloodlust or by any god who might wish to set it free. Her enchantments would hold, and she would be trapped in an everlasting state of drowning and electrocution, locked inside a sea of storms.

When Oriana made it back to the Phantom Wood, she vowed that she would bring this place that had been her only refuge–a sliver of salvation–to an end and allow the people she had come to love freedom after almost seven hundred years.

She had watched generations of families born. Known the many great grandparents of those who currently resided in Sardorf, and for all that she had caused them to endure, they were happy. Everyone within that small town nestled in her forest of enchantments was happy. She was grateful for these people more than they knew, and she would forever be indebted to them.

A sudden sadness settled over her. She had made it to the cliffs she knew so well with a few hours left before sunset. Oriana sat, reminiscing on her time in this world, on the humanity she had gained from these people, and on the friendships that had made the curse an easier burden to bear.

She would be lying to herself if she didn't admit to feeling like a failure in her inability to break the curse. But the more she thought of it, the more it seemed that Anthes had made it impossible. There was no way out of the curse. The only way to end it would be to agree to return with him, becoming his right hand in the war of the worlds once again. That would never happen, and she had come to terms with the consequences of that decision. She much preferred the thought of being locked inside herself, the bloodlust free but trapped for eternity, then going back to unleash it on any unsuspecting beings that Anthes wished to eradicate from existence. She preferred it as long as the bloodlust was contained and unable to harm anyone else.

The cold wind swept up from the ocean, lashing out at her face and hair. Oriana squinted against it as she raised her hands and pushed them out toward the sea. A massive bubble of water shimmered out over the ocean. Waves, winds, the spray of the storms, thunder, and lightning all wrapped around the orb of seawater so fast and loud that no one would be able to see or hear her once she was inside. Her cage was ready.

She lowered her hands, placing them upon the rocky cliff's edge and then pulled them upwards as if conducting an orchestra from the depths of the ocean. Sandy platforms glistening with seaweed and scattered bits of coral pushed through the ocean's surface, stretching out toward the storms in a long row and forming a walkway of steppingstones to her prison.

Oriana took a deep breath, and without looking back, she stepped onto the first platform.

24

GARREN

31ST DAY OF THE TWELFTH MONTH, 1774

"I wish to break Oriana from her curse, and I need your help," Garren said as he sat heavily at the stone feet of Hylda, Oriana's mother.

Orrick sputtered a malicious cackle. "My help? That curse is the best thing my father has done in centuries. Why in the cosmos would I want to help you break it?"

"Because it will anger your father. Anthes wishes for Oriana to come back to her rightful place as goddess and if she doesn't do that, he wishes her to destroy this world as her bloodlust. If we break the curse, neither of those things will happen. Anthes will be furious, and with the three of us combined, we can imprison him the same way he did you and Oriana. We can be the punishers for once." Garren searched for the words that would keep Orrick interested.

"You know nothing of the Gods, halfling," he spat, kicking a piece of stone skittering across the atrium floor. "Anthes cannot be tricked. He is the god of trickery. It is a fool's errand."

Garren remembered Oriana's words once again: *the Gods only care for themselves and their own power and glory.* "Think about it. You will go down in history as the god that tricked the trickster god. You will be worshiped as one more powerful than Anthes himself. You might even be his replacement within the High Council of Vanriel."

"I see my sister has told you much of our world. But you are wrong. The High Council does not just simply replace an eternal. The Six Eternal have been on their thrones since the beginning of time, when they were the only beings in existence with the Zydells. They cannot be replaced. Will not be replaced. Anthes is one of them. They will not accept any other in his stead."

"How do you know? Has anyone ever tried? Perhaps they have just never deemed anyone worthy of a seat beside them." Garren was reaching, tugging gently on strings in an attempt to pluck one that might turn Orrick in his direction. That would make him agree to help save Oriana. "Perhaps their feelings of Anthes are similar to yours, and they are searching for a way to get rid of him. You said it yourself that your father would kill both the Gods and the Zydells without even a thought to gain full control of the cosmos."

The god said nothing. His gaze had wandered off to some distant world in obvious contemplation of Garren's words. Garren took it as a small beacon of hope.

"Do you know how to break the curse he has placed over Oriana?" Garren tentatively asked.

Orrick turned his back to Garren, staring up at Anthes's menacing stone form, but answered, "Without knowing the exact words he cursed her with, I cannot answer that."

"I know the words to the curse. I have them memorized."

Orrick's head swiveled like an owl. He raised one eyebrow in interest. "I'm listening."

Garren recited the words of the curse just as Oriana had said them, word for word.

"In the cover of night's celestial glow,
A lust for blood left hidden will grow.

Two halves at war, broken apart,
Each vying for command over the heart.

The weakness of man your only satiation,
A single choice made will be your salvation.

When the power of crimson reigns free ten times,
Only one can survive and take over the mind."

Orrick picked up a piece of stone from the pile that had once been Zanos, his true father, he realized. Garren flung that thought away; he couldn't let his mind go there until he saved Oriana.

"I myself have never been subject to one of my father's curses, but I have enjoyed playing a hand in causing him to inflict them upon others. Each time, there has been a specificity to his words." He threw the piece of stone up and caught it again, continuing the movement for a long while as he paced the circular room, deep in thought.

Garren thought Orrick almost looked human–sane–as he paced. Yet there was something about the way he had worded that statement, *'playing a hand in causing him to inflict them upon others'* that made Garren's skin crawl. How many curses had Orrick instigated his father into performing?

Garren stared down at the pile of rubble between them. Orrick was mischievous and ruthless, and he seemed to hate the Gods just as much as Oriana, but in a different way. A more destructive way. He was surprised no one had heard the crumbling statue of Zanos shattering upon the atrium's floor.

Zanos, god of life and death, Garren thought. He couldn't fully grasp what that meant, or how he could possibly be the offspring of not only the king of the Gods, but a Zydell as well. And somehow it made perfect sense. He felt as if the mystery that was his life had finally been solved. He finally had an answer for why he was stronger, faster, and could heal so quickly. And everything else strange that had happened in his life. It all made sense now. He was immortal.

He was a god.

Garren's thoughts wandered back to what he had done to Orrick's arm just moments before. If he was capable of something like that, what else could he do? He shivered at the thought.

He thought back to each of the demons, the creatures from other worlds he had conquered over the years. Their remembrances sparked something else in his memory. If he was a god, or possibly even more powerful than one, how had that creature he fought before entering the Phantom Wood wounded him so severely? What had Orrick called that creature again?

"What is a Martok?" Garren asked.

Orrick stopped, catching and holding tightly onto the rock he had been tossing before turning to Garren. "Ah, yes. My Martok. Ruthless creatures from your home world."

"Wouldn't that also be your home world?"

"Not Vanriel. That creature came from Velhaven, the Zydell world."

"But how did you get it here if you are not permitted in their world?" Garren questioned. Was the fact that the creature had come from the world of the Zydells why it had affected him so badly? He had thought Oriana's forest had slowed his healing, but maybe it was the Martok's doing all along. A creature from his own world. With every answered question, ten more piled up in its place.

"I've never been one for following rules, just like your dear old dad, I suppose." Orrick winked at Garren before throwing the rock at Zanos's decapitated stone head, hitting it square between the eyes. "Enough," he said, stalking closer to Garren. "Are you sure those were the exact words of Oriana's curse?"

"Yes, those are the exact words she told me."

Orrick placed his thumb and forefinger on his chin, rubbing his jawline. "Hmm, I find the specific phrasing of *'the weakness of man your only satiation'* to be particularly odd. All the other phrases just seem like the usual grumpy old Anthes pouting about the fact that Oriana won't embrace her gift of bloodlust. He wishes only for her to be back at his side, which is woven through each line of the curse." Orrick's eyes flashed purple, and his features changed into an emotion that Garren could not discern. The corners of his mouth pulled down slightly before he added, "He has always been fonder of her."

A hint of sorrow laced Orrick's words and caught Garren off guard. It was bizarre to see such a raw and human emotion on his face. Garren had assumed that Orrick had no feelings outside of malicious intent, anger, and delight in seeing others suffer.

"What is so odd about that piece of the curse?" Garren asked, feeling uneasy at the thought of Orrick having real feelings.

"It is too specific in its wording. He knows Oriana's bloodlust and what it can do. She has unleashed it many times for him in battle, nearly single-handedly annihilating entire worlds. So why not just leave it at the first verse. '*In the cover of night's celestial glow, a lust for blood left hidden will grow?*' That already implies that her bloodlust will be unleashed upon the world. Why would he specify it, adding it into the curse a second time? There must be a reason for it."

Garren furrowed his brows. He wasn't sure he completely understood Orrick's thought process, but he began to analyze the words. Anthes hated the weakness of this world and many others. It was worlds like these that he wished to destroy.

"Well, it doesn't matter anymore. Her time is up. You're better off just forgetting about her," Orrick said, looking up toward the atrium's roof.

Garren followed his gaze to the hole in the domed ceiling. The sky was darkening; they didn't have long.

"What if we could somehow convince Anthes to break the curse?"

"Again with this tricking of the trickster god. It can't be done." Orrick pushed himself up from where he had been lounging on the mountain of stones.

"It's possible, between the three of us. I know it is," Garren pleaded. He was growing more anxious and desperate with each passing second. He would not lose Oriana.

"Three?" Orrick questioned, looking bored once again. Back to his old self.

"You, me, and Oriana."

"Two godly children and a halfling who can barely use his powers?" Orrick laughed a wholesome snorting sound that seemed genuine for once, although still slightly mocking. Not that Garren would expect anything less from him. "Gods, they will write sonnets about us. It's poppycock."

"You will never know if you could unless you try," Garren queried. "What's the worst that could happen? You can't die. Anthes would just lock you back into the Dark World and you would simply escape again. No harm, no foul."

Orrick gave Garren a sidelong look, his eyes narrowed into slits. "Fine, but we do it my way. I am the smartest of us, after all." He began making his way down the long corridor and toward the entrance of the monastery.

Garren took one more look around the atrium, shaking his head at the crumpled heap of stone that had scattered its way across the room. "Where are all the monks?"

"I locked them in their rooms," Orrick called from down the hallway.

"You what!? Why?" Garren yelled after him, jogging to catch up to the god.

Orrick turned, bringing both hands up with his fingers splayed and his palms facing toward Garren, shaking them in a showy fashion. "Chaos."

Orrick had devised a plan that Garren thought was exceedingly far-fetched. He didn't think it was going to work, but as Orrick had mentioned many times on their trek through the Phantom Wood, Garren knew nothing of the Gods.

And that was the only reason that he had conceded and put all his faith into Orrick. The god knew about Gods.

The plan depended on a few things and would go terribly wrong if it didn't work, but the biggest part of it required Garren to disarm the almighty god of war of his battle-axe.

Orrick had explained that Anthes had channeled an extreme amount of his power into the weapon, and without it, Anthes would be considerably easier to overcome. But with his axe, he would be near unstoppable.

The axe was named Balthar, meaning god killer in the old language. It was aptly named for being the only weapon that had killed a god.

The High Council nearly confiscated the weapon from Anthes, but instead, the god of war was sworn to never use the axe against another god again. Doing so would result in his own death by the weapon.

With Anthes disarmed of his battle-axe, Orrick would attempt to trick him into reversing the curse in exchange for the weapon, and then take him to Morial, the Dark World, to rot for the rest of eternity.

Garren had agreed to the plan, but he couldn't see any of it actually succeeding, and the worst part was he did not know if Orrick would choose to betray him instead, leaving both him and Oriana at the mercy of Anthes and Balthar.

Garren knew that Orrick would enjoy watching Oriana become the demon and watch her tear her way through Svakland. If that happened, Garren wasn't sure he would be able to stop her. She was the one demon he wouldn't be able to kill, not only because she was an immortal goddess, but because he loved her.

Fuck the Gods. He was going to break her curse. His chest grew tight as the sky grew darker. The plan would work. It had to.

Garren knew exactly where Oriana would be.

Orrick and Garren pushed through the trees and out onto the cliffside, and Garren's eyes widened as he took in the scene before him.

Oriana was halfway out to the Storm Sea, walking along a sandbar that jutted up from the sea and joined with the edge of the cliffs.

"Oriana!" Garren called out to her, but she didn't turn.

He sprinted after her, the waves of the churning sea crashing over the sand and spraying him with water that was cold as ice. He gritted his teeth and charged on.

The masts of broken ships creaked and groaned as he passed them. "Oriana!" he called out once more.

This time, she turned. "Garren?" he saw her mouth his name, the ocean's roar too loud to hear it over. And then she began running toward him. Tears glistened upon her cheeks and his chest ached at the sight of her pain. He wanted to take it away, needed to.

They crashed into each other, locking in a deep embrace. "Garren," she sobbed. "What are you doing here?"

"Saving you," he whispered against her ear. "I can't lose you, Oriana. Not when I've just found you."

"Garren." She broke free of their embrace. "It's too late. My fate is set. Y-you need to forget me."

He was about to tell her that he could never forget her when she caught a glimpse of Orrick standing on the rocky cliffs behind them, looking like his usual, bored self. Her eyes frosted over instantly as she speared Orrick with her gaze.

"What is going on? Why is Orrick here?"

"We've come to help you. I've asked for his help to–"

"You did what?" She cut him off. "Are you daft? He does not want to help, Garren! He helps no one but himself."

"Exactly." Garren put his hands on either side of her face, forcing her to focus on him. "That's exactly the leverage I used to solicit his help."

She scrunched her brows together. "What do you mean?"

"Come, and we will explain everything," he said, grasping her hand to pull her back toward the land.

She pulled out of his grip. "I can't."

"You can. We can fix this; we can break the curse."

"No!" Her voice was booming and final.

It was then that Garren looked behind her, to the ball of swirling sea hovering at the end of the sandy walkway. "What have you done?"

"It's a prison. It will hold me, locking me within the storms, so that I will never hurt another soul."

"No," Garren breathed. "Please, Oriana, let us help you."

She remained quiet, but she didn't turn to walk away either.

"Please," he said again.

Oriana closed her eyes, chest rising and falling in one large breath before she opened them again and nodded once. Intense relief washed over Garren as he grabbed her hand once more and led her back to the cliff side.

"Sister!" Orrick exclaimed, opening his arms wide for a hug. "So good to see you."

"Whatever you have convinced Garren to do, un-convenience him, brother. We both know you would like nothing more than to see me as a monster for the rest of eternity."

"Always so dark and lacking in faith, sister." Orrick rolled his eyes. "Your little halfling is quite the masterful manipulator. He is the one who has convinced me."

Oriana narrowed her eyes. "Halfling?"

"Oh yes. Your dear Garren is the son of the almighty Zanos. Can you believe it? That sniveling, irksome blighter has been going around and doing the same thing he has forbidden us all from doing. He even had me locked in Morial for it. Well, he will feel my wrath soon enough." Orrick continued to prattle on about all the things he would like to do to Zanos when he next saw him, but Oriana didn't seem to be listening; she was just looking at Garren.

"Are you alright?" he asked.

"Yes. It's just, it all makes sense now. I'm not sure how I didn't see it. I suppose I didn't think any half Gods were left after...well I just didn't put it together. But now I understand why you were able to see through my enchantments."

He gave her a small smile, attempting to hide the heaviness that had settled inside of him even since Orrick had dropped the news.

Oriana touched his arm and said, "I'm sorry. I'm sure that was hard to hear and quite a lot to take in."

"You don't even know the half of it," Garren started, about to tell her that not only was he half god, but that he wasn't even mortal at all, but then Oriana stiffened, cutting him off with a hand over his mouth.

"Stop. You have to go." She pushed him back toward the forest. "Go!"

Orrick snatched Garren's wrist and pulled him into the trees. "Oriana." It was the first time Garren had heard Orrick call his sister by name. "You don't back down. Fight."

A single tear rolled down her cheek at her brother's words. Garren wanted to say something, to ask what was going on, but Orrick pushed him behind a tree trunk and held him there.

The air grew thicker, hot and stifling, making it hard to draw breath. Garren peeked around the trunk of the large evergreen and saw a being that he could only describe as a true god, standing almost as tall as the statue of himself in the monastery. He was walking toward Oriana.

Anthes.

25

ORIANA

31ST DAY OF THE TWELFTH MONTH, 1774

She knew he would come to see her doom. That her father would not miss the opportunity to once more try to coerce her to join him in his quest for destruction.

"The final blood moon has come, daughter. I give you one last chance to put your foolishness aside and ascend once again to your place beside me."

"Why are you so desperate for me to come back? Centuries have gone by and I have continued to refuse, yet you still think I might change my mind. Why?"

"I see a greatness in you that rivals those on the High Council."

She laughed. "And what? You wish for me to join you on the High Council? They have ruled for millions of years.

If there was any chance of them adding a member to their court, they would have done so by now."

Anthes took a step closer to his daughter. "We can overthrow them, together. We can rule the cosmos. Control the realms."

"You are insane. What makes you think that I want that? That I want any of it. I don't wish to live among the Gods. I do not wish to be on the High Council. I wish to be here. To live forever in this world."

His hand shot out to wrap around her throat, but it was intercepted by a pale, long-fingered hand.

Orrick. Oriana was awestruck by her brother's interference. Not once in their long existence had he gone between her and their father. She narrowed her eyes at him, wary of what game he was playing.

"Father, I believe Oriana made her point very clearly. There is no use in forcing the issue. You know that not everything can be solved with brute force." Orrick's voice was laced with venom. Oriana's eyes widened. Orrick had never used such a biting tone with their father, especially not to defend her.

Anthes growled. "Orrick, you conniving serpent! Who let you out of Morial?"

"Let me out? Well, no one let me out, father. I let myself out." The corner of Orrick's mouth quirked in a prideful, mischievous way.

"You are the foulest of our kind. I am ashamed to call you son. This"–Anthes motioned toward Oriana and her surroundings–"is all your doing. I will take you back to the dark pits of Morial when I am finished here."

Oriana snorted.

This time, Orrick didn't stop the hand that wrapped itself around Oriana's neck. "Something funny, daughter?"

She grabbed her father's wrist with both hands, but it was as if she were trying to reach around a barrel. Her voice came out in shallow rasps. "I think it funny that both of your children have disappointed you so much. How very unfortunate for you."

Anthes snarled, tightening his grip around her throat. She sputtered, but only laughed more as she looked down at Anthes's feet.

A snake as thick as Anthes's own torso began to coil its way up his legs. His eyes shot down in surprise, something Oriana didn't often see on her father's face. He shook his leg angrily, trying to dislodge the serpent, but it only strengthened its hold, moving further up to his waist. He grabbed the scaly creature with his free hand and yanked. Still, the serpent coiled tighter.

Oriana's laughter continued even as she gasped the last of the air from her lungs. Orrick simply watched with a devilish smirk. "My, my sister. I never thought I would see such outright defiance. I mean, you've stayed in this place against father's wishes, endured his curse all these years, but to use your magic against him? I never thought I would see the day. Dare I say it, but I'm proud of you, sister."

Anthes's eyes were spitting flames as he cast his gaze back upon her. "Stop this!" he commanded, but she did not comply. Her breath wheezed as she sputtered another laugh. The snake twisted its long body around Anthes's arms and chest, stopping its ascent and resting its head on his shoulder. It squeezed even tighter and finally, Anthes's grip released from Oriana's throat. She fell to her knees, coughing as she breathed in heaping lungfuls of air.

Suddenly Anthes's red eyes widened. The snake locked around him, forcing his arms against his sides. Anthes clenched his fists, muscles and veins bulging through the gaps between the curled snake's black scaled body. Oriana looked around him to see Garren lift her father's battle-axe from the sheath across his back. The wind stilled, and the ocean ceased to move. Time stood still as the power of the weapon enveloped him; a brightness surrounded him, and for the first time he looked like a true god. Her eyes widened in awe and disbelief at how she had not seen it before. Garren twirled the weapon in his hand as if it were built for him before narrowing his eyes on Anthes.

Anthes squirmed in place, but Oriana willed the snake to coil higher around his throat. "Release Balthar at once, mortal!"

"How weak do you think mortals to be now, father?" Orrick taunted from his nonchalant stance, leaning up against a tree.

"Reverse the curse," Garren's voice rang out as if amplified. The force of it pushing against her. It was at this very moment that Oriana wondered if he was more than just a half-god and if he was, then what powers of his own did he possess?

Each born god or goddess was given two gifts–one from their mother and one from their father. If Zanos was Garren's true father, then Garren likely possessed a power far greater than hers or Orrick's, for Zanos was King of the Gods, more powerful than any on the High Council. Was Garren's mother truly the woman who raised him? Or had she been some other higher being? The way the axe seemed to sing in his grip as if it was finally in its rightful place, proved him to be something more. Much more.

Oriana took a quick glance at Orrick, but her brother's devilish smile was trained on Garren.

Anthes's laugh was spiteful. "You cannot command a god, mortal."

Garren took three long steps toward Anthes, angling the blade of the axe at his throat.

Oriana could have sworn sweat beaded on her father's brow.

"Reverse the curse." Garren's voice was lethal. It caused even Oriana to quake where she stood.

"It is not up to me to reverse it, boy. The curse must be fulfilled or broken by she who bears it."

Garren pressed the axe further into Anthes's throat, where golden blood began to well. Anthes did not flinch away from it, the warlord that he was. He only trained a hard eye on Garren.

"Garren," Oriana broke the tension between the two Gods. "He speaks the truth. There are powers at work that you do not fully understand. When Anthes cursed me, he set a fixed destiny. The curse must be fulfilled. It is now up to fate and destiny alone."

Garren growled in a way that Oriana had never heard him do before. It was the sound of pure, powerful rage.

"Release him," Garren said.

"What?" Oriana gasped. "No, if I release him, he will–"

"Release him!" Garren roared.

Oriana flinched at his fury and looked to Orrick, who gave her a barely perceptible nod before training his eyes intently on Garren.

Her heart slammed against her rib cage as she released the snake's hold around her father.

Anthes shot forward, but before he could grab his battle axe from Garren's grip, Garren tossed the weapon at him, pulling his long sword free from where it lay sheathed on his back.

"Garren!" Oriana screamed, but she was too late. Anthes was already swinging the axe at Garren's head. But to her utter surprise, Garren brought his sword up and blocked Anthes's swing.

The clang of steel echoed around them. Garren's blade held firm, against all odds. It didn't shatter into a million pieces around them. The blade had blocked Balthar. *Impossible,* Oriana thought, but the memory shot through her mind of that same blade drawing blood from her own finger.

Anthes drew his brows together in baffled astonishment.

Garren pulled back, and then pushed forward with his attack, moving through the motions with fluid grace just as she had seen him practice all those weeks ago at this very cove. He forced Anthes on the defensive, pushing him further and further toward the cliffside. But before Garren could push him any further, he spun, slashing his axe at Garren's side. Garren dodged with fluid ease but lost the upper hand. Anthes came back at him with god-like speed until Garren was dancing dangerously close to the edge of the cliffs. Just when Oriana was about to scream out his name to warn him, he dove and rolled to Anthes side and slashed his blade. Anthes grunted, swinging his axe to parry the strike, but the curved edge hooked onto Garren's sword. Oriana saw the flash of victory in Garren's silver eyes just before he yanked his blade upward and Anthes's axe went flying in a spiraling arc through the air. It was caught not by Garren, but by Orrick, who had come to stand by his side.

"Who are you?" Anthes growled at Garren.

The tip of Garren's blade dug into the god's chest and broke through his flesh, where a light trickle of blood began to soak into his leather armored vest.

"I am the man who never wants to see your hideous face ever again. You will leave this place and never set foot here again. For if you do, I will know it and I won't be so kind the next time we face one another." Garren's voice was deathly calm. "You will never see your daughter again. Never even think her name, for she is no longer and will never be your pet again, god of war and trickery."

Anthes seethed at Garren. They looked like two towering giants ready to tear each other limb from limb.

"Dearest father," Orrick sauntered forward, "Might we take a little journey to one of my favorite realms?"

Anthes didn't break his stare with Garren. "What are you, boy?"

Orrick looked quickly to Oriana. "Might you...you know," he said, making a coiling motion with his finger. With a snap of her fingers, the snake coiled tightly around her father once again.

"Oriana, release me!" Anthes boomed, struggling in the snake's hold.

Her eyes found Orrick's once again, and he gave her a small nod of approval.

Orrick's arms wrapped around his father. In all their years growing up together, they had never thought to team up against Anthes together, but Oriana saw it clearly now. Their combined powers could defeat him–*had* defeated him–for they were stronger together than apart.

Orrick graced her with the most genuine smile she had ever seen spread upon his lips. She mirrored him with a nod of respect.

"Release me at once, children!" Anthes squirmed within Orrick and the serpent's hold.

Orrick ignored his father, instead turning to Garren. "Halfling, do not allow her to *find satiation in the weakness of men.*"

Garren furrowed his brow, opening his mouth to no doubt ask what Orrick meant, but Oriana cut him off. "Why are you helping us?"

An uncharacteristic sadness settled over Orrick's features. "The Gods cast me off long ago, sister. It's time I pay them back for their harsh judgements. Tootles," he said, wiggling his fingers in a small wave and plastering that mischievous smirk back upon his lips. And then he was gone, taking Anthes and Balthar with him.

Oriana and Garren turned to each other, both opening and closing their mouths in unison, wanting to say so much, wanting to ask so much, but the crimson moon shining high above had other plans.

26

GARREN

31ST DAY OF THE TWELFTH MONTH, 1774

The world around them looked as if it were bathed in blood. A cold wind picked up, rustling through the trees. The final blood moon had finally descended upon them. This was it. They had failed–he had failed. This couldn't be the end.

Garren could do nothing but watch as the love of his life transformed for the final time into the deformity of her bloodlust. She speared him with her yellow gaze as her features contorted, molding into the creature. She cracked her neck back and forth as the change overtook her, opening her mouth wide with a growl as her teeth lengthened into daggers.

"Oriana, fight it." Garren didn't want this to happen, didn't want her to have to live this way, but the demon roared, fully emerged.

Garren looked out at the sea, at the sandbar she had created. It was all there, her power and enchantments were still there, which meant that *she* was still there, and how could she not be? A goddess could not be killed; not even a piece of her could be.

Haldis's words came to the forefront of his mind, '*Oriana is not truly gone when the monster emerges, she is just lying dormant, ruled by the curse.*'

"Don't you see, Oriana!" Garren yelled at the creature snarling before him. "You are still there! You are not separate! You are both the good and the evil. You can stop it; you can break free!"

"Oriana is gone." It hissed in response. "She cannot hear your desperate pleading, boy."

How could this thing be a piece of Oriana? She was so pure of heart, her kindness and loyalty expressed through everything she did, everything she had done to save this world from her bloodlust. Goodness always prevailed over evil. It had to, for that was where hope stemmed from.

The monster lunged for him, but he moved quickly, narrowly missing contact with her talon like claws. His shoulders ached from the remembrance of those nails digging into his shoulders. She stumbled past him, but did not fall, rounding on him once more.

"Oriana, please!" His voice quavered. The curse was not final until the blood moon disappeared, replaced by the morning light of the new day. He had time–*they* had time–to make things right, to overcome the curse.

Snow began to fall around them, showering them in flecks of shimmering red under the moon's eerie glow.

"You can still break the curse, Oriana. You must fight, overcome the bloodlust! You are stronger than it is."

A cackle came from the beast. "She cowers in fear, just as she always has. She will never hear you."

"Oriana!" Garren yelled again. This time, when the monster dove for him, he let it tackle him to the snow-dusted forest floor. Her nails dug into his forearms as she pressed them above his head against the cold mossy earth of the cliff side. "Oriana," he whispered, a single tear trailing down one cheek. And then he saw it, just as Haldis had said–a flicker of green against the monstrous yellow, for just a fleeting moment, but it was all he needed to see. She was there. She was still there.

Garren pushed, rolling the two of them until he was looming over top of the deformed creature. Her nails still dug into his forearms, piercing through his tunic and into the flesh below where fresh blood seeped through white linen.

The monster wailed, flailing like a fish out of water beneath him. "Filth!" she screeched.

Why did she hate his blood so much? Each time she had said the same thing, not wishing to be near him when he bled. "Why does my blood repulse you, demon?"

She rolled back on top, forcing him against the soft earth that was slowly turning to a glistening white as the snowfall thickened. Garren brought a leg up between them and kicked her off.

They both rose, squaring off toward one another. "Your blood is tainted by the Gods," it said, spitting upon the powdery snow in repulsion.

The monster took one quick glance at the forest toward Sardorf. It squirmed where it stood before Garren, practically itching to tear flesh from bone, to drink the blood of its kills.

"I will not allow you to harm those people."

"Well, come and stop me then," it said before sprinting into the wood.

Garren barreled after it, feeling a strength and speed, fresh and new course in his veins. It came in a rush, spreading through him like wildfire. He caught up to the creature in ten swift lunges, tackling it to the forest floor. "Oriana!" he roared, desperate to draw her out. "I know you are there! I saw you! Please, fight it! Fight the bloodlust!"

A high-pitched, malicious laugh came forth from the horrendous creature. "She will not come. She knows we must feed on the weakness of these mortals."

That one sentence, that single phrase took Garren's breath away. He knew how to break the curse.

Orrick had given it to him in his parting words. *Do not allow her to find satiation in the weakness of men.* It had been right there the whole time, in the center of Anthes's curse. The god hated weakness above all else, annihilated civilizations and worlds simply because of their supposed weakness. But Gods were not weak; they were the most powerful beings in the cosmos. And Garren had the blood of the Gods in his veins. It was the reason why the bloodlust hated him. His blood was not weak.

"Oriana! You need to fight! It's my blood! It's the key, please! You must drink my blood!" Garren pressed against the beast as it screeched and squirmed relentlessly beneath him. Its features shuttered, revealing Oriana's silken flesh and bright eyes before the monster returned.

"Oriana," he breathed, fresh tears falling unbidden down his face. "I know you are there, please. You must overcome it, take back control over the bloodlust. You are stronger than it, Oriana, you always have been. Let go of your fear and be in control of your own destiny. You cannot stay locked within yourself forever. Fight."

Suddenly, the creature cried out in excruciating pain. It jerked, gripping Garren's arms hard, but it did not dig its nails into his skin or try to crush his bones beneath its grip. He looked into its eyes, to see not a hint of yellow left. It was her. The deformity of her face and body began to melt away like the wax of a candle. Her forehead smoothed into supple skin, her nose and eyes altering back into the woman he had come to love these past weeks. Each malformation changed until they were all replaced by the soft, breathtakingly beautiful features of his love, his divine goddess. She brought her mouth up to meet the skin at the nape of his neck and bit down, teeth breaking through the thin layer of flesh. She drank deeply.

Pain seared through him like a bolt of lightning. It was hot and blinding. He could feel his limbs growing weak, but he held onto her as if at any moment he might lose her forever. With each gulp Oriana drank of his blood, his vision blurred, and his body sank in exhaustion. He hadn't felt like this since the Martok had wounded him, but if it was to save Oriana, he would give her all that she needed. He would give her everything.

Just as Garren thought he might pass out, wind and snow began to swirl around them, lifting them from the earth. He closed his eyes against it as they hovered in the air, gripping Oriana to his chest tightly while she continued to drink. Until the wind, the snow, and all the elements that had circled around them pushed out in a rippling wave across the land.

They returned to the solid ground once again, and Oriana's brilliant green eyes stared up at him. Within them, he saw all the tenderness in the cosmos. "You saved me," she whispered, still encircled in his arms.

"You saved yourself." His voice gave way to the emotion he knew she could see on his face. "Haldis knew. She always knew you were there hidden within the bloodlust."

They stood, locked in each other's embrace

"I thought I had lost you," Garren whispered into her hair, swaying slightly.

"I don't think I could ever be lost from you, not truly, for I know you will always be there to find me."

"Until the end," he whispered, his lips descending onto hers in a gentle kiss.

"Until the end," she said back to him. Her face was alight, for what he believed to be the first time in a long time, with hope.

SIX MONTHS LATER

Oriana looked out over the growing city around her. The moon was full overhead, peering down like a sentinel at the new city of Elscar, keeping watch over its new beginning. Its silvery haze bathed the world in a shimmer of warmth, offering good tidings.

In the months since the curse had been broken, Oriana had found a new zest for life. She had brought down her ominous Phantom Wood and reached out to the neighboring towns and villages, helping Sardorf to establish new relationships and trade–a foreign thing to a community isolated for five centuries.

The people of Sardorf rejoiced in the disappearance of the Phantom Wood. They dictated the 31st day of the twelfth moon to be a day of rebirth, celebrating the day with spiced drinks, food fit for kings, and presents for their family and loved ones.

Haldis had ventured out to Elscar, wishing to build a new civilization to honor those who once lived there. And so the city began to grow. Garren traveled throughout Svakland, spreading word that the ruins of Elscar had been rebuilt–the Bad Lands were no more. People flocked from far and wide, some seeking a better life and others searching for a new beginning.

In the city's center, Oriana recreated the freshwater spring with a new sculpture at its center to honor those who perished all those years ago–the old city of Elscar. Each and every one of their names were chiseled upon the surface of the stones, never to be forgotten.

Garren and Oriana eventually etched her story into Haldis's book of *Gods and Curses*, spreading the knowledge of other Gods and goddesses in the cosmos, as well as showing Svakland who their true guardian and overseer was. It also provided a remembrance of the centuries that the people of Sardorf had suffered because of the curse and of how the curse was ultimately broken. A god's curse was impenetrable, except to those who believed there was a way. It was the ones who never gave up, who read between the lines, that could overcome any obstacle. Those like Garren, who had broken through the embodiment of her bloodlust against all odds.

Up until then, Oriana had never truly understood the bloodlust. She had spent her entire life denying its existence, attempting to lock it away and forming it into a separate consciousness. She forced it to be on its own, splitting herself in two. She had created the thing she feared most.

It wasn't until the curse was broken that she saw clearly for the first time in her life, finally realizing what she had done. Evil cannot be suppressed; that only feeds it. Evil must be left to exist alongside goodness. The hatred for that part of herself grew until it was able to attack and hold power over her.

As Oriana accepted it, acknowledging the bloodlust as a piece of herself, it evolved, changing shape into strength, power, and protection.

No longer was she the meek goddess that had fallen victim to the fate that was thrust upon her. She was in control of her full self; she always had been. She was the maker of her own destiny.

Oriana looked up at the man standing beside her. Garren gazed out over the city, admiring what she had brought back to life from ash and rubble. Whether or not he liked to admit it, he had saved her. He had opened her eyes and helped her discover that she had always been in control, but was just too afraid to take it. She would forever be indebted to him for that.

"Do you ever wonder what Orrick did with Anthes and Balthar?" Garren asked her.

"Honestly," Oriana said, "I don't want to know as long as we never have to see them again." She could only hope her brother had done the right thing. One thing they did know for certain was that Orrick had not stopped filtering his creatures into Svakland.

"There is talk of a demon laying waste to ships venturing into Coral Cove." Garren turned his admiring gaze on her, reaching out a hand in question with an unmistakable twinkle in his eye. "Are you ready for our next adventure?"

A wicked smile played upon her lips as she placed her hand in his. "Let's go see what you can really do, Zydell."

ACKNOWLEDGMENTS

First, I want to thank you, the reader, for picking this book up and reading. I appreciate you. Thank you.

Troy - I love you, always. You are my biggest supporter. Thank you for all you do. Life is better with you in it.

J.L. Vampa - My Nadia. I love you to the moon and back. Thank you for always being there for me and for reading through every draft of this book! I truly couldn't have finished it without you there every step of the way.

Alex, Katelyn & Megan - Your constant support and excitement means the world to me! Thank you for reading the early drafts and being such loving friends.

Emma Hamm – Thank you for always answering my questions and helping me get this novel out into the world. We may have bonded over circumstances that really suck, but I am glad it brought us together.

Tank – My trusty companion and sweetest munchkin. Thank you for sitting by my side every night until the early hours of the morning while I wrote this novel. (Yes, this is my dog.)

Alyse Bailey - This book wouldn't have been what it is without your direction and encouragement, thank you.

My Street Team - All of your support, enthusiasm, and encouragement keeps me going. Thank you for helping me spread the word for this book! I adore you all.

ABOUT THE AUTHOR

K.C. Smith developed a love for fantasy at a young age, which only grew as she got older. Katelyn works as an Accountant in Baltimore, Maryland where she lives with her husband and their chihuahua, Tank. Writing allows her an escape from the corporate world at the end of the day. When not writing she can be found rock climbing and traveling the world.

Visit her on the web:
https://www.kcsmithbooks.com/
https://www.instagram.com/balancingbooksandcoffee/
https://www.facebook.com/kcsmithbooks
https://twitter.com/kcsmithbooks
https://www.tiktok.com/@balancingbooksandcoffee

See all of Katelyn's titles on her amazon page:
https://www.amazon.com/author/kcsmithbooks

CPSIA information can be obtained
at www.ICGtesting.com
Printed in the USA
BVHW052038021122
650798BV00002B/11

9 798986 459004